Praise for the novels of LuAnn McLane

Trick My Truck but Don't Mess With My Heart

"There's . . . an infectious quality to the writing, and some great humor." —*Publishers Weekly*

"[A] quick-paced, action-packed, romantic romp . . . hilarious." —Romance Designs

Dancing Shoes and Honky-Tonk Blues

"Abby shines as the sweet and loveable duckling turned swan. Lighthearted comedy and steamy romance combine to make this a delightful tale of a small town that takes Hollywood by storm." —Romance Junkies

Dark Roots and Cowboy Boots

"This kudzu-covered love story is as hot as Texas Pete, and more fun than a county fair."
—Karin Gillespie, author of *Dollar Daze*

"An endearing, sexy, romantic romp that sparkles with Southern charm!" —*New York Times* bestselling author Julia London

"Charmingly entertaining . . . a truly pleasurable read."
—*Romantic Times*

"A hoot! The pages fly in this sexy, hilarious romp."
—Romance Reviews Today

continued . . .

Wild Ride

"*Wild Ride* is exactly that—a thrilling, exhilarating sensual ride. I implore you to jump right in and hold on tight!"   —A Romance Review

"Scintillating romance set against the backdrop of a tropical island paradise takes readers to new heights in this captivating collection of erotic novellas. The three tales are steamy and fast-paced, combining descriptive romance with creative love stories." —*Romantic Times*

Hot Summer Nights

"Bright, sexy, and very entertaining. An author to watch!"   —*New York Times* bestselling author Lori Foster

"Superhot summer romance . . . a fun read, especially for fans of baseball and erotica."   —BellaOnline

"Funny, sexy, steamy . . . will keep you glued to the pages."   —Fallen Angel Reviews

DRIVEN
by
Desire

LuAnn McLane

A SIGNET ECLIPSE BOOK

SIGNET ECLIPSE
Published by New American Library, a division of
Penguin Group (USA) Inc., 375 Hudson Street,
New York, New York 10014, USA
Penguin Group (Canada), 90 Eglinton Avenue East, Suite 700, Toronto,
Ontario M4P 2Y3, Canada (a division of Pearson Penguin Canada Inc.)
Penguin Books Ltd., 80 Strand, London WC2R 0RL, England
Penguin Ireland, 25 St. Stephen's Green, Dublin 2,
Ireland (a division of Penguin Books Ltd.)
Penguin Group (Australia), 250 Camberwell Road, Camberwell, Victoria 3124,
Australia (a division of Pearson Australia Group Pty. Ltd.)
Penguin Books India Pvt. Ltd., 11 Community Centre, Panchsheel Park,
New Delhi – 110 017, India
Penguin Group (NZ), 67 Apollo Drive, Rosedale, North Shore 0632,
New Zealand (a division of Pearson New Zealand Ltd.)
Penguin Books (South Africa) (Pty.) Ltd., 24 Sturdee Avenue,
Rosebank, Johannesburg 2196, South Africa

Penguin Books Ltd., Registered Offices: 80 Strand, London WC2R 0RL, England

First published by Signet Eclipse, an imprint of New American Library,
a division of Penguin Group (USA) Inc.

First Printing, October 2008
1 3 5 7 9 10 8 6 4 2

SIGNET ECLIPSE and logo are trademarks of Penguin Group (USA) Inc.

LIBRARY OF CONGRESS CATALOGING-IN-PUBLICATION DATA:
McLane, LuAnn.
Driven by desire / LuAnn McLane.
p.   cm.
ISBN 978-0-451-22504-7
1. Motocross—Fiction. 2. Motorcycle racing—Fiction. I. Title.
PS3613.C5685L68 2006
813'.6—dc22   2008011978

Set in Sabon Roman
Designed by Alissa Amell

Printed in the United States of America

This book is for Gary. God bless the broken road.

I would like to thank motocross racing for providing the excitement that brought this book to life. I am in total awe of the fearless racers who defy gravity while pushing their minds, bodies, and spirits to the limit.

A special thanks goes out to Supercross legend Jeremy McGrath for his entertaining and informative autobiography, *Wide Open*. McGrath's personal account of his rise to fame is inspirational to anyone reaching for a dream.

This book would not have been possible without the insight and support of my editor, Anne Bohner. Thank you for pushing me into new territory. I'm now a huge motocross fan. I would also like to acknowledge Liza Schwartz for keeping me on track. Thanks for all that you both do from the beginning stages until the book hits the shelves.

As always, I owe a special thanks to my agent, Jenny Bent, who is the driving force behind my career. Your continued encouragement keeps me motivated and challenges my creativity.

Chapter One

"*T*ake your nuts out of your pocket and jump the creek," Jayden told himself as he gave his motorcycle some throttle and roared across the open field before entering the hushed darkness of the woods. Even though it had been a while, Jayden knew the worn trail well, and easily snaked in and out of tricky, tree-lined turns while ducking beneath low-hanging branches. Stiff fall foliage licked across his helmet and slapped against his goggles, but Jayden barely noticed as he raced up the hillside leading to the creek.

Ever the daredevil, Jayden had first jumped Willow Creek as a ten-year-old kid while riding a BMX bike, taking to the air like a scene in a Spielberg movie. Now, pushing thirty, Jayden Michaels was a Supercross legend with nearly a dozen championship titles under his belt. Normally, flying over the creek wouldn't be a big deal, but with a recently banged-up shoulder, Jayden knew that the jar of the landing was going to hurt like hell. Pain, though, wasn't really the issue. Jayden was no stranger to broken bones and dislocated body parts.

He was, however, supposed to be resting and babying his shoulder instead of training for the upcoming Super-cross series beginning in a couple of months.

So . . . with just a few indecisive seconds left, the question remained as to whether he would leap over the creek or make a hairpin turn and head back down the hillside. "Ahhh, screw it," Jayden growled behind his helmet, knowing all along that he would make the jump.

Bracing himself for the pain upon impact, Jayden inhaled a deep breath and took to the air. "What the hell?" Just as his tires left solid ground, a woman came from out of nowhere and hopped onto a flat rock in the middle of the gurgling water. Upon hearing the whine of his engine she turned and gave him a deer-in-the-headlights look . . .

And then she screamed bloody murder but stood there frozen in place.

"Shit!" Jayden grabbed a handful of brake and somehow managed to avoid crashing into her. She screamed again while flapping her arms. Still airborne, Jayden saw her stumble backward and tumble with a splash into the middle of the rocky water just before he flipped over the handlebars and sailed through the air. A heartbeat later, Jayden smacked into the ground with a bone-jarring, breath-stealing thud. Pain, white-hot and gut-wrenching, shot up his arm, spreading fingers of flame that gripped his sore shoulder.

"Ohmigod . . . *ohmigod*, are you okay?" Her voice . . . breathless, throaty . . . drifted into his foggy brain. "Oh, *please* be okay."

While trying to clear his head Jayden blinked up through mud-splattered goggles into wide, impossibly blue eyes. She had a sweet face framed by fringy golden hair and a full, sexy mouth that even in his befuddled state turned him on . . . Wait a minute.

God. *Alexia?* No . . . it couldn't be.

Damn, the spill really rattled his brains. Alexia was married to some rich bastard and lived up East. She was not kneeling next to him with concern in her eyes.

"Are you okay?" she repeated, and her incredible mouth trembled a bit. She swallowed and, *God help him*, licked her bottom lip. It *was* Alexia and he damned well knew it.

Jayden tried to answer but was mortified that all he could manage was a pathetic wheeze, which pretty much meant that he wasn't okay. His shoulder throbbed and it hurt to breathe.

"Let's get this off," she, *Alexia*, said, and gently lifted his head to remove his helmet.

Jayden would have protested with something like *leave me the hell alone*, but he still couldn't breathe. It didn't help matters that the flannel shirt she wore unbuttoned revealed a wet T-shirt molded to her breasts like second skin.

"There," she said after removing his headgear. Her eyes widened slightly and her lips parted, making Jayden wonder if she recognized him. Surely she did. Although he was still a bit dazed with his helmet and goggles off, there was no doubt that the woman hovering over him was Alexia Spencer, the woman who had cruelly made him choose between her and his motocross career. He had chosen racing . . . well, sort of. All along he had hoped that she would follow him on the circuit, but less than a year later he had heard that she had married a filthy-rich dude twenty years her senior. Crushed like an empty beer can, Jayden had raced like a maniac, without fatigue or fear. In a twisted way his meteoric rise to the top was driven by his desire to purge her betrayal from his system.

Shit. And now here he was lying on the ground like a damned rag doll. Digging deep and ignoring his aching shoulder, Jayden tried to sit up but his body failed to cooperate.

"Hey, whoa there. Try to catch your breath," Alexia pleaded in that husky voice that made even normal everyday conversation sound sexy. "I think you got the wind knocked out of you." With a frown she leaned closer, bringing that body, that *mouth* within striking distance . . . if only he could move. Not that he would actually touch her . . . or wanted to touch her for that matter. Okay, he admitted to himself when he eyeballed her breasts and swallowed hard . . . maybe not that last part.

"Do you think anything is broken?"

Jayden managed a curt, negative shake of his head even though he wasn't at all sure.

"Good," she said with such relief that you would have thought she cared about him. Of course Jayden knew better. A dry chuckle bubbled up in his throat but came out sounding pretty much like a moan. *Well, hell.* "Ohmigod, you're *not* okay, are you? Should I call 911?" Her husky voice trembled a bit around the edges.

"No," Jayden was able to croak.

"Are you sure?" A damp lock of honey blond hair, a softer shade than her teenage platinum in-your-face shade, clung to her cheek and caught on her bottom lip. She reached up and tugged it away, causing Jayden to focus once again on her full mouth . . . a mouth that could work magic like no other woman's. God . . . he could barely breathe, his shoulder might be dislocated, and he was becoming aroused, something that would be difficult to hide in his Thor motocross pants.

And here he thought that after all this time, he was over her.

Apparently he wasn't.

But, then again, he knew that too. The ten years that he had lived as a Supercross stud with piles of money and droves of women meant nothing. He wanted Alexia by his side at the podium and he wanted her now. It royally pissed him off. Red-hot anger blew past the haze of pain and after inhaling some much-needed oxygen, Jayden managed to sit up. "Fuck!" He grabbed his shoulder and swallowed hard.

Alexia's eyes widened even more. "Jayden, is there something I can do?"

Well, at least she knew it was him. For a moment there he wondered. He was no longer the wet-behind-the-ears kid who roared out of Braxton, Tennessee, all those years ago. "Too late for that," he said with more underlying meaning than she would ever know. No one, not even Colin, knew how much her quick marriage had torn him up. "Why the hell did you jump out in front of me?"

Her blue eyes narrowed a fraction or two. "I was hiking." She jammed her thumb over her shoulder. "I live up there in the cabin on the ridge. I hike here all the time and never once has a dirt bike tried to mow me down."

You live here? The question slammed into his brain. "But that cabin belongs to Colin McCord."

She shrugged, causing some jiggle beneath her wet shirt. "I bought it from him this past summer." When she shivered, Jayden realized how cold she must be. As if trying to get warm she folded her arms across her chest, causing her breasts to all but spill out of the V-neck shirt. He didn't remember her breasts being that big, but then again she had been just nineteen . . . little more than a girl when he left.

"Well, head on up there before you catch your death."

Her brows drew together. "But you're hurt . . ."

"I'm fine," he lied, gritting his teeth against the pain as he pushed up to his boot-clad feet. To his horror he weaved and had to brace his hand against the tree that he had narrowly missed crashing into.

"Right," Alexia replied tightly as she grabbed his arm and looped it over her shoulders.

"What the hell do you think you're doing?"

"Jayden, you're in no shape to ride. I'm taking you up to my cabin."

"I'm *fine*, Alexia," he growled, but just saying her name rattled his already scrambled brain. That . . . and the familiar floral scent of her perfume that cut right through the damp earthy smell of the woods. "And I'm not about to go to your cabin."

"The hell you're *not*!" To prove her point Alexia tightened her grip on his glove and tugged him forward.

"Yeah, well, we'll just see about that," Jayden protested, and would have yanked his arm away and stormed off, except for one thing. She was right. He was in no shape to walk. The thought that he might have reinjured his shoulder had his knees turning to water and his stomach in knots. At his age, his motocross-racing days were numbered and he didn't want to cut his career short. The throbbing pain was actually making him feel queasy . . . well, that and the thought that Alexia's husband might be waiting on the front porch to greet them. Great . . .

When they reached the log cabin, Jayden stopped at the steps leading to the wraparound porch. "Your husband might not like you bringing me inside his house," Jayden commented with a little more bite than he intended. He felt her shoulders stiffen and then she shivered.

"That won't be a problem."

"Really? So he allows you to bring in stray men?"

"Allows me?" she muttered darkly and shook her head. "I no longer take orders."

Okay, so that sounded like he was a caveman, Jayden thought with a wince. He opened his mouth to apologize but then snapped it shut. Who cared what she thought of him? Jayden racked his rocked brain for something jackass to say in reply because he was becoming increasingly pissed off that he *did* care. And damn it, he didn't want to.

"I left him," she stated flatly.

"Left him?" Her sudden admission slammed into his head, scattering his thoughts like dry leaves in the wind.

"Yes," she bit out sharply. "Now, let's get you inside."

"For good?" Jayden persisted and then felt like a fool. "Not that I give a flying fuck," he added, which of course sounded as if he did.

"Don't be so crude."

"Sorry," he said, and meant it. "I should have kept

that last part to myself." He pretended not to care what she thought about him, but crudeness toward a woman wasn't his style and he would challenge anyone who dared to go that route.

"Forget it," she answered firmly but softly, and despite everything Jayden almost smiled. Even when Alexia was pissed, her smoky voice would arouse him. It wasn't fair. Jayden remembered never winning an argument, because she never screamed and cursed . . . just was her damned sexy self until he was putty in her hands.

"Can you make it up the steps?"

"Huh?" He was distracted by the fact that she hadn't really answered his question. Had she left her husband for good as in divorced? *Not that he gave a flying fuck* . . . Hey, he could say it in his own head, damn it.

Alexia motioned toward the porch. "Do you think you can make it up the steps?" she repeated.

"Sure," Jayden scoffed, but then gripped the handrail like a lifeline even though it shot pain up his arm. He hated leaning on her . . . showing weakness . . . but his damned shoulder throbbed in tandem with his accelerated heartbeat and if he really wanted to admit it, he was shaken in more ways than one. Gritting his teeth, he promised himself that the moment he felt he could ride he'd get the hell out of there. While inhaling a deep breath he made a mental note to avoid this section of the trail at all costs. He'd find something else to jump . . . *Like her bones* popped uninvited into his head. "Not in a million years," he muttered beneath his breath.

"Excuse me?" Alexia tilted her head and looked up

at him. She was of medium height but in his boots he towered over her. With his shoulder-length hair and two days of not shaving he knew he must look rough around the edges, but if he intimidated her, she hid it well.

"Nothing," he replied tersely. He was getting increasingly pissed at himself for the train his thoughts kept taking . . . like whether she tasted the same. She sure smelled the same: a soft floral scent that was warm and alluring. Alexia's mouth parted as if she might say something, but then she inclined her head and assisted him up the fieldstone steps.

When they reached the porch, she led him to a decorative wooden bench flanked by a pot of bright yellow mums. "Have a seat and we'll get those boots off you."

"Yeah, wouldn't want to track dirt into your place," Jayden agreed as he eased onto the bench. While Alexia started unbuckling his muddy Fox boots, Jayden almost managed a grin. He had been to this cabin with Colin countless times, but it had been strictly a guy's environment, a place to crash after a day of fishing, riding, or sometimes just to hang out playing cards in the dead of winter. Never had there been potted flowers on the porch or a grapevine wreath hanging on the door. He'd just bet that it was decked out inside as well. Alexia always did have a sense of style even as a teenager. Judging by the silver Beemer SUV parked in the driveway, she could certainly afford it.

That last thought drove home the fact that Alexia might have left her husband, but God help him, imagining her with another man even after all these years still burned in his gut. But even if *left him for good* meant that she was divorced, it didn't make one damned bit of difference, he told himself firmly. Alexia Spencer had made her choice ten years ago, and he had come out on the short end of that stick. Okay, so she had an issue with the danger of the sport; hell, he could argue that taking a hike in the woods could be dangerous. Jayden chuckled dryly at that thought, drawing a frown from her, but unwilling to divulge his thoughts, he remained silent.

After arching a questioning eyebrow, Alexia bent her head back to her task. Jayden would never in this lifetime let her know that she could still get to him, he thought as he watched her working on getting the racing boots off. Hell no, he would pretend indifference if it killed him. But then, looking down and seeing her blond head bobbing between his legs made Jayden squirm on the wooden bench.

"Oh, are you in pain?" When she looked up with unexpected compassion in her eyes, it hit him as hard as the sexual pull. Maybe harder.

"Yeah, I've got a banged-up shoulder," he admitted gruffly, letting her believe that his discomfort was from his injury.

"From today's spill?" Alexia asked as she scooted the tall, stiff boots off to the side. When she looked up at him he shook his head.

"No, I had my throttle stick wide-open during a jump a few weeks ago. Shot me into the air like a rocket, and I landed hard on my shoulder."

"Let me guess, you're supposed to be babying it?" she asked softly.

"Yeah, well, you know me . . . ," he answered, and then trailed off. What was meant to be a flippant response brought back old memories. She did know him . . . once. Inside out. And God, he had known *her* . . . every inch of her youthful body that had now blossomed into a gorgeous woman. But damn it, he didn't want her concern. She gave up the right for that, he thought darkly, and then realized that he needed to get his emotions under control before he said or *did* something stupid.

A heartbeat ticked between them before she sighed. "I suppose some things never change," she commented in what sounded like a tired voice.

"Yeah, you got that right." With a shake of his head Jayden inadvertently grinned at the irony of her statement. When she frowned Jayden realized that she must have been thinking that he was being a flippant jackass.

"Don't I, though?" she muttered, and glanced away. Her reaction should have suited him just fine, but then a sudden shadow passed over her features . . . such sadness that despite his resolve to remain aloof, it clawed at Jayden's heart.

"Alexia . . . ," he said softly, but when her head whipped up to look at him expectantly he didn't know what to say. Alexia swallowed hard and, God help him, if she cried Jayden knew it would turn him inside out. He suddenly ached to reach down and touch her cheek. He almost did . . . but then she inhaled a sharp breath as if clearing her head and pushed up to her feet. When a cool breeze rustled through the trees she rubbed her hands up and down her arms and shivered.

"Let's get you inside so you can get out of those clothes," Jayden suggested as he stood up. When Alexia's blue eyes widened a fraction, he could have kicked himself in the ass. *Okay, bad choice of words.* Jayden rarely if ever blushed but he suddenly felt heat creep up his neck. "You're, you know, *wet*," he explained, but of course that only made him want to shove his foot into his mouth even farther.

"Thank you, Captain Obvious," Alexia muttered with a hint of mirth in her voice that reminded Jayden that she once had a quirky sense of humor. God, how he had loved to make her laugh . . . that and other things that he dared not think about. Difficult, though, when her T-shirt seemed to be shrink-wrapped to her body. He was glad, however, that her mood had shifted. He could take her anger, deal with her indifference . . . *whatever*, but not witness her sadness.

After she removed her own muddy boots, Alexia offered him her shoulder to lean on, but Jayden declined. "I'm okay," he assured her, and was in fact feeling better. Although his shoulder throbbed and his cut lip smarted, the dizziness had subsided enough that he felt confident to walk without assistance.

"Come on in," she offered after opening the heavy wooden door without using a key.

"You shouldn't leave your doors unlocked," Jayden commented firmly as he entered the foyer.

Alexia looked up at him in surprise but then gave him an it's-none-of-your-concern look.

It really was none of his business but the thought of harm coming to her made him persist. "Look, I know I'm overstepping my bounds but this cabin is secluded. There aren't any phone lines and cell phone reception is sometimes spotty."

"I appreciate your concern," she said in a tight tone that meant the opposite of her statement. "But I think it's pretty safe up here." She folded her arms across her chest and gave him a classic stubborn Alexia expression that he remembered all too well. It also drew his attention to her breasts . . .

When Jayden took a step closer, her eyes widened a fraction but she stood her ground. "Look, you've been away from Braxton for a long time. Yeah, it's still a small town but rowdy kids, mostly guys, hang out up here in the woods and party."

"So I should be afraid of some teenagers sneaking up here to drink beer?" She lifted her chin in defiance. "Come *on*, Jayden."

"It's not as innocent as when we were kids, Alexia. There are some drug problems here just like everywhere else. It's one of the reasons Colin wants the motocross club to fly. Extreme Machines will give the kids here in town something to do instead of getting into trouble."

"So you're not moving back here but just in town to promote Colin's new club?" She raised her delicate eyebrows and Jayden could have sworn she was holding her breath.

"Don't worry," Jayden answered with a little more bite than intended, but it pissed him off that she seemed to want him gone as soon as possible. It pissed him off even more that it bothered him so much. "I'm only here to help Colin get the club rolling and to train for the Supercross circuit." When she shivered again he added tersely, "Go change, Alexia. I'm feeling fine now so I'll see myself out," but then he made the mistake of turning too quickly. A wave of dizziness engulfed him. He fought the darkness closing in on him, but it was a losing battle and he felt his legs buckle . . .

Chapter Two

"Jayden!" Alexia shouted, and rushed forward when he crumpled to the hardwood floor with a sickening thud. "Ohmigod!" After dropping to her knees beside him, she placed a cold hand to his forehead as if that could tell her anything or even help . . . but at least it seemed nurselike. "Jayden!" she repeated and racked her brain for her CPR instructions file, but was in such a state that her brain drew a blank. She was normally a fairly calm person except when it came to medical emergencies. She supposed that her phobia stemmed from the childhood trauma of having a mother who suffered from epileptic seizures. One minute her mom would be fine but then without warning would slide to the floor and convulse. Try as she might, Alexia would *freeze* with terror and had never been able to shake her fear when faced with someone's injury or illness.

Like now. *What should she do?* Her heart pounded and cold sweat rolled down her back.

When she gently tapped his cheeks and he failed to respond, Alexia brushed his long hair to the side and felt beneath his jaw for a pulse. "Thank God," she muttered when the steady beat drummed against the pads of her fingertips. She placed a hand on his jersey and blew out a sigh of relief when the rise and fall of his chest indicated that he was breathing normally.

"Hey," Alexia tried again in a more gentle tone when she really wanted to scream. With trembling fingers she brushed back a lock of dark hair that had fallen over his brow. "Please wake up." When his eyelids flickered Alexia blew out another breath of relief, but instead of waking up, he moaned. "God . . ." Her heart skittered in her chest when she suddenly wondered if Jayden's injuries were more serious than she thought. While wringing her hands she stared down at him wondering if she should loosen his clothing, smack his cheeks harder . . . use smelling salts? "I don't *have* smelling salts," she muttered. "Damn, why don't I have smelling salts?" She shook her head and was teetering on the verge of terror, thinking that maybe he was bleeding internally or something equally horrible, when a tiny voice in the back of her head whispered, *"Kiss him."*

Kiss him?

"Oh, right, like he's Sleeping Beauty," Alexia mumbled, but then thought that perhaps pressing her cold lips to his warm mouth might just shock him awake. Yeah, that's what she would do, just brush her mouth against his . . . not a *real* honest-to-goodness kiss. *Fine.* She answered her argument with her pesky internal self that needed to just shut up! "I'll do it," she whispered, and inhaled a deep breath before leaning down and . . .

"Oh!" When he suddenly opened his eyes Alexia jerked her head back so fast that she would have toppled backward but Jayden's hands shot out and saved her from falling over. Instead, she fell forward and flopped against him chest-to-chest and cheek-to-cheek. When her hands smacked the hardwood floor on either side of his head, she let out a little squeak.

"Easy there," Jayden murmured. He sucked in what was probably a breath of pain from her body-slamming his sore shoulder.

"S-sorry." Alexia quickly tried to pull her cheek from his cheek, but his hands on her back held her close. Her mouth brushed against his bristly jaw and then slid over his soft lips, sending a jolt of pure heat sizzling through her wet, frozen body like a lightning bolt.

"Jayden . . ." Alexia opened her mouth to tell him to let her up, but his lips brushed against hers again and she fought the strong urge to lean in and kiss him senseless. She pushed up with her palms on the floor when her pesky internal self screamed, *no, don't do this. Are you crazy!* But his warm, soft lips moved against hers, teasing and then coaxing. *Nooo.* Sensing her surrender, Jayden slid his hands, warm and firm, over the damp cotton shirt, making Alexia want to peel the fabric from her body and give him access to her bare skin. With a moan he tangled his fingers into her hair and pressed her head closer. Desire unfurled, edgy and potent, but she fought her feelings and resisted.

Sensing her withdrawal, he tugged her shirt from her jeans. His hands felt hot and hungry against her cold skin and he pressed her closer so that she could feel the steely hardness of his arousal. "Let's get you out of those clothes and into bed," he suggested into her ear.

"No . . . this is . . . *God*," she protested, but then

arched her back when he sucked her earlobe into his mouth. "Insane."

"Who cares?" He licked the shell of her ear.

"Jayden, you're hurt."

"I'll manage, believe me."

Alexia knew she was playing with fire and she was going to turn to toast, but when he started to nibble on her neck, her powers of reasoning short-circuited. How often had she fantasized about how her young lover would feel as a hard-bodied man, especially recently when her world had come crashing down around her ears and her past had come back full circle to haunt her?

But sudden anger balled like a fist in her gut. Even after all these years she blamed Jayden for her accident . . . the tragic event that still caused nightmares. A horrific night he knew nothing about and yet she blamed him . . . still. Maybe she needed this . . . something wild and wanton. And perhaps she could purge him from her system and finally feel a sense of closure.

"Alexia?"

She swallowed and then shook her head. "No," she said firmly while clinging to her anger and pride. "You can rest on the sofa." She pushed up from his body and walked on unsteady legs toward her bedroom, half hoping that he would follow her. But at the same time praying that he wouldn't, because she wasn't sure how much longer she could resist his touch. Even after all these years and so much between them, it was evident that Jayden Michaels could still make her burn with desire. Oh, how Alexia wished that she could read his mind and know what he was thinking . . . feeling. Even though her legs trembled, she held her head high and her back stiff, but she could feel the heat of his gaze. She supposed he wanted to extract his own revenge against her as well, for something he thought he knew but in truth didn't.

With her heart pounding, Alexia walked through the great room, past the two-story fieldstone fireplace, and down the short hallway leading to the master bedroom. Trying to chase away her jittery nerves, she inhaled deeply, letting the soothing scent of burned wood and spicy candles calm her fears. For months now this cabin had been her haven, her safe place where she left the rest of the world behind.

And now this . . .

Resisting the urge to look over her shoulder, she paused in the garden bathroom to remove her damp clothing, tossing the garments to the terra-cotta tile floor with a wet plop. Clinging to her anger, she chased away her nerves and then considered getting back into her get-him-out-of-my-system, kick-ass mood. Why not? Okay, she could think of about a dozen reasons right off the bat, but she pushed them from her mind. Maybe this was what she needed to get back her lost confidence. With a grin that trembled at the corners— but hey, it was still a *grin*—she considered walking boldly into the bedroom stark naked, but then made the mistake of looking into the mirror. "Well, hell . . ." Her reflection hammered home the fact that she was no longer the slender girl Jayden once knew intimately. "Damn, damn . . . *damn*," she whispered, and narrowed her eyes, seeing each and every flaw. "What in the hell am I doing?"

She got pissed at Jayden all over again as she decided to get dressed and stop this madness. But of course her clothes were wet, meaning that she would have to venture into her bedroom in defeat. "Damn him," she hissed through gritted teeth. Until today she was doing fine . . . well, not *fine* but making strides, and now . . . *this*! She decided that she should wrap herself in a towel and was all set to stomp into the room and show him the door when her eyes met his in the mirror.

"Stop second-guessing yourself."

Alexia whirled around and sucked in a breath. With one shoulder leaning against the door frame, Jayden gave her a slow, sultry smile. Of course he had the nerve to stand there in nothing but skintight black boxer briefs, looking all tanned, buff, and even better than ten years ago. And God, with his shoulder-length hair, dark-shadowed jaw, and, holy crap, an armband tattoo, he looked . . . dangerous. Deliciously so.

"So you think you can read my mind, do you?" she asked coolly, trying to keep her eyes above his waist and succeeding . . . almost. He was hard. He was ready. And he was impressive.

"As a matter of fact, yes."

Pretending indifference when she wanted to throw herself at him, she arched an eyebrow as she reached for a towel and wrapped herself in the fluffy warmth. "Really? Then why aren't you gone?"

"Because you don't want me to leave."

"Is that right?" She lifted her chin but tucked the towel tighter. "You always were full of yourself, Jayden Michaels. Go back to your motocross groupies." She wiggled her fingers in a dismissive gesture. "This was a mistake."

Something flickered in his brown eyes, something vulnerable that Alexia didn't want to see, but then he said, "You're absolutely right."

Shock, then disappointment, quickly turned to blazing anger. "So, this was your plan? To get me naked and turn me down?"

His dark brows drew together and then he laughed. "Right. And first I thought I'd mow you down with my bike. Yeah, I planned this whole thing."

Okay, so it had made sense in her head.

"Besides, you started this by kissing me." He pointed at her for good measure.

Alexia hated to be pointed at. She took a step forward and slapped at his offensive finger. "*I* kissed *you*?" His comment was like a match to dry hay and the flames engulfed her. She wondered whether smoke was coming out of her ears like a cartoon character. She wouldn't have been surprised.

"Uh . . . *yeah*." When he arched one dark eyebrow she thought about grabbing her razor, holding him down, and shaving the damned thing off.

"You," she said low and lethal while pointing at him, "kissed"—she jammed her thumb at her chest—"me."

His other eyebrow joined the first one. Okay, she'd shave them both off. "When I opened my eyes you were on top of me." He mimicked her pointing gestures, sending her into orbit.

Alexia wasn't one quick to anger, but she was seeing red. "I was trying to arouse you!" Oh, poor choice of words! "To . . . to wake you up!" she hastily added. *God.*

"Do I look like Sleeping Beauty?"

"Well, you sure as hell aren't Prince Charming." Had Alexia not been so pissed this would have been almost amusing. But she was pissed. Royally. She was also somehow totally turned on, so much so that she was going to have to tell him to leave or she would surely drag him into bed and have angry sex with him. In order to save what was left of her dignity, which wasn't much, she needed to point him in the direction of the door. Alexia opened her mouth to do just that, but when Jayden pushed away from the door frame she noticed a painful-looking raw scrape that ran down his side. A nasty bruise on his injured shoulder reminded Alexia that he really was injured and in pain. He shouldn't have been riding before and certainly not now.

"I'm outta here," he growled. A muscle jumped in his jaw, making Alexia wonder if it was from pain or anger, or perhaps both.

"You're not going anywhere." She wasn't about to let him go until she knew he was safe to ride his bike.

His brown eyes widened. "The hell if I'm not. I'm fine."

"Yeah, I've heard that before—just a few minutes ago, as a matter of fact. And then you crumpled to the floor."

"Kiss my ass," he snapped.

"In your dreams." From the looks of him, he wasn't steady on his feet either physically or emotionally, but she knew he would be an idiot and leave anyway unless she did something to stop him.

"I'm outta here," he growled again, but then swayed.

"Jayden, for God's sake just go crash for a while on the sofa. You're in no shape to drive."

"I've driven in worse shape than this, believe me.

Why do you care anyway?" He looked at her with turmoil in his brown eyes, and she once again saw a vulnerable side that clawed at her heart. But when she couldn't bring herself to tell him that she never stopped caring, he took a step but had to place a steadying hand against the wall.

Alexia pictured him smashing into a tree and her stomach clenched. "You are not going anywhere!"

"Watch me!"

"Don't do this!" Panic gripped her and she walked over and placed a restraining hand on his shoulder, but he shook her off. "Then let me give you a reason to stay . . . ," she said, and did the only thing she could think of to keep him there.

Jayden sucked in a breath when Alexia let her towel slip to the floor. His first thought was that she was beautiful. His second thought was that he wanted her so badly that he could taste it. But then it hit him: She was afraid he'd kill himself tearing back down the hill and she was pulling out all the stops to keep him from doing just that. "Alexia . . ." was all he could manage to say, knowing full well he shouldn't take advantage of this bizarre situation they'd somehow managed to cook up. But the sight of her full breasts, her rosy, erect nipples sent all his blood draining from his brain and flowing south. His already hard erection turned to granite.

Raising her chin a notch, Alexia let him look his fill, but her eyes appeared wary as if she felt insecure about her appearance. She probably thought she was overweight, but the word that sprang to his mind was *goddess*. She appeared toned and yet lush . . . curves and shadows, peaks and valleys that he wanted to explore . . . taste. High, firm breasts tapered to a trim waist but flared to womanly hips and, God help him, her skin had a soft, golden glow that begged for his touch.

Yeah . . . she was a goddess.

Alexia swallowed hard and licked her lips as if nervous but she stood her ground while Jayden slowly let his gaze travel the length of her body and then back up again to meet her eyes. She had her pride, and Jayden knew what it must have cost her to hold him there by offering herself. He should stop this insanity now, but he just couldn't bring himself to end something he had dreamed about whenever she had crossed his mind. Of course, there were other emotions at play here, lots of them, but even after what had gone down between them all those years ago, he couldn't bring himself to crush her pride by turning her down.

Not that he could. No, he didn't have that much willpower.

Inhaling a deep breath, Jayden stepped forward until he was close enough to touch her. "You're even more beautiful now than I remember."

"Maybe that's because you never thought of me."

Jayden laughed softly without humor and then tucked his knuckle beneath her chin. "Not true. But are you forgetting that you were married, Alexia?" He gazed down at her for a long moment. "Why?" He shook his head. "Why in the hell did you marry him? Money?"

"No! You know me better than that!"

"I thought I knew you." His eyes searched her face for answers when she remained silent. "Did you love him?" The words tumbled out of his mouth before he could stop them.

She frowned and glanced away. "I was young. Confused. Made *mistakes*."

Her voice cracked, and although Jayden sensed there was so much more for her to tell, he backed off. "I shouldn't have asked you that," he admitted, but God, he wanted to know the answer.

She shrugged. "He was there when I needed . . . ," she began, but then inhaled a deep breath and seemed to get her emotions under control. "And let's not forget that you roared out of town without looking back."

The pain in her eyes got to him and he cupped her chin in his palm. "I was young and made mistakes too." He wanted to tell her how often he had regretted his rash behavior, but the fact that she had turned to someone else clawed at his heart. She had betrayed him and yet he couldn't stop from leaning in and capturing her mouth in a kiss.

She braced her palms against the marble sink and let him run his hands up her arms and then oh so lightly over her breasts. "What's going on here, Jayden?"

"I can't seem to stop myself. I've thought about this too often and now that you're here in front of me . . ."

When her eyes closed, he cupped her breasts and then circled his thumbs over her pebbled nipples. She sucked in a sharp breath and caught her bottom lip between her teeth as if fighting her response. While continuing to caress her breasts, he started a moist trail of kisses, beginning with her shoulder and traveling up her neck. With a soft moan she angled her head to the side, giving him better access to the long column of her throat. He paused to lick the rapidly beating pulse and then bent his head to kiss the soft swell of her breasts.

"Ah . . . *Jayden.*" Her sigh was low, throaty, and sexy as hell. Hearing his name on her lips was his undoing and made him want her to cry out louder with heated passion. With that thought in mind, he circled one nipple with his tongue and then feasted on the other, licking, nibbling, and then sucking until her breathing became shallow and ragged.

With a groan she gripped the edge of the countertop and Jayden knew she was giving in to the intense passion that still burned between them. He wanted to taste and explore, drawing this out until her legs trembled and she had to cling to him for support. He pulled back, kissed the soft skin of her inner thighs, first one and then the other, pausing to blow hot breath on her mound. She quivered, sighed, and when she groaned in impatient protest he eased his middle finger inside, caressing hot spots to drive her wild.

"I . . . shouldn't let you do this."

"Too late now."

"No . . . I . . ." She pushed at his head but then gasped when he caressed her hard and fast. When she was on the verge, he pulled out, parting her folds until she was completely exposed to his gaze. Jayden drew in a shaky breath. She was pink, swollen, glistening, and gorgeous. With a groan of his own, he bent his head and captured her with his mouth and then laved her with his tongue.

"God . . . no, you can't!" she groaned.

"I have to." He needed to show her what she had given up by marrying someone else. He had once known how to drive her wild and he was determined to do so again. She felt soft, slick, and tasted of sex and woman.

He ate her up, cupping and kneading her ass, pulling her closer, licking deeper, harder, faster until she threaded her fingers through his hair and arched against his mouth.

"Oh!" Her cry was hoarse, throaty as if coming from someplace deep within that had been dormant for a long time. Her thighs trembled and she clung to him. Jayden paused just long enough for her to crave release desperately and then he covered her with his mouth once more, licking and then sucking the climax from her throbbing body. "God!" When her knees gave way, Jayden grasped her waist and held her up, kissing her and nuzzling her while she rode the aftershocks.

Alexia was limp, trembling, and Jayden wished he could pick her up and carry her into bed, but his shoulder hurt like hell and he didn't want to risk not being able to lift her without doing any more damage to his body. Instead, he wrapped his good arm around her waist and assisted her into her bedroom. With a sigh Alexia tumbled onto the bed, blond and golden against the deep, rich colors of her comforter. Pillows of all sizes surrounded her, making her appear small and feminine in the large, four-poster bed. The shades were drawn, letting in muted sunlight that filtered through the trees, and the overhead paddle fan hummed lightly, stirring the wood-scented air. Other than that, there was silence in an atmosphere thick with anticipation.

For a long, delicious moment Jayden gazed down at Alexia, drinking in the sight of her luscious nude body. He felt ready to burst just looking at her and hoped to God he didn't immediately come like a horny teenager. Jayden's heart pounded and his dick throbbed, but he was an athlete, *disciplined*, he told himself. Taking a deep breath, he calmed his raging libido.

Alexia's eyes, still a bit dazed, widened when he took a step toward the bed. Jayden knew he looked different from the lanky youth she remembered. Years of racing had left him hardened and laced with scars from various falls and wrecks. Once short and spiky, his hair had grown long while he was laid up from an accident, and since everyone had given him such shit about it he had decided to keep it that way. The Celtic armband tattoo was added to enhance his badass look, but the moon and stars inked just to the left of his groin was done because he loved to ride at night.

Alexia swallowed, shivered, and Jayden wondered if she was cold or scared shitless. God, he must appear almost frightening to her. A part of him wanted to soothe her with soft words to let her know he wasn't as fierce as he appeared, but damn her, she had been his first love . . . hell, maybe his only true love and she had trampled on his young heart, causing more agony than he had thought possible. His emotions became a tangled mess of guilt and anger.

Sure, as she said, they were young, and he supposed he should cut her some slack, but seeing her, *wanting her* this damned much suddenly brought back the pain as if it were yesterday. As he was looking down at Alexia, it hit him like a sucker punch to the gut that it was because he had never stopped missing her, loving her, which was precisely why he should put his clothes on and get the hell out of there. Torn, he closed his eyes and inhaled a deep breath, but then turned away from temptation.

"What are you doing?" Alexia came up to her elbows and looked at him expectantly.

"I'm leaving." He didn't mean for his tone to sound so flat, angry. Her eyes widened, she swallowed hard, and then her lips trembled. If she cried, he would come undone. He needed to hightail it out of there before she did.

Chapter Three

Humiliation hit Alexia like a blast of icy water. Here she was, stark naked, offering herself on a damned silver platter, and Jayden all of a sudden seemed absolutely desperate to leave. Frozen in place, she watched him search for his clothes. Moisture filled her throat and her nose twitched, but she willed herself not to cry. No, he would not see her tears, damn him, damn him, *damn him*!

Alexia was torn between begging him to stay and telling him not to let the door slap him in the ass as he left, but she didn't trust her voice. This brought her attention to his tight butt, looking mighty fine as he tugged on his racing pants, and it pissed her off even more that she could find him attractive when he was being a jerk. He winced as he pulled his jersey over his head, but she hardened her heart. If he wanted to kill himself going back down the hill, then let him. She had done her best to keep him there . . .

And she hadn't been enticing enough.

Alexia forced herself not to grab a pillow and cover

her nakedness. She was pushing thirty and the tight body she once had was long gone. Not only that, but she had put on weight after she caught her college professor husband in bed with a student. Classic. Chocolate-chip cookie dough had become her friend, but she figured it had been better than pills or alcohol. She was trying to get back in shape, which was why she had been hiking in the woods when Jayden had almost mowed her down. Give a girl a break! Tears welled up in her eyes, but she blinked and sniffed as silently as she could, trying not to draw his attention while he tugged on his socks.

She would not cry.

When Jayden turned around, though, Alexia couldn't stop from grabbing a fluffy, fringed pillow and hugging it in front of her body. So she had thrown herself at him like a sex-deprived loser. At least she had a higher motive, like, *hello*, saving his sorry-ass neck. But, truly, what had she been thinking? She could have offered to drive him back into town or fixed him lunch . . . anything but *this*. The fact that she had allowed him to bring her to a mind-blowing, bone-melting orgasm added to the humiliation factor, but even though she knew her face must be glowing beet red Alexia managed to lift her chin and hoped that her watery eyes resembled a glare. Fat chance, but she tried anyway.

"I'll make it back down the hill," Jayden quietly assured her. "I've been banged up worse than this and finished entire races."

Not trusting her voice, Alexia nodded. *Just go*, she silently screamed. But no, he had to stand there clothed and confident while she played with the gold fringe on her pillow.

"Alexia . . . ," he began in a soothing voice, and then trailed off as if not sure what to say. In his defense, what exactly did you say in a situation like this? *Nice to see you again after all these years?*

Alexia prayed for her sense of humor to surface. It was there . . . and had gotten her through many a tough time . . . she just couldn't reach that deep at the moment. She supposed it was the pity in his tone that got to her. Anger, *passion*—she could take just about anything from him and survive, but not pity.

His pity pissed her off.

But instead of her ranting or yelling as she so wanted to do, a hot, fat tear escaped the corner of her eye and rolled down her cheek. *Well, damn!*

"Alexia," he said again in that same I-feel-sorry-for-you voice. He even took a step toward the bed.

"Just go," Alexia croaked, and angrily swiped at the tear. She hugged the pillow closer and blinked up at him. "Go and . . . stay . . ." She paused for a pitiful sniff. "A-*way.*"

"Listen," he began in that same soothing tone that only succeeded in offending her further.

"Go!" she warned, but he ignored her command. When he took another step closer, she glared and said, "I'm warning you!" Amusement flashed in his brown eyes and she supposed her threatening him was rather funny because what could she possibly do? Would the humiliation ever end?

Apparently not.

Well, she'd . . . she would . . . *throw* something!

When Jayden dared take another long-legged stride closer to the bed, Alexia let out a little growl and winged the big pillow at him. She didn't think she had all that

much oomph on it, but she supposed her anger chan-
neled some adrenaline, because the plump pillow smacked
him in the chest and knocked him backward. The surprise of her spontaneous toss probably had something
to do with it, but suddenly the mighty Jayden Michaels
was on his ass. Alexia lifted her chin and added a defiant so-there purse of her lips, but when he grunted
and grasped his shoulder she immediately regretted her
action.

"Jayden!" She scrambled from the bed so fast that
she all but tumbled to the floor and then kneeled beside
him. His eyes were closed and he sucked in a breath.
"Are you okay?" She cupped his cheek and waited for
his answer.

Jayden inhaled a deep painful breath, not knowing
what emotion was going to surface this time. Alexia
had succeeded in making him angrier than he thought
possible, more turned on than he could remember being
in a long-ass time, and now he thought he just might
have to laugh even though his shoulder was killing him.

"Jayden, I'm so sorry." Her soft apology went
straight to his heart, and he groaned.

"I didn't mean to hurt you."

"Too late for that." His tone was flippant, meant as
a joke, but their past was suddenly in the room like a
damned white elephant. The one emotion he wasn't going to explore was love, he firmly told himself, but when
he opened his eyes and found himself gazing into her
soulful ones, he knew it was a lost cause.

Hell yeah, he had never stopped thinking about
her . . . loving her.

But he'd be damned if she'd ever know it . . . fool
me once and all that. "You're more dangerous than the

whoops at *Rock Star*," he complained, and almost made her smile. Her mouth was entirely too close for comfort, and the gentle hand on his cheek made him want to lean into her palm and let her kiss the pain away. But instead, he jerked his head away from her touch.

They didn't speak, didn't move.

He ached to pull her into his arms, rub his hands over her soft skin, and hold her close, but he reminded himself that this was Alexia . . . the same woman who had turned her back on him and married another man. It had nearly destroyed him and he wasn't about to give her that power over him once again.

Angry with himself that he had allowed this to happen, he shifted, ready to leave the cabin and get the hell away from her.

"Don't go," she said in a husky voice that turned his heart over in his chest. But just when he was ready to slide an arm around her she added, "Until you feel safe to ride."

Jayden fisted his hand and clenched his jaw hard. Alexia still had the power to mess with his head and to hurt him. "Okay," he answered tightly, "I'll rest awhile before I head out." And then he was never coming back. He'd stick close to the motocross course at Extreme Machines, hang out with Colin and the other racers, and avoid Willow Creek at all costs . . . because the price was too damned high to pay.

Jayden inhaled a deep breath in an effort to clear his head, but his thinking power became clouded by the enticing floral scent of her perfume and the heady scent of sex. He closed his eyes and promised himself that he'd chill just long enough to gather his scattered wits and then he was out of there. Jayden forced his tense muscles to relax and rested his head against a fancy little pillow while trying to ignore the fact that Alexia was warm and naked and just inches away. A heavy sense of sadness settled over him when he suddenly wished that things were different, but he couldn't change the past, so why go there? If he wanted to be fair, and he didn't, he would acknowledge the fact that although Alexia had forced him into an impossible decision, she really didn't understand. Unless racing is in your blood, you don't know the drive, the absolute need to do it. Of course there had been his near-fatal crash that scared the crap out of her . . .

Okay, he had been the one who had left town without so much as a good-bye, but he had expected her to eventually follow. He had been brash, too young, way too confident, but Alexia, in the end, had committed the ultimate betrayal by marrying another man. Up until then he had been her first and, he had always thought, her only. It made his blood boil just thinking of her with someone else. To this day, Jayden had a hard time understanding why she had married a man so much older, a college professor so far removed from Braxton, Tennessee, that it still blew his mind. Now more than ever he thought that there was a piece of the puzzle still missing, but for the life of him could not figure it out.

Anger washed over Jayden in a hot wave, and once again he was all set to leave, but then Alexia sighed, shifted, and the blanket slipped. The curve of her neck, her bare shoulder somehow seemed vulnerable, almost fragile. Once again he had to clench his fist in an effort to keep from touching her. Swallowing a frustrated growl, Jayden vowed to simply close his eyes for a few blessed minutes and then slip from the bed, away from the cabin, and out of her life.

After a deep sigh, Jayden tried to wrestle his tender thoughts into submission. He was actually drifting off to sleep when a sudden thought hit him hard: *To hell with staying away from her.* Not many people knew it, but he was a silent investor with Colin McCord in Extreme Machines. Jayden had maybe a year or two left in him before retiring from motocross, and he fully intended to return to Braxton. He'd be damned if he'd allow the fact that Alexia had returned to change his carefully laid out future and drive him away. *Screw that.* No, he needed to do the exact opposite and find a way to be in her presence on a regular if not daily basis. Then he could get over Alexia Spencer once and for all, and he would do it not by running or hiding but by facing and confronting his feelings for her head-on.

But then he heard her soft breathing next to him and inhaled the light floral scent of her perfume and once again had to fight the strong urge to drag her into his arms. Deep down he realized that he might not ever be able to get over her. So that left getting back together. Jayden instinctively knew it had to be one or the other or he wouldn't be able to live in Braxton. Even now, thinking of her in the arms of another man made his jaw clench.

Of course, how to become a fixture in her life became the next question. Jayden thought about it for a few minutes, and the answer came to him out of the blue. *Perfect.* He smiled as he drifted off to sleep and vowed to put his plan in motion first thing tomorrow.

Chapter Four

"*Y*ou want me to do *what*?" Alexia placed her palms on her sister Brianna's antique desk and leaned in just shy of nose to nose.

"You heard me, Alexia." Brianna folded her slim arms across her chest and tilted back in the squeaky chair. "It's not easy to snag Jayden Michaels for an interview. The fact that he wants to do a series of motocross articles with our little publication is an honor."

"Fine." Alexia pushed away from the desk and made a flipping motion with her hand. "But choose another reporter to do the story instead of me."

Brianna shook her strawberry blond head so hard that her curls bounced. "No can do," Alexia's younger sister, who also happened to be editor of the *Braxton Times*, replied. "Jayden requested *you*."

"Well, I refuse."

"Then you're fired."

"You won't fire me," Alexia sputtered.

"Watch me."

Alexia narrowed her eyes at her twenty-five-year-

old baby sister and drew in a deep breath. This sucked.
Petite little Brianna was cute as a button and a sweetheart . . . until it came to running the paper. Although
the *Braxton Times* was a small-town, weekly publication, it had a reputation for excellence and wide circula-
tion across three counties. Bri took her job seriously
and would indeed fire her on the spot if she refused to
write the story. While Alexia's pay as a staff reporter
wasn't big bucks, money wasn't much of an issue.
Thanks to the lack of a prenup, her jackass cheater ex-
husband had to cough up some substantial cash for his
sordid little affair. But although Alexia didn't need the
income, she loved the job and didn't want to lose it.
"Come on, Bri. You know my history with Jayden.
Have a heart."

Brianna had the decency to appear sympathetic. "I
understand how this would be a bit awkward."

"Right." Alexia nodded hopefully while her face
grew warm, thinking that Brianna had no idea. After
yesterday, awkward didn't even begin to cover it. She
had thrown herself at him . . . begged him to stay, hoping he would finish what she had shamelessly allowed
him to begin. Instead, when she had woken several
hours later, Jayden had been gone . . . taking her pride
with him.

Brianna tucked a lock of red-gold hair behind her
ear and quietly laced her fingers together on top of her
old-fashioned desk blotter. Inclining her head in an I'm-
the-boss way, she said, "But you're a professional. You
can handle this."

Without thinking, Alexia closed her eyes and sucked
in a breath.

"Wait a minute. Oh . . . my . . . *God*," Brianna

suddenly blurted out, totally forgetting to use her serious editor voice. "Alexia!"

"What?" Alexia raised both eyebrows and tried for innocence, but she knew her sister's I-know-you're-hiding-something radar was up.

"Have you . . . have you seen Jayden since he's been back in town?"

Alexia widened her eyes and raised her palms upward. "How could I have seen him? I've been up at the cabin all weekend." There, that was a question and not a lie. Well, not exactly a lie anyway.

Brianna's mouth formed an O and she put a hand to her chest. "You *did* see him!" She forgot all about business and gave Alexia her undivided attention. "So spill. How did it go?" she asked, and when Alexia hesitated she continued. "Don't even bother to deny it. I'm your sister, remember?"

"Hmm, I thought you were my boss."

Brianna wrinkled up her nose. "Whatever. Come on, now, what did Jayden say when he saw you?" she persisted but then frowned. "Wait a minute. If you've been up at your cabin all weekend, then"—she put her hands to her cheeks—"he came up to your place?" Her voice became a very noneditor but very Brianna squeak. When Alexia's cheeks heated up even warmer, Brianna's eyes rounded. "He did!"

"He didn't come to my place," Alexia corrected, but at Brianna's confused expression continued. "Well, not intentionally."

"Oh, just quit talking in circles and explain to me what happened." Brianna, trying to get back into her "boss" mode, folded her hands and waited.

Oh, how Alexia wanted to spill her guts, but didn't.

"Okay, at least admit to me that seeing him shook you up, didn't it?"

"Yes." Alexia nodded but refused to give details even though she knew her sister would take her secrets to the grave.

Brianna sighed. "All right, I won't pry until you have a bottle of wine under your belt."

Alexia smiled. She had missed her sister terribly. Although her parents had migrated south, living near Brianna was a bright spot in an otherwise dark and twisty year. Alexia hadn't been sure at first about moving back to Braxton, but now she was glad that she did . . . well, until yesterday. "So now you understand, right?" Alexia asked hopefully, and then quickly interjected, "Hey, why don't you do the story, Bri?" She wiggled her eyebrows at her sister. "I know you always had a thing for Colin McCord. This would give you an excuse to hang around Extreme Machines."

"Oh, for goodness' sake," Brianna scoffed. "I'm way over my schoolgirl crush on Colin. Need I remind you that he's ten years older than me?" But then Brianna put a hand over her mouth before saying, "God, I'm such a ditz. Not that there is anything wrong with falling for an older man . . ."

"Except when they cheat on you," Alexia responded dryly. She reached over and patted her sister's hand. "You don't have to walk on eggshells around me. Look, I know now I never should've married a man twenty years older than me, especially after . . ." Alexia felt tears well up in her eyes. Perhaps she should tell Brianna what had happened. Then maybe she would understand and not make her write the damned story. Alexia had to wonder just what Jayden was trying to prove by requesting her anyway. Was he trying to win her back or prove that he was over her?

"Listen." Brianna's tone turned serious. "I don't know what all went down between you and Jayden that drove you into Mitchell Parkwood's arms. All I know is that . . ." She trailed off and then glanced away.

"What?"

"I was only in the eighth grade when you broke up with Jayden," she said slowly, and looked back at Alexia. "All I remember is wishing that someday a boy would look at me with such adoration as Jayden used to look at you."

"We were kids," Alexia stated flatly, but then unexpected sadness washed over her. "Raging hormones and all that . . ."

Brianna looked down at the weathered hardwood floor and shrugged. "Maybe."

"I hear a but."

For a moment Brianna hesitated but then looked over at Alexia with tears swimming in her eyes. "But does a love like that, so pure as only young love can be, ever die?" She paused and then gave Alexia a dreamy shake of her head.

"Oh, would you listen to yourself? You're a reporter, not a romance writer. You're talking mushy *nonsense*."

She sniffed. "Am I?" Brianna's blue eyes were so full of wistful longing that it brought tears to Alexia's own eyes. She remembered once feeling the same way about life, and now all she felt was bitterness. Alexia hoped to God Brianna, always good-hearted and idealistic, never became jaded like herself.

"No, Bri, you're not spewing nonsense. I did love Jayden with all my heart. That's why I freaked when he almost died in the motorcycle accident. But I thought he loved me enough to give up something so dangerous." Alexia shook her head. "Instead, he rode out of town without so much as a good-bye," she answered with more anger than she knew still existed. When her comment was met with silence, Alexia narrowed her eyes at her sister, who was nibbling on her bottom lip. "Okay, now *what*?"

Brianna winced. "You're not going to like what I have to say."

"Tell me anyway. You know you want to."

"You promise you won't get angry?" Brianna asked in a small voice, sounding younger and less tough than she wanted to portray herself. She really was a sweetheart, and Alexia would have to kick the butt of anyone who ever dared to hurt her sister, because Brianna could have her heart broken easily.

"No, I can't promise that, Bri. You obviously know whatever you are going to say is going to tick me off or you wouldn't preface it with asking me not to get angry."

After chewing thoughtfully on the cap of a pen, Brianna said, "Okay, I might as well tell you, since I'm not going to relent on having you write Jayden's story." She tossed the pen down. "So you're going to be mad at me regardless."

"Ohmigod, would you please get to the point!"

Despite being an excellent, no-nonsense journalist, Brianna was an expert at beating around the bush when it came to conversation.

"Okay, here goes. No matter how much I loved someone, I couldn't give up writing." She patted her chest for emphasis. "It's in my blood. I can understand how Jayden couldn't have given up racing. It's too much a part of who he is. He would have been miserable and you know it."

Alexia felt a flash of anger. "I watched Jayden's motorcycle stall in a midair jump. I witnessed his body slam into the ground and crumble like a helpless rag doll. At the age of twenty he almost died. *Died*, Brianna!" Alexia's voice shook with pent-up emotion. She swallowed the hot moisture clogging her throat. "I hoped and prayed for him to quit after that. But he didn't. God, how I tried . . . really tried to be supportive, but I was petrified each and every race. And then . . ."

Brianna looked at her expectantly. "And then what?"

"Nothing." Alexia shook her head hard. "I gave him the ultimatum and he chose racing over me. You know the rest. End of story." No one except for Colin knew about her pregnancy, and she had sworn him to secrecy. To this day she couldn't talk about the tragic ending that had altered her life forever. Even now the memory of it made her hands tremble.

"Is it the end of the story, Alexia? Or is there something I don't know?" Brianna leaned forward with her palms on the desk. "I'm your sister. You can tell me anything and it stays here. You know that, right?"

"Of course I do." She could talk to Brianna now, but back then her sister had been too young to confide in, and her mother had been having health issues that sent her parents south. So after the car wreck that had taken the life of her unborn child and the ability to have another, Alexia had run off to college and into the arms of a man whom she thought she loved but soon found out otherwise, wasting years of her life living with loneliness and despair. She shuddered at the memory.

"Alexia, for goodness' sake, what is it?"

"The past is over." Alexia forced a smile, knowing that if she told Brianna the tragic story and Jayden's role in it, Bri would relent about her writing the article, but then what if Jayden really did refuse and went to another, bigger publication? This meant a lot to her sister and Alexia was just going to have to buck up and do it. "Call Jayden and tell him to let me know when he wants me to begin interviewing him."

"Alexia," Brianna began, "you don't really have to do this if it's too difficult. Screw Jayden and his damned story," she said so fervently that Alexia had to chuckle. Bri rarely used foul language and it just didn't sound right coming out of her mouth.

"I should wash your mouth out, baby sister."

Brianna rolled her eyes. "Yeah, right," she said, but a pink blush stained her cheeks. "You've been gone too long. I'm all grown up and say bad words and everything."

Alexia laughed again. "Did you just say *bad words*?"

"Oh, stop! Just because I don't have a potty mouth like you!"

Alexia laughed harder and was more than glad to lighten the moment. "Could you be any cuter?"

Brianna scrunched up her nose. "What you really mean is, can I be any nerdier?" She shook her head, making her curls bounce. "Just once I want to be the life of the party like you."

Alexia's moment of levity evaporated. "Honey, I haven't been the life of the party for a long, long time."

"Really?" While angling her head Brianna tapped her pen against her cheek. "Then we need to have one."

"Wait a minute . . . one what?"

"A party!" She wiggled her hands in the air, obviously warming to her idea. "When Mom and Dad thought I was sleeping, I used to sneak out and watch you and your friends hang out in the woods behind our house. I *so* wanted to be older and cool like you." She smiled brightly. "Now I *can*. Well, not the older part."

Alexia pulled a face.

She giggled. "Maybe not the cool part either."

"I'm not so cool anymore," Alexia joked, but then felt sort of sad. She missed those younger, carefree days. And longed for what she once had with Jayden, also popped into her head, but this time she didn't try to internally deny it. It was true. She missed the feel, the smell, and the taste of him. But most of all she missed the intensity of their young love and ached for the years lost.

"So let's start planning. You need a welcome-home party. Whadaya say? Let's get your mojo back. And get me some while we're at it."

Well, damn. Alexia didn't want to burst Brianna's bubble, but she did not want a party, especially in her honor.

"We'll have it at Mom and Dad's. A barn dance and a bonfire! Maybe roast a pig and—"

"Bri, I really don't want a party," Alexia interjected gently but firmly.

"Why?"

Okay, that was a fair question for which she had no real answer. "I like my quiet, private life."

Brianna looked at her for a long, thoughtful moment. "Do you? Really?"

Alexia raised her eyebrows and put her fists on her hips. "Of course. I enjoy . . . um . . ." She had to think for a minute. "Long walks in the woods." Except for when a motorcycle tried to mow her down. "And . . . ah . . . reading. Old classic movies," she insisted, but sounded a little too defensive even to her own ears. "I've even thought about taking up . . . ," she began, but trailed off when Brianna put her palms to her cheeks.

"Knitting?" Bri squeaked.

"No!" Alexia protested. She was going to say needlepoint but now decided to keep that information to herself.

"Ohmigod," Bri breathed. "You have officially become more boring than me."

"You're not boring!"

Brianna rolled her eyes. "Mom has a more active social life than me. Alexia, I walk and read too, but my TV of choice is the Food Channel for some weird reason, since I rarely cook. God, we are so lame." She put her index finger and thumb to her forehead. "Losers!"

"We are certainly not losers!" Alexia sputtered, but then thought sadly that maybe they were.

"Ohmigod, the Spencer sisters are . . . spinsters!"

It was Alexia's turn to roll her eyes. "Bri, first of all,

I've already been married and you are only twenty-five, so neither of us can be spinsters . . . *Ugh,* I can't believe you used that outdated term anyway. There's simply no such thing anymore. Today women have choices."

"Okay, then we're not spinsters, just plain old losers." She shrugged and although Alexia knew Brianna was mostly joking, it was hitting a little too close to home. "We need to . . ." She leaned forward in the battered leather chair that she refused to get rid of because it was their grandfather's, looked left and right even though they were the only two in the office, and then mouthed, "Get laid."

Alexia might have laughed at another uncharacteristic comment if visions of Jayden naked hadn't just slammed into her head. Schooling her features into what she hoped was a nongiveaway expression, Alexia sputtered loudly, "We are not losers and we do not need to get laid!"

Brianna's eyes widened and she put her index finger to her lips.

"Oh, come on, Bri, we're the only two in here," she said equally as loud, but come on, Bri was getting under her skin. "And you don't have to mouth or whisper *laid,*" she scoffed just as a cool rush of air blew into the office. When Brianna blinked rapidly and bit her bottom lip, the hair on the back of Alexia's neck stood at attention. *Oh . . . crap.*

Then, confirming her sudden realization that they were no longer alone, a deep voice said, "I have to say that I disagree with at least one of the comments, but by all means don't whisper on my account."

"Sorry!" It was Alexia's turn to mouth to Brianna

before pivoting around. "And just which comment are you referring to, Colin?"

"Well, you two certainly aren't losers," he said slowly while flashing a friendly grin. Blond and buff with shaggy Owen Wilson hair, Colin always looked as if he just stepped off a sunny beach. In fact, he had lived in California while on the West Coast motocross circuit before recently retiring and migrating back to Braxton.

"So, what brings you here? An ad for Extreme Machines, I hope?" Alexia asked, only half joking.

Colin pursed his lips as if considering the notion and turned his attention to Brianna. "Your sister here has been houndin' me to do an ad." He rubbed his chin that had a generous amount of sexy dark-blond stubble. "You know, I think it's a great idea, especially with the upcoming series you're doing on Jayden's career."

"We can certainly arrange that," Brianna said in a businesslike voice that Alexia noted was a tiny bit breathless. Apparently Bri wasn't quite over her crush on Colin McCord. Not that Alexia could blame her sister. Colin was even better-looking now as a rugged thirty-something than he had been as a kid. When he removed his leather jacket, the indigo denim shirt sporting the Extreme Machines logo brought out his light blue eyes and golden tan. He wore a woven hemp choker and wristband that most guys in Braxton wouldn't be caught dead wearing, but Colin pulled it off. "Here's a price list," Brianna offered.

"Thanks." Colin stepped closer to the desk and took the sheet from Brianna with a polite smile. While he might appear blond, buff, and laid-back hip, Colin was actually a good ole Southern boy at heart, with a bit of a reckless wild streak that helped make him a motocross champion. But while the other racers were intense, Colin's method of training was more play than work. Alexia knew that it used to drive Jayden crazy that Colin was so successful but somehow made racing look almost effortless.

"If you have any questions, just let me know," Brianna offered.

While shaking his head, Colin looked down at the paper. "The pricing seems pretty self-explanatory. I do want to place a series of ads, so I'll put something together and get it to you before the official grand opening." He looked up from the paper to gaze at Brianna. "We need to set up a time to get together and go over some ideas I have in mind."

"Certainly," Brianna answered crisply, and handed him her card. "I'll be happy to be of assistance."

Oh, I bet you will, Alexia thought, and had to hide her smile behind her hand. Colin seemed slightly amused by her no-nonsense little sister, but his gaze lingered on Brianna's face long enough for Alexia to wonder if there was a bit of an attraction on Colin's side as well.

"Great, then we'll have to set something up," Colin said to Brianna, and nodded.

"I'm here long hours, so it will be easy to do."

After a quick glance around, Colin said, "Maybe in a more relaxed atmosphere than this office to spark some creativity."

Brianna's eyes widened a fraction, but she quickly recovered. "Of course. Excellent suggestion."

Alexia watched the exchange with interest and hoped that Colin wasn't toying with her sister. He wasn't the type—at least she didn't think so—but maybe years of living in California on the motocross circuit had changed him. Fame and money could do that to even the most grounded of people. Alexia hoped it wasn't true of Colin.

"Good," Colin said, and his smile seemed genuine. "I'll check my schedule and we'll set something up real soon." He gave Brianna another warm smile and then turned to Alexia. "Here," he said, and handed her a large envelope. "This is Jayden's training schedule at Extreme Machines. I thought you'd want to come up and watch him work out and get some interview time while he's in his element."

There was nothing Alexia wanted to do less, but she nodded as she took the envelope. "Thanks. When does he plan on getting back?"

"Getting back?" Colin glanced down at his watch. "He's up there as we speak, trying out the new whoops we added."

"What?" Alexia felt a sizzle of alarm. "But he's injured. The whoops will jar his sore shoulder."

Colin shrugged. "You know Jayden. I tried to reason with him, but he seemed to be in a restless mood and wouldn't listen."

"Yeah, I know Jayden. Some things will never change," she remarked with such bitterness that both Colin and Brianna looked at her expectantly. Alexia, however, wasn't about to explain that Jayden had run off that morning when she had foolishly anticipated waking up in his arms. Trying to shift the focus from where she knew they were thinking, Alexia said, "The danger of this sport still blows me away." And so, unfortunately, did Jayden, but she purposefully left that part out.

Colin reached over and put a hand on Alexia's shoulder. "There will always be risk involved in motocross."

Alexia pursed her lips. "Hmm, a gravity-defying extreme sport. Ya think?"

"Just keep an open mind, okay? One of the goals I have at Extreme Machines is to preach using proper equipment and taking safety precautions to the riders, especially the kids. Knowing what you're doing makes all the difference."

Alexia arched an eyebrow while shaking her head, but when she opened her mouth Brianna interrupted. "I'm sure that Alexia will write an excellent series of motocross articles, including the one about Jayden. While of course the danger of the sport will have to be mentioned, she'll focus on the positive impact Extreme Machines will have on Braxton and the surrounding community." Brianna gave Colin a polite, businesslike smile before shooting Alexia a pointed *are you insane?* look.

"Need I remind you both that I'm not the right person to write this story?" She pulled a face at Brianna and then looked up at Colin. "And that's putting it mildly."

"Well, need I remind *you* that Jayden made it clear that he wouldn't let anyone else do it?" Brianna said with such apology that it made Alexia even angrier with Jayden. While Brianna might try to be a tough cookie as editor in chief, Alexia knew it was hard for her sister to force her to do the story.

Alexia thinned her lips. "I don't know what he's trying to prove other than he's still a jerk."

While squeezing Alexia's shoulder, Colin said, "Maybe you should give Jayden a chance. You might not know his motivation as well as you think you do."

"Give him a chance to hurt me again? I don't think so."

Colin remained silent but his level look made Alexia feel a little guilty. She supposed that Jayden really did deserve to know the whole story, but she didn't think she could ever reopen that old wound especially since, right or wrong, she held him at least partially responsible for the accident. The thought hit her that the wound never really healed and never would unless she talked to Jayden about that night, but she pushed it aside.

"Just do me a favor and give it some thought. Jayden has changed, Alexia . . . matured."

"Right," Alexia said tightly, and was having real trouble holding back her emotions. "That's why he . . . ," she began, but then stopped herself.

"Why he what?" Colin asked, and gently shook her shoulder. "If there's something I should know, then tell me."

Alexia forced a smile but knew her eyes were stormy. "No, Colin, there isn't. Let's just say that I should have learned my lesson ten years ago. Jayden still likes to cut and run."

"Alexia . . . just what went down between you two? If he—"

"No." She shook her head firmly and put a hand on Colin's chest. She would never want to ruin the friendship that Jayden and Colin shared. "There's nothing you need to know. Look, I'll do the damned story for Brianna's sake." She glanced over at her sister. "Jayden will leave town soon anyway. I'll just have to gut it out."

"You don't have to," Brianna said.

"Yes, I do," Alexia told them both. "I don't know what game Jayden's playing, but I'm not going to let him win."

"I don't think . . . ," Colin began, but then stopped himself. "I should just go," he said, and gave her shoulder one last squeeze. "Brianna, I'll get back to you soon, okay?"

Alexia watched her sister give him a brisk nod, but then her gaze lingered on Colin while he walked out of the office. Alexia smiled, thinking that her sister was definitely smitten with the shaggy-haired motocross champ. As soon as the door shut, Brianna stood up from behind the desk and said, "Why do I get the feeling there's something—no, make that a lot of things—going on here that I don't know about?"

While Alexia hated the hurt and concern that was evident in Brianna's tone, she didn't want to get into this conversation . . . not now and maybe never. "Oh, Bri, I'm sorry, but I don't want to dredge up the past. I came back to Braxton to move on with my life."

While leaning her hips against the desk, Brianna nibbled on her bottom lip. Finally, after a sigh, she said, "Fair enough. But, Alexia, if you ever need to talk and I mean about anything, you can come to me, okay?"

Alexia leaned over and gave Brianna a quick but fierce hug. "I will, and the same goes for me." Then, to lighten things up, Alexia said, "Colin was looking pretty freakin' hot, don't you think? Could his eyes get any bluer?"

Brianna waved a dismissive hand in the air. "I didn't notice."

"Sure you didn't," she countered. "Admit it, he gives you butterflies."

"He does not!"

"Liar."

Brianna looked at her for a defiant moment. "Okay, the man makes me melt. Are you happy now?"

"Yes."

"Good, now get busy. We have a paper to put out."

"Okay . . ." But when Alexia sat down at her desk to work, thoughts of Jayden filtered into her head and continued to plague her all morning long. When she should have been writing, the memories of the smell of his skin, the warmth of his touch kept distracting her until she finally gave up and called it a day.

As she gathered up her things, she put the envelope that Colin had given her in her leather case. She wondered again just what Jayden was trying to prove by requesting that she write the article . . . but whatever his reasoning, she wasn't about to lose her head where he was concerned ever again. Oh, yeah, she'd be aloof, distant, and deal with him on a strictly professional basis. If he *ever* thought he'd land his sorry self in her bed again, he was sadly mistaken.

"If you think you can still get to me, Jayden Michaels," she muttered as she tossed her leather case into the passenger side of her SUV, "well, then, just bring it on. I'm ready."

Chapter Five

*I*n an effort to blow off steam and get the kinks out after spending hours doing paperwork, Colin hopped on his street bike and raced across the open road, going faster and faster until the passing scenery became nothing more than a passing blur. He grabbed a handful of brake around a hairpin turn, leaning close to the pavement, but when the road straightened out he twisted the grip and hit seventy miles per hour in an instant. He took to the air over a series of hills, allowing the exhilaration of screaming speed, oddly enough, to calm him down.

When he came closer to Braxton, he eased off the throttle and slowed down but couldn't resist popping a wheelie for a passing pickup truck that blew its horn in recognition. Even now riding remained a reprieve from reality, but in his youth taking to the road had been an escape from bickering parents and backbreaking chores on his farm. His mother and father never did take seriously his desire to compete and even now waited for him to grow up and land what they called a *real job*. To his parents, racing had been a waste of time and money, with his dad wanting him to work the farm while his mother preached college. But in the end, their lack of support and faith in him had been Colin's catalyst for winning races. Having never been taken seriously, he had been determined to show them that he could succeed.

But even after he won the National Amateur MX Championship title at Loretta Lynn's ranch in nearby Hurricane Mills, Tennessee, the biggest honor in amateur motocross racing, his parents remained, for the most part, unsupportive. Hurt and angry, Colin had left Braxton for good and struck out on his own. Now he knew that his wild ways, including a nearly naked spread in *Playgirl*, were in rebellion. While the media made him into a superstar stud, and he had played the role well, what he always craved was parental approval.

Colin laughed inside his helmet, thinking that he was in his midthirties and still trying to impress his mother and father. At first he didn't intend to ride all the way back to town, but the urge to see Brianna had him rumbling down Main Street toward the *Braxton Times* office. Sure enough, her sensible little sedan remained parked in front of the old building. As Colin pulled up to the curb he tried to think of an excuse as to why he was dropping in on her. When he couldn't think of anything plausible, he decided he'd have to wing it.

The bell over the door jingled as he entered, drawing Brianna's attention. When she looked up, her eyes widened but she quickly recovered. "Why, hello there."

She greeted him with a soft smile that alone made him glad that he returned. "What brings you here, Colin?"

He hesitated but decided to go with honesty. "I was driving around to blow off steam but I really wanted to see you."

"To talk about the ads?"

"No." He took a step closer to her desk. "I've been thinking about you all day and . . ." He shrugged and ran his fingers through his hair wondering if he was coming on too strong. "Look, if I'm interrupting . . ."

"You are, but I'm grateful for the break." She laughed, a throaty, sexy sound that contrasted with her sweet face.

"Good." He supposed that pulling her to her feet and kissing her senseless wouldn't be wise. But damn, he wanted to.

"I bet you're cold. How about a cup of hot chocolate?"

"That sounds good." He tried to remember if a woman had ever offered him hot chocolate before, and grinned. She was so damned cute that he wanted to gobble her right up. When she scooted from her desk, Colin unzipped his jacket and hung it from a hook on the wall.

"I'll even share my secret stash of Oreos." She produced a bag from beneath the coffeemaker where water was heating up and offered him one.

"Thanks." Colin munched on the cookie while he watched her make the hot chocolate. She had changed from work clothes to hip-hugging white sweatpants and a matching hoodie, and when she bent over he tried without success not to stare at her sexy little ass. He imagined cupping her cheeks and pulling her close, and suddenly didn't need the hot chocolate to warm him up.

"Careful, don't burn your tongue." She handed him the steaming hot chocolate and then picked up her own. When she cradled the cup and blew on the steam, Colin's imagination ran wild. He wondered how something as innocent as drinking hot chocolate could suddenly be an erotic adventure, and tried to reel his wayward thoughts back in. But then, after Brianna took a small sip, she licked a drip from the rim of the cup with the tip of her tongue and he had to swallow a moan.

"Would you like another cookie?"

It took a moment for her question to sink in since he was still thinking about her tongue. When she raised her eyebrows, Colin had the sense to shake his head. "No, I'm good."

Oh, I bet you are, Brianna thought, and fought back a hot shiver. The mug seemed small in his big hands, and she suddenly wondered what those long fingers would feel like against her bare skin. She had been thinking similar thoughts about him all day, interrupting her concentration, which was why she was still at the office. To suddenly have him here in the flesh made her heart beat faster. She gripped the warm mug tighter and tried to come up with something intelligent to say, but the fact that he had been thinking of her as well turned conversation into a challenge. To fill the silence, she tried, "So, how is your hot chocolate?" Okay, that was lame.

"Good."

"Aren't the minimarshmallows cute?" Worse!

"Yeah." He looked down at his mug and nodded,

bless his heart. "What's hot chocolate without marsh-mallows?"

"I like whipped cream too."

"Mmm, so do I."

"Hey," she said brightly, "I think I have a can of it in the minifridge. I drink hot chocolate a lot when I'm here late," she felt the need to add. "Want some?"

He swallowed hard but nodded. "Sure."

"I'll get it," she offered with enthusiasm, and then bent over to open the little door. But as she was retrieving the can of Reddi-Wip she heard Colin clear his throat and realized that in a room already filled with sexual tension, she was introducing a potential sex toy.

Holy cow.

But it was too late to take back her offer, so she straightened up with the can and shook it vigorously before popping the lid off. "Here you go," she said, trying to keep her imagination from running wild, but her brain conjured up a much better place to squirt the frothy concoction, causing her trigger finger to malfunction. "Oh!" Instead of a mere dollop in his cup Collin ended up with a swirling mountain that quickly became the leaning tower of Reddi-Wip. "Sorry! Lick it quick before it lands on your shoes."

Colin complied, lapping the melting froth with quick strokes of his tongue. Brianna watched with a kind of fascination and was a bit disappointed when he had the situation under control.

"Did you do that on purpose?" he asked with a grin.

"No!" she fervently denied, but wished that she had the nerve to do something spontaneously sexy and fun. "I swear." He had a little dollop on his chin. God, how she longed to ease up to her toes and lick it off. "Um, you have some on your chin," she sheepishly informed him, and knew her face was flaming.

"Where?"

"There." She pointed but instead of using his own finger, Colin took her hand in his and used her finger to wipe the cream from his chin.

Colin gazed at her finger as if making a decision. Then, while her heart about thumped out of her chest, he sucked it into his warm mouth and licked the cream off. "Gone?"

Brianna's voice had left the building. All she could manage was a slow nod.

"I should let you get back to work," Colin said in a husky voice that felt like a caress.

She bobbed her head again.

He still held her hand in his but before letting go he kissed her palm. "I'll call you about getting together to discuss the ad."

Another nod.

"Don't work too hard."

She gave him a negative shake this time while thinking that she must resemble a living, breathing bobble-head.

"Lock the door behind me," he advised, and then kissed her lightly on the cheek.

Rooted to the spot, she watched him walk over and tug on his leather jacket. When he reached the front door she finally managed, "Drive carefully, okay?"

He gave her a slow smile. "You bet."

It wasn't until after he left that she looked down at the can of Reddi-Wip that she clutched in her hand. "Holy smokes," she mumbled, and then smiled. Arching her eyebrow at the red and white can, she said, "Someday . . . you and I are gonna have a lot of fun with him."

She watched him rumble away on his motorcycle and let out a long sigh. "And I hope that someday is soon."

$\mathcal{A}$fter a warm-up lap, Jayden decided to go for the maximum amount of speed and really had his bike cooking on the course. The more he had to concentrate on riding, the less he could think about Alexia. He took the next jump as low to the ground as he could, but winced when the tires hit the dirt, causing white-hot pain to shoot up his shoulder, but he gritted it out and kept on riding. But when Alexia filtered back into his brain his front end almost washed out on him just before the sand whoops. "Shit!" He almost pile-drived into the face of a jump but recovered in the nick of time. Knowing he should stop or he would eventually crash, Jayden pushed on for another lap until he lost his concentration again and missed a foot shift. "Damn it!" He bobbled in the dirt and cursed a blue streak.

"Just what the hell kind of stunt are you trying to pull?" Colin yelled as soon as Jayden brought his bike to a stop.

Confused, Jayden removed his goggles and helmet. While pushing back sweat-dampened hair from his forehead, he said, "My shoulder's too messed up to do any stunts. You know that."

"Quit playing dumb-ass with me," Colin growled, and took a threatening step closer. "You know what I'm talking about."

"No, bro, I don't." Jayden tossed his helmet to the grass and raised his gloved hands in the air. "What the hell is up with you, Colin?" He was trying to keep his cool, but a muscle jumped in Colin's clenched jaw, confusing Jayden further. Colin was a fierce, fearless competitor who broke the law of physics by landing a double backflip, earning numerous FMX and MX titles. But off the track he was usually pretty laid-back.

"Did you sleep with Alexia?"

"Did she tell you that?"

"Answer me."

Jayden felt his own anger rise. "I don't have to tell you shit, man."

Colin inhaled a deep breath and blew it out. "What the hell are you trying to do to her, Jayden? Get back at her? Huh? What? You know, I was trying to defend your sorry ass, but maybe I've been wrong about you."

Jayden took his gloves off and tossed them near his helmet. "Are you into Alexia, Colin? Is this what this is all about? I always knew you two had this . . . I don't know . . . *thing*."

Colin raked his fingers through his shaggy hair. "No, dude, not like that. Alexia is like a sister to me. When I talked to her earlier, she admitted that she had seen you and sounded shook-up. I care about her, Jay, and so help me if you hurt her again I'll kick your ass. So, tell me, what the hell are you up to?"

While gazing up at the cloudless blue sky, Jayden

blew out a long breath, which turned to steam into the chill air. He looked back at Colin. "I wish to hell I knew, bro. Ya know, after she married that old son of a bitch I thought I was done caring about her, but *damn* she still has the power to tear me up inside." He pinched the bridge of his nose. "I guess I'm trying to face my fucked-up feelings for her head-on, ya know what I'm sayin'? Do or die or what-the-fuck ever." He picked up a rock and threw it. "It pisses me off that she can still get to me."

"Sounds to me like you still love her."

Jayden looked over at Colin in surprise, but then again his friend always had an uncanny way of reading people. "Yeah, well, like that dumb ass that I am, I probably fucking do, but I want some answers and having Alexia write the story was the only way I could think of to force her into my company." He shrugged. "I know . . . pretty lame."

"Um, I have to warn you that she's not liking it one bit."

"Too damned bad." He picked up another rock and threw it harder.

Colin silently watched the rock land. "But, Jay, what if you find out there really is still something between you two, other than the obvious? In a few weeks you'll be leaving town again to race. Déjà vu? You can't do that to her, bro."

A cool gust of wind lifted Jayden's damp hair from his neck, causing a chill to run down his spine. Or maybe it was the memory of what he had done to Alexia that caused the shiver. Yeah, she had married that old dude, but maybe she wouldn't have had he not run out of town without looking back. In his youthful arrogance he had expected her to follow, and then male pride had kept him from calling her or returning home even though there were times when he ached with missing her. Instead, he had raced like crazy, letting fame and money go to his head. Had he handled the situation differently and not put himself first, what might have happened? Jayden looked over at Colin, who had been his friend and motocross inspiration over the years, and said, "You're right. I let my emotions . . . hell, my damned desire almost get the best of me." He inhaled a deep breath and then said, "I'm going to contact Brianna and call the whole thing off."

"Well, shit!" Colin kicked the dirt with his boot. "Jayden, you can't do that!"

"What the hell, Colin? Isn't this what you wanted?"

"No! Brianna is counting on this interview. You can't back out on her *now*," Colin insisted so forcefully that he actually appeared embarrassed and jammed his hands into his jeans pockets. "It wouldn't be professional on your part," he added in a more normal tone of voice.

"Whoa . . . are you Brianna's knight-in-shining-armor guy too?"

"Shut the hell up."

"Wait a minute . . . you're really into her, aren't you?" Jayden gave Colin a shove.

"I don't know, man. She's, like, in her midtwenties or something. Way, way . . . *way* too young for me," he protested a little too hard.

Jayden laughed. "Brianna? She's been an adult since she was, like, five. Much more mature than her age and a hellava lot more levelheaded than we ever thought of being. I bet she still is," he added with a grin.

Colin rocked back on his boots. "She's just so genuine, you know? Doesn't have a clue how damned sexy she is."

"So you are into her . . ."

"Hell yeah. But there's the age thing and she's so . . ." He shrugged and jammed his hands in his pockets. "I don't know how to explain it. Smart. Driven."

"Sounds like you're describing yourself," Jayden began, but Colin waved him off.

"Me? Smart?"

"Fuck yeah. You gonna ask her out?"

"I want to. She's just so different than I'm used to."

"You mean no agenda? Not some airhead after your money? Dude, give it a shot. Just treat her right. She is a sweetheart. I'd hate to have to kick your ass."

"That's the thing, Jayden. She's girlfriend material . . . not a one-nighter. I don't know, man."

Jayden put his hand on Colin's shoulder. "She's a grown woman. Give her some credit. We're back here in Braxton and have a different outlook on life."

Colin inhaled a deep breath and blew it out. "Yeah. I hope you're right, because if I hurt someone as amazing as Brianna, I'll kick my own ass. You won't have to. So, what are you gonna do about the article?" he asked, changing the subject.

Jayden scraped his fingers through his hair. "You're right, I can't back out. My publicist would have a frickin' cow. I guess I'll let Alexia off the hook and allow Brianna to do the story. Think that will work?" he asked while hoping that Colin would suggest otherwise.

"Yeah, that would be the right thing to do, Jay. Hey, you know, maybe Alexia will do the story anyway."

"Fat chance," he replied, and felt a sense of loss that

his plan was falling through. "Okay, enough talk about chicks. Let's get back out there on the course."

Colin shook his head. "You should rest that shoulder."

"Screw my shoulder. I need some speed." He reached down and retrieved his gloves.

"So, what did you think of the added jumps?"

While tugging on his gloves, Jayden said, "The course is pretty well laid out. The twelve jumps and sharp turns are challenging enough for the seasoned rider, but a novice can still find his rhythm and handle his bike. I was totally digging the straightaway."

"Cool. Anything you think we need to add?"

"Maybe adding some gypsum and sand to improve the texture of the dirt."

"I was thinking the same thing. And I want to eventually add a peewee course and more jumps at the back of the property."

"Awesome ideas. Now let's ride."

Jayden quickly found his rhythm now that the course was becoming more familiar to him. He rode hard, took the straightaway fast, while keeping the jumps as low to the ground as possible in an effort to minimize the jarring pain plaguing his shoulder with each landing. As usual he got in the zone until an hour later when he stepped off the bike and then suddenly felt as if he had hit a brick wall. Luckily, the rustic A-frame on the far end of Extreme Machines property where he was staying had a kick-ass hot tub on the back deck. And that was exactly where he was heading.

"Hey, you wanna come over for a soak in the hot tub and grab a couple of beers?" Jayden asked while trying to flex the kinks from his neck.

"Na," Colin answered after removing his helmet. "I've got a mountain of paperwork to deal with. I'm going to put some ads together for the *Braxton Times* and maybe call Brianna."

Jayden arched an eyebrow.

"Strictly business, dude."

"Sure it is." He gave Colin's shoulder a shove. "All right. Give me a shout if you change your mind. My ass is in for the day."

"Gotcha," Colin said, and gave Jayden a wave as he rode away and headed for the cabin.

After heating up the hot tub, Jayden shed his riding gear. Wrapped in a towel, he headed to the fridge, glanced at the beer with longing but snagged a sports drink instead, thinking that the potassium and electrolytes would help bring his tired and battered body back to life.

Jayden guzzled half of the drink and then padded out to the back deck, noting that the wood was rough and weathered beneath his bare feet. Secluded by dense woods, Jayden didn't have to worry about swim trunks, and after ditching the towel he sank into the gurgling, hot, frothy water. "Ahhhh, damn, this feels good," he mumbled after finding a jet to massage his sore shoulder. Propping his arms up above the water, he leaned his head back and let the swirling water work its magic. After a few bone-melting moments Jayden closed his eyes and was hovering between sleep and thoughts of Alexia when a female scream jarred him awake. "What the hell?"

Jayden blinked, trying to get his bearings in the waning light, thinking he had been dreaming, but another equally loud scream had him scrambling from the water. Hot tubs, though, he quickly found out, were not made to scramble from. "Shit!" Jayden lost his footing on the slippery surface. He flopped sideways on the first step, slamming his leg on the side of the tub, and then landed with a rolling thump on his sore shoulder. "Ouch . . . damn!" Sharp, hot pain snaked down his arm and throbbed in his leg. With a quick intake of breath he ignored his discomfort, pushed to his feet, and ran around the side of the A-frame.

He came to a skidding stop in the cold, damp grass. "Alexia?"

"Jayden!" Her mouth formed a big O and her eyes widened. She pointed and said, "Y-y-ou're naked!" She glanced down and then quickly raised her eyes to his face.

Moot point, Jayden thought, since she had already seen him up close and personal, but he somehow didn't think this was the time to point that out. "Thank you. I hadn't realized until you happened to notice," he commented dryly, but then did his own quick glance down and thanked God he didn't have a boner from his earlier thoughts of her. "Yep, I'm naked as a jaybird. The real question is, why are you *here*, followed closely with why were you screaming bloody murder?"

"Oh!" Her face turned a pretty shade of pink. "There was a . . . frightening, um, big, hairy, beady-eyed . . . scary thing that spooked me."

"Big and hairy?" he asked skeptically while rubbing his shoulder.

"Yes." Her chin came up and she wiggled her fingers. "But forget about it. No big deal."

"You screamed like the hounds of hell were after you."

"I was taken by surprise," she said defensively.

Jayden would have smiled if he hadn't been naked and starting to freeze . . . Oh, crap, he was going to shrivel up to nothing! He looked toward the trees, barely resisting the urge to cover his package, or what there was of it. Thank God the sun was starting to set, Jayden thought, but really wanted to get his towel. He tried not to shiver like a girl, and said through clenched teeth, "Well, I guess you scared the big, hairy, beady-eyed scary thing off. You sure startled me. Um, this scary thing didn't happen to be a mouse, did it?"

Alexia pulled her gaze back from the woods as if looking for more beady eyes. "Oh, okay, *yes*. But hey, he ran right in front of me! I was a little spooked, okay? And you know there are black bears in these parts too. Have you forgotten that?"

When she reached up to brush a lock of hair from her eyes, Jayden noticed that her hands trembled and decided to cut her some slack. He suddenly recalled that although she loved the outdoors, wild animals used to freak her out, even little ones like field mice. "Hey, you wanna come inside for a drink or something?" When her eyes widened he wished he hadn't said the *or something* part.

"Um . . ."

"I promise to put clothes on."

"Oh . . . w-well . . ." When she made the mistake of looking down again Jayden had a very hard time not covering himself.

What brought her here anyway?

"Alexia? Is there something I can do for you?" Okay, that sounded suggestive, especially given his lack of clothing. He reached up and threaded his fingers through his cold, wet hair. "I mean . . . is there something you wanted?" *Well, shit.* He lowered his hands, nonchalantly covering as much as he could, which was pretty doggone much given the chill circumstances. This wasn't going well at all, and to make matters worse he just couldn't hold back a girly little shudder. He started to backpedal toward the towel.

"Oh, you're cold!"

"Uh, yeah, I'm sorta naked."

She frowned. "Why?"

"It's Naked Day in Braxton. Didn't you get the memo?"

"Um . . . no." For a second he thought she was going to smile and a part of him wanted her to smile . . . to laugh. She used to laugh all the time.

"Too bad," he said, trying again.

Instead of smiling, she sucked her bottom lip between her teeth and nibbled. God, she looked sexy in low-slung jeans and a snug hooded sweater. If his balls hadn't been starting to frost over, he just might have gotten other ideas.

"I—I should go. I shoved an envelope under your front door. Sorry that I screamed."

Somehow that ticked him off even though he had no real reason to be angry. But come on, she had left something knowing full well he was there? It managed to hurt that she wanted to avoid him that much. Okay, it was a bit awkward after what had happened, he'd give her that, but still . . . "Okay, Alexia, but I'm freezing my ass off . . . literally. I'm going inside." He turned and started walking back to the hot tub.

"Ohmigod, you're bleeding!"

"What?"

"I swear, Jayden, you're bleeding!" She stepped closer. "Ohmigod, did you injure your sore shoulder? It's scraped."

Jayden reached down and wrapped the towel around his waist. "It's nothing."

"Let me see!"

"No!" He knew it was stupid, but he hated showing her weakness yet again.

"You're hurt!"

"No!" Jayden said, and cringed when he realized that he sounded like a little kid. "I'm fine," he added more calmly as he slid open the glass door and entered the blessed warmth.

"Oh, like I haven't heard *that* before. Sure you are." She followed him inside. She narrowed her eyes at him and said, "I'm not leaving until you show me your shoulder."

Jayden swallowed and although he considered taking a step back, he held his ground. She wasn't very big but could be a force to be reckoned with when she got fired up. He used to like getting her fired up . . .

"What happened anyway?"

"After you screamed, I fell getting out of the hot tub."

"Oh . . ." She gave him a so-that's-why-you-were-naked look that turned to a guilty wince. "Sorry about your luck, but that stupid rodent scared the daylights out of me. His eyes were *beady*." She shivered at the memory.

"It's okay. Don't worry, I'll live," he said casually, but the statement hung heavy in the air between them. It was the first thing he had said to her after his near-fatal motorcycle crash, which prompted her to make him choose between her and his career. When their eyes met, Jayden knew that she remembered too, but Alexia's eyes suddenly turned stormy and she abruptly looked away. For a horrible moment Jayden feared that she might cry, and he wanted to pull her into his arms and hold her close. It hit him then how poorly he had handled things all those years ago, and he wanted to finally tell her how sorry he was. "Alexia . . . ," he began, but when she lifted her gaze to his face he didn't know how to convey his feeling and the words he longed to say were left unspoken.

"Let me check out your shoulder," she said gruffly. "You're scraped and bleeding. Do you have a first aid kit?"

"Probably," he answered as he reached down to secure the loose towel tighter around his waist. He didn't want to remind her that his lodging was temporary and he didn't know where everything was located.

"Hydrogen peroxide?"

"I guess," he said, but then backpedaled. "Look, I'll be fine," he insisted, but then grabbed his shoulder when hot fingers of pain clawed at his injury.

"If I can't take a look, then perhaps I should just drag you to the hospital."

"I'm not going to the hospital," he scoffed, and dropped his hand from his shoulder, but then realized that he was caught between the proverbial rock and a hard place. And speaking of hard place, Jayden was starting to react to the smell of her perfume, the feminine curve of her neck, and a soft-looking lock of golden hair that kept brushing against her cheek. There shouldn't be anything so ultimately sexy about a sweatshirt and jeans, but Jayden had the urge to unzip her hoodie and cup his hands over her soft curves.

"Well, then?" Alexia shrugged and folded her hands over her chest as if reading his thoughts. "Lead me to the bathroom."

Jayden hesitated but then realized he should probably have the scrape attended to since he didn't want an infection and it was burning like hell. The last thing he needed was more shoulder problems. "Okay," he muttered darkly. His upper thigh hurt like hell too and he hoped he hadn't pulled a groin muscle.

"I promise to be gentle." Alexia's lips twitched and for a moment Jayden thought she might actually smile, but she cleared her throat and remained stoic. He wondered if she would ever let down her guard against him, and he realized in that moment that it was important to him that she did. She used to be so carefree and uninhibited, and now she seemed wary and tense. Life had obviously dealt her some blows, and that knowledge clawed at his heart. He wished that she would open up and tell him about her marriage.

"This way," he said, and padded across the nubby Berber carpet leading to the short hallway. The rustic A-frame cabin was a bit worn, but the slight musty smell was finally gone, replaced by the woodsy scent of the fireplace mixed with outdoor pine. Although it wasn't luxurious, Jayden was coming to enjoy the quiet, peaceful setting that was such a contrast to his fast-paced lifestyle. For the first time he contemplated that settling down wouldn't be so bad.

A sudden vision of him and Alexia curled up in front of a crackling fire while sipping brandy went through his head . . . not that he ever sipped brandy, and it was a romantic image that he shouldn't even be considering . . . but then *why not?* slammed into his brain. Perhaps he should stop fighting his feelings for Alexia and explore them instead. After all, how many times do you get the chance to make something right that you screwed up so royally the first time? Didn't they owe it to each other to at least try?

Jayden stopped in his tracks in front of the bathroom door and his heart pounded when the realization hit him that he would never be content with his life if he didn't at least attempt to win Alexia back. Jayden knew because of their past that she would fight him tooth and nail, but facing a challenge had never been a problem for him.

"Are we going to stand here in the hallway all day?" Alexia asked from behind him. "Let's just get this over with, Jayden."

"You're right," Jayden announced while pushing the wooden door open and flicking on a bright light. "Why fight the inevitable?"

"Now you're talking," she said in that matter-of-fact tone that he was going to change.

"And I hope you're listening." When she gave him an odd look, he merely smiled, knowing that he meant something entirely different from tending to his shoulder. He wanted emotion from her . . . and by God, one way or another, he was going to get it.

"Okay, now let's get a good look at that shoulder," Alexia said briskly while trying not to dwell on how amazing he looked wrapped in nothing but a towel. She tried even harder not to think of what was beneath the fluffy white cotton that contrasted with his golden skin.

He had a gorgeous, defined chest covered with a wedge of dark hair over his pecs that narrowed nicely to an enticing happy line heading south.

When Alexia realized where her thoughts were heading, she pushed past Jayden, hoping that her hardened nipples didn't show through her sports bra and hoodie. Her intention had been to drop off some interview questions for Jayden to look over and then hightail it out of there before he even knew she was around. Well, so much for *that* plan, she thought with a sigh.

Alexia entered a rather spacious bathroom that had been updated with a double sink and an open tiled shower stall. She glanced over at another door that stood ajar to the master bedroom, revealing a bed that was rumpled and unmade, but instead of messy it somehow seemed intimate and sexy.

When Jayden cleared his throat from behind her, Alexia wondered if his imagination was heading in the same direction. She quickly averted her gaze and prayed not to blush, but the visions she suddenly had in her head were hot enough to set her hair on fire. She eyed the sink but she supposed that blotting her forehead with a cool washcloth would be a dead giveaway, and she wanted to keep her wayward thoughts hidden from Jayden at all costs.

After rummaging around in a linen closet, Jayden reached to the top shelf and retrieved a small first aid kit. "Here you go," he offered, but looked a bit nervous.

While hiding a smile, Alexia popped the lid and was glad to see the stuff she would need. While she wouldn't wish bodily harm on him . . . well, and really mean it . . . she couldn't help but get a little satisfaction from his embarrassment. After he left her bed without so much as a *see ya later*, he could use a little humiliation. "Fool me once . . . ," she murmured under her breath with a slight shake of her head.

"Excuse me?" Jayden's dark eyebrows rose in question.

"Um . . . I said, let me see that scrape."

"Okay." He did as ordered. Their eyes met in the mirror.

"You're too tall. You'll have to lean against the sink."

"No problem." He cut a fierce figure with his long, dark hair, lean, muscled physique, and armband tattoo. Alexia thought that he looked as if he belonged on the cover of a historical romance novel, wielding a sword. The image struck her as funny and she almost smiled. Then, just as quickly, sadness washed over her when she recalled the days when she had shared her innermost thoughts with him. Jayden had been the only one who truly understood her quirky sense of humor and the way she viewed things a little off center.

God, how she missed that connection and wondered if it would be the same with him now. Of course first she would have to find her sense of humor, which had been lost for quite a while.

"Alexia?"

"Hmm?" she asked, and was embarrassed when she looked at his half-naked reflection in the mirror. Although she carefully kept her gaze on his face, Alexia felt the familiar stirrings of desire and had to physically squelch the urge to run her hands up his chest and feel his warm skin and silky chest hair beneath her fingers. She fisted her hands at her sides and inhaled a deep breath.

"Now what do you want me to do?" he asked, and had the nerve to sound suggestively sexy.

"Oh . . ." Alexia had so many delicious answers to that burning question, but then she reminded herself he wasn't her romance novel hero and she sure as hell wasn't a damsel in distress . . . well, strike that . . . she was sort of in distress, at the moment anyway, and come to think of it, being rescued and whisked off into the sunset certainly had its appeal. Alexia swallowed a groan. Too bad she gave up on fairy tales and happily-ever-after a long time ago. *Yeah, screw that notion.*

Alexia inhaled a deep breath in an effort to clear her head. She really needed to patch him up before getting the hell out of there. Jayden Michaels represented pain, regret, and heartbreaking loss. In fact, the scrape on his shoulder wasn't too bad. Perhaps she should just let him tend to himself, she thought . . . but then his towel gaped open.

"Ohmigod, Jayden!" She picked up the edge of his towel and peeked beneath.

"Hey," he protested, "what are you doing?"

"We need to take care of that."

Chapter Seven

"*T*ake care of what?" When his eyes widened at her she let the towel drop back in place.

"Jayden, you have a really nasty scrape on your upper thigh. Doesn't it hurt?" Although Alexia put on a brave front, she really wasn't very good at anything remotely medical. The mere sight of blood had her dinner doing a tap dance in her stomach.

Jayden gingerly rubbed his thigh and winced. "I must have done that when I hopped out of the hot tub. Actually, I'm glad. I felt a burn and I was afraid it was a pulled groin muscle."

"I should clean you up and get some antiseptic on that." She rummaged around in the first aid kit. "Looks like you have what I need," she said, and then felt a blush coming on at the implications of her innocent comment, or then again perhaps it was a slip of the tongue. She had gotten a pretty good peek beneath the towel. Clearing her throat, she removed a pack of antibiotic towelettes. "It might sting a little." Or a lot . . .

and inflicting pain on him had her hands trembling. She caught her bottom lip between her teeth and then looked up at him. "Ready?" When he nodded, she opened the packet and decided to start with the abrasion on his shoulder, which was raw but thankfully not bleeding much. But when she gently dabbed at it, he flinched and pulled away with a hiss. "Sorry, did that hurt?"

"Not really, but it was cold!"

Cold? And here she thought he had hurt him. "Oh, suck it up!" she said more sharply than she had intended, but she was becoming frustrated in more ways than one.

"Your bedside manner leaves a little to be desired," he said in a joking tone, but hit a little too close to home.

"Yeah, well, so does yours!" Alexis blurted out without thinking. Their eyes met in the mirror and Alexia felt seriously close to crying . . . and it pissed her off that he still had that power over her.

He should not have that power! Unable to help herself, she glared at him.

"I shouldn't have left like that," Jayden quietly admitted.

His confession was unexpected and sounded so sincere that the urge for Alexia to cry became stronger, so she clung to her anger like a suction cup. "Ya *think*?" she tried to spit out, but the emotion clogging her throat made her reply come out a croak. Embarrassed, she looked away. "It doesn't matter."

"Yes, it does," Jayden firmly disagreed.

Surprised even more, Alexia looked back at him with wide eyes while her heart pounded. She wondered if he was referring to the first time he left her as well. Sudden hope spread like warm honey in her chest, but then she became annoyed for getting sucked back in by Jayden again. Would she ever learn? *He'll just leave me again*, she thought. With a lift of her chin, she turned her attention back to his shoulder. "If you say so," she muttered as she gently dabbed at the scrape. His body stiffened at her offhand remark, and she felt a bit rotten at her callous response but knew she had to use her anger as a shield or leave herself exposed and vulnerable. After gently blotting the blood she reached down and picked up the little tube of ointment.

With his head bent, Jayden watched her but remained quiet while she smoothed the salve over his raw skin. Alexia tried to keep her concentration on her task, but his warm breath tickled her cheek and the heat from his body had other thoughts sneaking into her brain. It didn't help that the towel gaped again, exposing a muscled thigh while barely shielding his package. When she averted her eyes, her slippery fingers brushed over his nipple and he sucked in a breath making Alexia wonder if he was becoming aroused as well. "I, um, need to tend to your . . . other area." She looked at him and felt such a strong pull of desire that she almost couldn't fight the urge to press her lips to his.

"Okay." His voice, soft, husky, washed over Alexia like a warm caress. They both knew that he could take care of his injuries himself, and it was as if they were using this as an excuse for her to stay with him . . . to touch him. He parted the towel farther and bent his knee, exposing the nasty scratch.

"I'm sorry the stupid mouse made me scream. A

doggone bear wouldn't have spooked me as much." She rolled her eyes.

Jayden nodded and then grinned. "I remember . . . mice and spiders scare the crap out of you."

"And bats!"

"Yeah, and bats." His smile deepened and she knew he was recalling incidents, most of which involved making love outdoors. They had shared such passion, passion that Alexia knew still burned deep within them. All she needed to do was lean in and kiss him and that same passion would explode . . .

Which was why she should go. *Now!*

But she simply couldn't.

Alexia opened another antiseptic towelette, but this time she warned him. "Remember, this is going to be cold."

After he nodded she gently washed and disinfected the scrape while trying not to inflict too much discomfort. She got through that part, but when she applied the salve her fingers gently rubbing his skin made her feel warm and tingly. She licked her bottom lip and tried not to think about what was beneath the soft white cotton just inches away, but when the bulge beneath got bigger, Jayden shifted, causing the towel to gape and expose way too much.

"Oh!" Alexia tried to cover him but tugged too hard. The knot at his waist gave way and suddenly Jayden's package was totally on display. Alexia got quite an eyeful including the sexy moon-and-stars tattoo. "Oh," she said again, and tried to cover him, but her bare hand brushed against the hard length of his dick. "S-sorry." She quickly withdrew her hand.

"Don't be." The husky timbre of his voice had her looking into his eyes. He gently took her hand and after kissing her palm said, "Touch me, Alexia."

"No."

"Why not?" His eyes searched her face. "Why fight this?"

She could name several reasons but her brain held them all hostage. When she hesitated, he took her hand and guided it to his hard length. With a sigh, Alexia enclosed her fingers around him and closed her eyes. He felt hot and hard and powerful beneath her cool hand. She knew she should withdraw, but when he moaned, Alexia moved her hand up and down, watching while he grew hotter and harder. When a pearly drop of pre-come appeared, she swirled the silky wetness over his head with her fingertip.

"God . . . ," Jayden groaned, and leaned back while gripping the edge of the sink. "Alexia . . ."

Inhaling a shaky breath, she hesitated once more, wanting him so much—and yet giving in to her desire meant risking her heart. Although she was trying so hard to restart her life, she was still too shell-shocked to offer him anything more than something physical . . . but she wasn't sure if she was capable of giving her body while withholding her love.

When Alexia stopped caressing him and went very still, Jayden gazed down at her. Knowing that he shouldn't but unable not to . . . he drew her into his arms and covered her mouth with his. She stiffened but then sighed and wrapped her arms around his neck and kissed him back with . . . the word that came to mind was *gusto*. He felt a surge of elation, the same as if he had just secured the hole shot at a race, but instead of adrenaline he felt a warm rush of desire. Threading his fingers through her soft hair, he slanted his mouth over hers, kissing her deeply. She tasted of mint and woman, hot and sweet. Their tongues met, swirled, tangled, and he drank her in until his head was spinning.

Jayden remembered her hot spots and decided now was the time to use every one of them and find new ones. Reluctantly pulling his lips from hers, he brushed her hair to the side and started a moist trail of kisses down her neck. She inhaled softly and tilted her head, giving him better access. Bold now, he tugged her shirt from her pants and slid his hands up her warm, soft skin while licking, nibbling, and sucking her earlobe until she moaned and pressed her body closer to his.

He cupped her ass, pushing her into his erection, and ground gently against her mound, wanting desperately to be buried deep inside her. Sliding his hands beneath her waistband, he sucked in a breath when he encountered barely-there lace and firm, silky skin. He kneaded her ass cheeks, pressing her even closer until he was so turned on that he trembled.

"Alexia, I want you," he whispered in her ear. "Let's go to bed."

"No," she replied, and his heart sank. "I want to stay in here."

"In here?" When she nodded, Jayden pulled back and looked down at her, but she avoided his gaze. He understood what she was saying. She would give him sex . . . but nothing more. He hesitated. He didn't want to fuck her; he wanted to make love to her. "Okay," he answered, trying to sound indifferent when he was hurt and a little angry. The anger was directed at himself for this weakness. Part of him wanted to turn her away, not accept her offer of hot sex and a cold heart, but he couldn't . . . because he loved her.

He loved her. It was evident. It was obvious. There was no sense denying it. And he was going to do everything in his power to win her back. He just couldn't let her know it. "If that's what you want . . ."

She nodded but looked down at the floor. He wasn't sure if she was trying to punish herself or him, but he was going to turn this into something different from what she expected . . . or at least try to.

"Alexia . . ." When she wouldn't look at him, Jayden tilted her head up. His intention was to kiss her tenderly to show her that he could make love to her even in a damned bathroom, but as if reading his mind, and she used to be good at that, she pulled his head down and kissed him hard, almost roughly.

Jayden held back, trying to kiss her slow and easy. She would have none of it and pulled his head closer, sucking his tongue, nipping at his bottom lip, kissing him wildly until Jayden's control snapped. He pushed her up against the wall, grinding against her with his bare, fully aroused body.

"The clothes gotta go," he growled into her ear, and then reached down to yank her jeans to her ankles. Holy shit . . . she had on a black thong that was a mere patch of silk with lace sides. Breathing hard, he tugged her hoodie from her arms and made quick work of her T-shirt and sports bra. He stepped back and drank in the sight of her mussed hair, swollen lips, flushed skin. Her breasts were full, firm with dusky pink nipples. She was rounded, *curved*, and standing there in nothing but the black thong she was his every fantasy in the flesh.

"You're gorgeous, Alexia. Baby, let me take you to bed."

"Why?" she asked in a husky but firm voice. "So you can leave me again?" Her eyes widened as if she wished she hadn't said that, but she held his gaze instead of looking away.

Jayden paused. He wanted to argue that it would be difficult to leave his own place, but she was a bundle of emotion and he knew that arguing would be pointless. It also occurred to him that unless she cared she wouldn't be so damned upset. He latched on to that thought and decided, for now anyway, to give her what she thought she wanted. He would fuck her senseless, make her come over and over until she was a quivering mass of sensation unable to walk, talk, or think.

Then he would carry her to his bed and hold her close for the rest of the night.

"Okay, lean against the wall and spread your legs for me." He would give her what she was asking for, but end up getting what he wanted in the end . . . he hoped.

With wide luminous eyes, Alexia did as he requested. She knew she was teetering on the edge of falling right back in love with him, but she was determined to keep her heart and body separate from each other. She'd give in to the exquisite pleasure of having sex with him, but keep her emotions under lock and key. No bed . . . no sweet tender words.

Just hot, amazing sex. That, she needed, craved, and she could handle . . . Well, maybe.

When Jayden leaned his hard, naked body closer, Alexia closed her eyes, thinking he was going to kiss her, but instead he said hotly in her ear, "Turn around, and put your palms in the air and lean your entire body against the wall."

She nodded. "Okay." Her heart pumped hard and her legs suddenly felt weak. The wall felt shockingly cool against her flushed skin and sensitive nipples. She knew that Jayden knelt down, but, unable to see what he was doing, she shivered in anticipation . . . and then she felt the damp tip of his tongue on her bare ass. He licked in circles and then blew on her damp cheeks, causing chill bumps to rise. He replaced the cool sensation with the heat of his mouth, kissing, nibbling, and then rubbing his rough stubble against her skin, lightly abrading, until she was squirming against the wall. With his teeth, he toyed with her lace thong, tugging, licking, and then parting her cheeks with his hands so that she was open and exposed. She could feel the moist warmth of his breath, the prickle of his five-o'clock shadow, replaced by the softness of his long hair brushing across her ass. She was hot, she was cold, and melting from the inside out . . .

Without warning he slipped his middle finger beneath her thong and into her wet heat. "God, you feel so good," he growled as he moved his finger oh so slowly in and out. Alexia gasped, but when she tried to turn around he put a gentle hand to the small of her back. "Stay there."

Her answer was a whimper.

He removed the thong with his teeth and then replaced his finger with the head of his penis. He teased, toyed, guiding his cock between her thighs. Desperate, with her hands firmly against the wall, Alexia perched her ass outward in blatant invitation. He teased with his hand, his dick, his mouth, and then . . . God help her . . . *his tongue.* Alexia moaned and then gasped when he stood up straight and covered her with the heat of his body.

"I want you," he said low and hot into her ear while rubbing his skin against hers.

"Then take me," she shamelessly offered, but when she tried to turn around, he pressed her against the wall. The smooth paint was a cool contrast to the heat of his body, making her want to turn around even more to warm her chilled skin. She shivered, both hot and cold at the same time. "Jayden . . . ," she pleaded when he scooted her to where the wall was even colder.

"Alexia, do I need protection?" he asked.

His question went straight to her soul, but she gave him a negative shake of her head. "Not necessary," she answered, letting him assume she was on birth control . . . oh, how she wished that she needed to be. Pushing that crushing thought to the back of her brain, she shivered again and was desperate to turn around into his warmth and melt into his body. Instead, he kissed her neck, her shoulders while his dick, hot and hard, pressed against her back.

Frustrated now, Alexia bucked and squirmed. "Let me turn around, damn you!" She arched her back and pushed hard until without warning he turned her around and entered her with a deep, delicious stroke. "God . . ." The heat of his body against her cold skin was shockingly wonderful and the coolness against her back was welcome. He stood very still as if savoring being inside her.

Then, bending his head, he took one nipple into his hot mouth and then moved to the other, licking, sucking, and nipping lightly until her breath came in short gasps. Alexia arched her back away from the wall, seeking more and more of his mouth, more of his dick. She threaded her fingers through his long hair, pushing him closer, filling his mouth. With a groan he pulled back and then kissed her with such passion that Alexia had to wrap her arms around his neck for support. While his tongue swirled, sucked, and licked, he moved slowly . . . almost all the way out and then back as far and as deep as he could possibly go.

While the slow, easy strokes were deliciously erotic, she wanted harder, faster . . . "Jayden . . . ," she pleaded.

"Mmm . . . yeah?" Knowing what Alexia needed, he lifted her left leg and wrapped it around his waist. "Press your shoulders against the wall," he instructed, and then with his other hand beneath her ass he arched her hips upward and pumped hard, fast, giving her what she needed, craved.

"Ohhh . . ." Desire coiled tighter and tighter until it was almost painful. Alexia needed release but held on, wanting to come with him. She tangled her fingers in his hair and pulled his mouth to hers, but when his tongue touched hers she became undone and spiraled out of control. Her climax was achingly sharp, reaching, grasping, and then it exploded in blinding intensity.

When Jayden arched his back and buried his dick deep, she felt him pulse and then violently come with a hot rush that had her wrapping her leg around his waist tighter. She arched up, took him in, and kissed him hard while squeezing every last drop from his dick. This felt so good, so right that a voice in the back of her brain whispered that there would never be anyone for her but this man.

Jayden stayed inside her and turned the hard kiss into something gentle and sweet that touched her in a way that she had not experienced since . . .

Since the last time she had been with him.

Noooo . . . She wanted him to pull out so that she could run away from these intense feelings that were gloriously wonderful but scary as hell. As if sensing her withdrawal, he threaded his fingers with hers above her head and continued to kiss her gently, sucking emotion from somewhere deep within her soul that had been buried for a long, long time. She ached with the beauty of it, but if anything it made the urge to run away even stronger.

But he would not let her.

Instead, he took one hand from the wall and placed her palm over his heart in a tender gesture made more powerful by the fact that Alexia knew that this wasn't something that came easily to him. A sob rose in her throat, but he kissed it away while the sure, steady beat of his heart sent a silent but powerful message.

He loved her.

And by God, *she loved him*.

But it terrified her because she didn't know if she could ever forgive him.

Chapter Eight

Jayden could feel the cold blast of her fear as if it were breathing down his neck. Damn! He wanted to kick himself in the ass for letting his emotions get the best of him. Putting her hand to his heart? What was he thinking? She probably thought it was some cheesy ploy, but he meant it. He loved her and if she asked him to walk away from racing . . . by God he would. He couldn't imagine that he would do that for anyone for any reason, but the intensity of his feelings for her was that powerful. He could not, would not lose her again. Before he could stop himself, he tilted her head up, looked into her eyes, and said, "I'll walk away."

Her blue eyes widened and then she swallowed. After a moment her lips trembled but she said, "I understand. You should. There's just too much hurt between us, Jayden."

"Wait . . ." Jayden began realizing that she had gotten the opposite message of what he had intended, but she was on a roll and wouldn't stop.

"You shouldn't walk. You should run."

"That's not—"

"I'm carrying some pretty heavy baggage from my divorce mixing in with our already messy past," she continued as her eyes darted longingly to her clothes. "Oh, right, this is your place. I get to run this time," she added with a nervous little laugh that sounded too close to a sob for Jayden's comfort.

"Alexia—"

"Listen, I brought a list of questions for you to go over for the interview. Let me know when you want to begin," she added, and tugged at her hands, which were suspended above her head, but Jayden refused to release her. She might be afraid, and something told him she was withholding something from him. He could see it in her eyes, so he decided not to tell her that he meant that he would walk away from racing . . . not from *her*. But it was too soon and he needed to back off since it was obvious that she was scared shitless. Someday he would get her to tell him everything about her failed marriage and whatever baggage she was referring to. But there was one thing that was still amazing between them that she couldn't deny and couldn't resist.

Sex.

And he wasn't above using it to his advantage.

"Jayden, let me go."

"No."

"What do you mean . . . *no*?" She tugged at her wrists.

Instead of releasing her, he moved one hand over so that he had her wrists captive in one of his hands, leaving the other one free to roam over her soft, supple skin . . . and so he did. Slowly, pausing here and there.

"What are you doing?" She tried to glare but her

eyes dilated and her breath started to come in shallow gasps.

"Touching you. I love the feel of your skin."

"Well . . ." She paused to gasp when he caressed the tender skin of her inner thigh. "Q-quit. I mean it," she insisted but in a breathless voice that lacked conviction.

"Really?" he asked with his mouth a mere fraction from her lips.

"Yes!" she said, but gasped when he bent his head and took one dusky nipple into his mouth. He circled his tongue and then sucked before rubbing his rough cheek over her sensitive skin. She squirmed and arched her back away from the wall. "Stop!"

"Okay," Jayden agreed, but he wasn't about to let her go until he had turned her every which way but loose. "In a minute . . ." He needed to have her coming back for more until he broke through the icy barricade she had erected around her heart. He did, however, loosen his hold so that she could easily break away if she truly wanted to, but she didn't seem to notice.

When she leaned her head to the side and sighed, he nuzzled her neck, licked the outer shell of her ear, and then captured her mouth with a hot, searing kiss. When she moaned into his mouth, he knew what he wanted to do . . . he wanted her to see how beautiful she was when she climaxed.

"Come with me," Jayden said low in her ear.

Alexia nodded, giving up all pretense of resisting. But when she thought he was going to pull her into his bedroom, he moved her in front of the bathroom mirror. "Wh-what are you doing?"

"Watch . . . look at us." Jayden stood behind her and cupped her breasts like a push-up bra before sliding down her rib cage to her abdomen. Her belly quivered when his long middle finger parted her lips and dipped into her warm, silky wetness. He brushed her hair to the side and kissed her neck while caressing her with lazy rolling circles.

Alexia was helpless to look away. The sight of Jayden's big hands roaming over her body was so erotic . . . almost as if she were watching someone else except that she was feeling each and every bone-melting sensation. His finger worked magic, dipping in for more sweet liquid before returning to his task.

"Reach up and lock your hands around my neck," Jayden requested, and Alexia was helpless to resist . . . Besides, she thought that any minute now her knees might give way, so she did as he asked. "God, you are so gorgeous. So damned sexy. Now watch and let your-self go . . ."

Alexia's eyes widened when she witnessed Jayden reach around her waist and part her sex to fully expose her pink folds. "Jayden . . ." She glanced up and saw him looking at her in the mirror.

She was shamelessly open, exposed, ripe, *ready*. But instead of feeling embarrassed, she felt sexy, powerful, and more aroused than she thought was possible. Her whole body felt alive and she was powerless to resist. He suddenly sank his finger deep and then caressed her intimately, slow and easy, while they watched.

With his long hair and his armband tattoo, he was fiercely masculine in contrast to her feminine curves. He took his time as if savoring the feel of her skin and spoke softly in her ear, whispering words of passion. He was right. Watching his long fingers dipping into her and then swirling, caressing . . . was beautiful and erotic beyond reason. When her climax washed over her, it was shockingly and achingly intense. Her mouth opened in a silent cry that ended in a throaty "God . . ."

"Look how lovely you are," he said in a low whisper that almost sounded as if he were inside her head, speaking directly into her brain so that it would be stuck there forever. She gazed at her flushed body and for the first time in a long while she saw the beauty instead of the flaws. Jayden's strong arms circled her waist and held her tight. She lowered her gaze from his warm brown eyes . . . eyes that saw too much and questioned more. Oh, there were scars from the inside out but for now she chose not to think of them and let herself just get lost in the moment.

Sex, just sex, Alexia thought. *Let this be nothing more.* Of course she knew she was lying, deluding herself, but he didn't have to know that.

"I want you in my bed," he said.

Although Alexia didn't want the intimacy of his bedroom, her legs were giving out and she was oh *so* depleted. She nodded without looking up and stumbled after him. He held on to her hand and she wondered if he thought she might take flight and run. She should. But the soft mattress, fluffy feather pillows, and snuggly comforter felt cozy and wonderful next to her body that still hummed with satisfaction. "I should go," she mumbled, more to herself than to him, but her eyes closed as soon as her head rested against the crisp cotton, heaven help her, that smelled like *him*. But instead of fighting it, she inhaled deeply and tucked her hands beneath the pillow with a long, blissful sigh.

Alexia's eyes fluttered shut until he eased into the bed beside her. Her body immediately tensed and she had the urge to scramble from the bed, but her heavy limbs resisted.

"Hey, just relax," he said in a low, soothing voice. "Get some rest."

"Okay," she whispered, but of course didn't relax one little bit. How could she with Jayden lying naked right behind her just inches away? She could feel the warmth of his body, the tickle of his breath on her neck, and she longed for him to pull her into his arms and hold her against his body. But he didn't. He probably thought she would jump up and run if he did. With her eyes wide open, she stared into the muted darkness for who knows how long. She was just about to get up and leave when he made some sort of noise, a cross between a growl and a sigh, and then wrapped his arm around her and held her close.

He didn't say a word but buried his face against her neck as if saying, "I just couldn't help myself."

The tension oozed from her muscles like whipped cream into hot chocolate. But if she thought the sex was amazing . . . well, this was even better. It felt so good to be held like this that she couldn't suppress another sigh. She could feel his smile and he hugged her even closer. Still, they didn't speak as if fearing that it would break the spell, this tentative truce that they both needed for just a little while.

Alexia closed her eyes and drank him in like a dry sponge to water . . . Once stiff and brittle, she now felt soft, full. She snuggled into him, loving his warmth, his strong arms, and the way he smelled of musky cologne and man. The scent of sex lingered between them, awakening languid desire . . . but first she needed sleep and soon drifted off into a deep slumber.

* * *

Alexia was sleeping so innocently, so blissfully that the nightmare took her by surprise. She hadn't had it in a while and fought hard to wake up, but couldn't. As always, it happened in murky slow motion as if she were underwater trying to swim . . . fighting for breath, wanting to surface and take in gulps of air. But the nightmare gripped her, held her down, sucking out her oxygen and filling her with terror . . .

Rain was pouring down in windy waves, pounding on the hood of her car and lashing against her windshield. Alexia knew she should pull over but she was too distraught to think straight, so she drove on in the blinding storm. Jayden had left town without so much as a good-bye and he didn't know . . . She had to catch up with him to tell him the news, to plead once again to stop racing for the sake of their child. She placed a protective hand over her abdomen and her alarm grew, quickly sliding into panic. She squinted her eyes in search of a place to ease off the road when her cell phone rang. Alexia reached over and pulled her purse onto her lap and instinctively reached for the ringing phone.

She glanced down at the glowing screen. "Jayden . . . ," she said, and in that brief, distracted moment, lost control of the car.

"No!" she screamed, pushing hard on the brakes, fighting for control as she headed on a bumpy, bone-jarring course directly for a tree. Putting her hands in front of her eyes, she waited for the crushing impact but thank God, it didn't seem all that bad, just a jarring crunch and thud, but the airbag blew up like a giant mushroom, pushing her purse into her tummy so pain-

fully hard that she screamed before the airbag smacked her violently in the face. Tasting blood, she screamed again until all was silent except for the pouring rain and her ragged breathing. For a moment she sat there shaking so hard that her teeth rattled, and then she started to sob.

I'm okay, she thought as she dialed 911, but as she waited for the police to arrive she felt something warm and wet on her jeans . . . blood. "No, please, no . . ." She squeezed her legs together, trying to stop the blood from gushing. After a few minutes cramps started at her back and gripped her abdomen and she knew—oh God, she knew—that she was miscarrying . . . losing the baby. "Stop! Please stop!" She put her hands between her legs, quit breathing in a desperate effort to slow the bleeding, but she could feel the life draining from her womb until she felt empty. So very, very empty.

"Alexia," Jayden said again, and gently shook her shoulder. "Wake up. You're having a bad dream."

"No . . . please . . . no," she moaned in such agony that Jayden shivered. She had also mumbled his name so he knew the dream—no make that her *nightmare*—had something to do with him. She trembled, and he realized with growing horror that she was crying.

"Alexia, please, wake up." He pulled her close and wrapped her into his embrace until she stopped the violent trembling. "It's okay. It was only a dream."

"Oh God, oh God, *oh God* . . ." She stiffened when she woke up and drew in a ragged, shaky breath but remained silent.

"Do you want to talk about it?"

"No," she croaked. "And . . . and I should go."

He held her tightly and kissed her shoulder. "No

way. You're too upset to drive," he insisted, and she immediately started sobbing. "What? Alexia, tell me. I want to help."

"It's too late." She shook her head and tried to get up.

"No! Please! Settle down. You don't have to talk but you're not going anywhere." When he gently kissed her head, she stopped struggling as if out of energy, breathing hard, sniffing. He gently brushed away tears from her cheek and said, "You don't have to say a word, but I'm here for you, understand?"

She nodded.

"You can cry, shout, cuss, talk, hell, even hit me if it helps, but let it all out if you need to."

"I can't," she said in a small, defeated voice.

"If that son of a bitch you married hurt you, I'll hunt his ass down . . ."

"No." She shook her head. "No. It was just . . . a . . ." She paused and shuddered. "A bad dream."

"Will you let me hold you, Alexia?"

She hesitated but then finally gave in and nodded slowly. "Yes, just hold me," she answered, and then surprised him by turning around and laying her head on his chest. He pulled her arm up securely around his neck and then stroked her hair until her shallow breathing became steady and normal. It hit him hard how much he wanted to comfort her, soothe away her fear, and he wondered how many times she might have needed him and he wasn't there.

Jayden longed to ask her about the nightmare but didn't push even though she seemed so fragile, so shaken that it twisted his heart. He hoped that she would eventually open up to him so that they could put the past to rest and discuss the possibility of a future. But for now he would settle for having her in his bed and in his arms. With that in mind he tightened his hold, not wanting to give her the opportunity to sneak away as he had done in the past. Jayden shook his head. God, he was such an ass . . . a selfish son of a bitch. He had some serious making up to do. He only hoped that she would give him the chance to try again.

Chapter Nine

The rich aroma of coffee brewing teased Alexia's senses, but she didn't want to wake up. She burrowed deeper in the covers, snuggled into the pillow, and sighed. Oh no, wait, did she smell bacon? Mmm, she thought with a sleepy smile. *Bacon.*

But then a jolt that had nothing to do with caffeine hit her and she opened her eyes wide. It was morning. She was at Jayden's cabin. In his bed. She peeked beneath the covers and winced. Yes, she was naked. For a moment she felt disoriented, but then the floodgate of memories from the night before burst forth and flowed into her brain. With another groan she covered her face with her hands. In a panic she looked down at the floor for her clothes and began plotting her disappearance out the back door. There was a back door, right? An escape hatch? Something?

All this was racing though her frazzled brain as she sat up in bed and weighed her options. But then Jayden suddenly appeared in the doorway holding a tray of food with a steaming mug of coffee that was calling her

name. Alexia nervously licked her lips and barely resisted the urge to reach up and smooth her bed-head
hair. She always had horrible morning sticking-up-
everywhere hair while he had the nerve to stand there
looking freshly showered and squeaky clean. He was
shirtless, wearing only flannel lounging pants, tied at
the waist, that were slung low on his lean hips. Just one
little tug . . .

Oh, heaven help her.

Jayden looked at her and held up the tray in invitation, but he appeared a bit nervous as if he didn't know
whether to smile, joke, or be serious. He opened his
mouth but opted for clearing his throat, and it was then
that Alexia realized with a horror that the blanket and
sheet were pooled at her waist, making her shirtless too!
With modesty getting the best of her she grabbed the
sheet and tugged it up to her chin. "You could have
at least knocked," she accused stiffly, and then primly
pressed her lips together as if she were some innocent
virgin and hadn't had steamy sex with him pinned
against the wall and then watched herself climax in
front of a mirror.

"Um, the door was open," he said, but was smart
enough not to grin.

"Then you should have announced yourself or
something," she protested while eyeing the coffee.

"Hungry?" he asked with raised eyebrows.

"Well . . ." Alexia briefly considered declining
breakfast and hitting the road before she did something
stupid yet again like de-pantsing him, but the food
smelled heavenly and God, she needed coffee. "A little,"
she admitted in the same prim little virgin voice when
there she was, *naked*, sleep rumpled, and salivating over

more than just the food. When her stomach growled, loudly protesting the unfair fact that the tray was over *there* and she was over *here*, Alexia couldn't keep from laughing at herself.

Laughter had kept her company and even in the darkest of times she had tried to retain her sense of humor. So now, when she was naked, hungry, and embarrassed at her behavior, her tears, and yes, even her need to be held and cuddled, she managed to smile and then laugh softly at the entire scheme of things.

"Here you go." Jayden gave her a tentative smile and looked at her with a wary expression wondering, she supposed, if she had gone over the edge, but it only made her laugh harder.

Perhaps she had reached her limit in trying to dodge another curveball life was hurling at her, but this time she didn't even attempt to duck. "Well, what are you waiting for? Bring that tray over here and feed me."

Jayden blinked and gave her a more relaxed smile while his long legs brought him over to the bed. He sat down on the edge of the mattress and handed her the coffee mug.

"Thanks," she said, and took a sip. "Strong and sweet with a splash of cream, just the way I like it."

"I remembered," he said, but avoided her gaze and picked up a slice of bacon instead. It occurred to Alexia that she wasn't the only who had suffered the loss of their love over the years. But then he surprised her further by saying, "I remember everything about you."

"So you thought about me over the years?"

"Yeah, a lot," he admitted, and then glanced away.

Alexia cradled the warm mug in her hands and asked softly, "Then why did you leave me without so much as a good-bye, Jay? You rode out of town and never looked back."

He laughed without humor. "I was arrogant enough to think you'd come running after me. But instead you up and married someone else."

Alexia was silent. Sad. But she wasn't ready to tell him the whole truth. She took another sip of hot coffee and changed the subject. "This looks divine," she commented, and forked a bite of fluffy scrambled eggs. Mmm, delish!" She crunched through a slice of bacon and licked her fingers. "I didn't know you were such a good cook."

"There's a lot you don't know about me, I guess. People change, Alexia. Mature. Learn from mistakes."

Alexia looked at him in surprise, but his gaze remained on the floor. The Jayden she knew had always been so cocky, so sure of himself, but here he was, this fearless champion looking as though he wanted to say something but was scared. Alexia wanted to reach for his hand and tell him that she knew exactly how he felt. Scared to death. Part of Alexia longed to tell Jayden that they should start anew and forget the past, but what would he say if she revealed her secret? Her anger? Her blame?

Let it go, echoed in her head.

But as she sat there looking at his profile the truth came from out of nowhere and hit her like a blow to the head . . . another curveball that she didn't see coming.

She didn't blame Jayden.

She blamed herself.

She should have pulled off the road out of the pouring rain and dangerous conditions. She never should have searched for her phone, especially under such circumstances. The baby, Jayden's baby, was in her care, was *her* responsibility and something Jayden wasn't even aware of when he made the call or that it was even raining or that she was driving!

It was her fault! Her damned fault and he had suffered a tremendous loss that he didn't even know about. She should have told him about the baby as soon as she knew she was pregnant, but she wanted him to stay off the circuit out of love, not obligation. Even so, she could have handled his absence, but after his horrific crash she couldn't handle the fear knowing they had conceived a child . . . and yet from the beginning he had the right to know. She had been wrong . . . so very wrong.

Alexia's heart ached and tears welled up from out of nowhere. Her appetite vanished and the eggs stuck in her throat. She swallowed a gulp of coffee but had to swipe at a tear.

Jayden frowned. "What's wrong?" He threaded his fingers through his hair and looked at her in confusion. "Was it something I said?"

"No." She gripped the mug so tightly that if it weren't so sturdy it would have shattered in her hands. "This just isn't going to work for so many reasons."

"Really?" He stood up from the bed and turned away with his hands fisted at his sides. Then, when he seemed to gain his composure, he whipped around to face her. "Name one."

"Okay, for one, you're leaving in a few months for the Supercross circuit."

"So what?" He shrugged. "Come with me."

"You know how I feel about racing."

He raised his palms in the air. "What? The danger?

Come on, Alexia. Men are cops, firemen, and construction workers, for Pete's sake. Men and women are losing their lives serving our country. I fell down the steps once. Should I never take the stairs again? Get behind the wheel of a car? Should you never walk in the woods again?" He started pacing the room but then stopped and pinned her with a look. "Hey, I know my accident freaked you out years ago, but get over it, Alexia. I'm alive and kicking. So give me a better reason, because that one sucks."

When she didn't answer he continued. "I left our relationship out of youthful pride, arrogance. The lure of fame, money. The chance to follow my dreams. We'll never know what might have happened between us had I given up racing or if you had come after me instead of marrying." He shook his head. "None of that matters anymore. I'm shoving all of that meaningless shit aside and handing you . . . make that *us* . . . the chance of a new beginning." He hesitated and then said, "Maybe we had to go through all that crap to bring us right here . . . right now. Are you willing to give it a shot?"

Alexia fisted the sheet in her hands. He looked at her with such hope that it tugged at her heart. He was putting it all out there, laying his heart on the line. "Jayden, there are . . . things about me that you don't . . ." She swallowed and then shook her head and finished softly. "Know."

He stood very still as he gazed across the room at her. "Whatever it is, tell me." When she remained silent he said, "Then how about this? I don't care. That's what new beginnings are all about. Leaving the past behind."

She picked up the coffee mug more to have something to do than to drink. She stared down at the brown liquid and said, "You don't know that."

"Then tell me."

Alexia felt a cold lump of panic lodge in her throat. Would he forgive her for a careless moment that cost them the life of their unborn child? Would he want a woman who couldn't bear his children? She stared down at the coffee as if it had all the answers.

"You know what, just forget it."

"Forget everything you just said?"

"No, remember what I told you. I wasn't handing you a line of crap," he said firmly. "I'm beyond playing games, Alexia. I hope you know that."

When he looked at her expectantly she nodded. "I believe you, Jayden."

He appeared relieved. "Good, but forget about giving me an answer. I'm pushing too hard." He back-pedaled a couple of steps. "Look, I'm going to the track to practice. You can take your time here. There's more coffee. Oh, and I answered the questions you had in that packet you shoved under my door."

Alexia looked up in surprise. "Already?"

He shrugged. "I couldn't sleep after . . . ," he began but then trailed off.

"Oh." She understood. The nightmare. It hung in the air between them for a moment and she knew he was hoping for an explanation in the light of day, but when she remained quiet he turned around. With a heavy heart she watched him grab his gear and head from the room, but when he reached the doorway, he paused and turned back around. "You know, I was going to call Brianna and tell her to let you off the hook."

"Really? Why?"

"For one thing, Colin warned me not to break your heart." Jayden grinned. "Said he would kick my ass." He arched one dark eyebrow. "Not that I'm worried or anything," he added in typical male fashion, but then his grin faded. "There are people here in Braxton who care about you, Alexia. I'll tell you right now that it's not my intention to hurt you, but you know what?"

Alexis shrugged. He was continuing to baffle her. "What?"

"I'm not about to let you off the hook. You're going to either hate me or love me by the time this motocross story is finished," he warned her with another warm smile that softened his features and reminded her of why she had fallen for him so many years ago. "I'm betting the latter."

"Thought you weren't cocky anymore," she challenged, desperate to lighten the moment.

His smile deepened. "Not cocky. Just confident." But then he shook his head. "Okay, maybe wishful thinking is more like it."

"Let's go with that one," Alexia suggested. She smiled even though her emotions were a twisted jumble of hope and fear. After he left, she sat there in the middle of his bed, cradling the coffee mug while wondering just what in the world she was going to do. Her heart beat faster at the prospect of starting over with Jayden. Could they really put the past to rest?

Alexia closed her eyes and sighed. A hot tear slid from the corner of her eye when she thought of the choices she made and the way their lives could have, *should* have been. And, oh, how she regretted the lost years living in a loveless marriage to a man who had treated her as a trophy wife and nothing more.

Mitchell had made it quite clear that he didn't want children interfering with their social life, so her infertility had never been an issue even though at times she had ached for a child in her arms and had prayed that by some miracle she would end up pregnant. In fact, she had often wondered if with medical intervention the scar tissue could be removed, making her chances for conceiving better.

The more Mitchell had withdrawn from their marriage, the lonelier Alexia had become. She had craved a gentle touch, a warm embrace, and the heat of passion. Even so, she had kept up appearances, entertained, *smiled*, laughed as if she didn't have a care in the world when in fact she was an empty shell of her former vibrant self. Another tear escaped and then another until she gave up the fight and let the tears flow.

Alexia ached with lonely sadness that seeped into her bones and made her want to curl up in bed and stay there all day. Now, when she was being given a second chance at happiness, she didn't know if she was courageous enough to take it. After sniffing loudly she shuddered, thinking that she would eventually have to tell Jayden about the baby. Would he put his arms around her in comfort? Or walk away in disgust?

With a low moan Alexia put one hand over her mouth and then shook her head. She couldn't do it. She might not be able to control her nightmares or have the power to stop the tears from flowing, but she didn't think she could speak of that unspeakable night ever again.

Thankfully, no one except for Colin knew about the accident or the baby. Her parents had been in Florida, so it had been Colin who had held her hand that fateful night. Her mother's health had been shaky at the time and Alexia didn't want to burden them after the fact. No, she had grieved and suffered in silence, and then eventually lost herself and her identity as Mitchell's wife. At first he had been attentive and charming, immersing Alexia in a fantasy world filled with parties, travel, and excitement. Material possessions, though, soon became a poor substitute for love and passion, so much so that she had been angry but then ultimately relieved when Mitchell had cheated. It had been her out.

Oh, how she had pretended but had never felt comfortable in her big house up East. Alexia shook her head. No, she was much more at home in her cabin, hiking in the woods instead of wandering aimlessly at the galleria. Moving back to Braxton had been the right decision, she thought with a sigh. She had just started to settle into a comfortable, peaceful existence when Jayden blew that all to hell.

"Now what am I going to do?" she mused out loud. After dabbing at her wet cheeks with the top sheet, Alexia suddenly felt weary. She shoved the breakfast tray out of the way and scooted beneath the covers. "I'll just close my eyes for a couple of minutes," she whispered, thinking that Jayden would be gone the better part of the day. She tucked her hands beneath the pillow and sighed. "Just a few minutes of rest and I'll be gone before he ever gets back," she mumbled as she scratched her nose and stretched like a kitten. "Mmm," she inhaled deeply, and couldn't help burrowing her nose in the Jayden-scented sheets . . .

His image, naked and aroused, slid into her brain like warm butter and then melted downward into her body, making her limbs feel heavy and languid. With a soft sigh Alexia recalled the taste of his skin, the heat of his mouth, the touch of his tongue. Semiasleep, she turned over and reached out across the bed hoping to turn her erotic fantasy into reality.

But he was gone, and she should leave his bed and hurry home, away from temptation. "In a minute," she mumbled, but her eyelids felt incredibly heavy and the pillow was so cozy . . .

Chapter Ten

*J*ayden wheeled down the tacky straightaway, enjoying the speed before plowing through the soft sand berms. The condition of the track was good, not too hard or stiffly packed. He went into the turn, careful not to chop the throttle but kept it on about a quarter of the way the whole time before gradually hitting the gas to build up some speed in a smooth movement that came as natural as breathing. He kept his body position loose and flexible while setting himself up for the next turn.

Jayden rode hard, trying to keep his focus and not think about Alexia. But he simply couldn't stop thinking about her, and when he encountered an unexpected slippery patch, he hit the gas too hard. "Damn!" When his rear wheel started spinning out he tried to pin the bike but lost control and went sliding into a stack of hay bales. "Shit!" he shouted when his shoulder hit the ground. Not good. For a moment he lay there stunned and cursing but thanked God for helmets.

"What the hell do you think you're doing?"

Jayden turned his head to see Colin looming over him looking none too pleased. "What does it look like? I fucking spun out."

"There's a group of kids over there observing your stupid ass. I told them to watch and learn, but what I should have said was 'watch and don't do that.'"

Jayden sat up and removed his goggles and helmet. "Sorry, man. Lost my focus."

"Well, dude, then get your ass off the track. You've got no business here if you can't concentrate. Wait, let me guess, you have Alexia on the brain."

"Shut the hell up."

"No, you shut up and get outta here. Go back to her."

"She's gone, man."

"She's got a Beemer SUV, right?"

"Yes." Jayden's heart kicked it up a notch. He thought she'd be long gone.

"When I passed the cabin a little while ago, it was there." Colin raked his fingers through his shaggy hair and grinned. "Man, you've got it bad. Go on back there and get her out of your system before hitting the track again. You getting yourself killed will *not* be good for business."

"Yeah, I guess you're right." Jayden absently rubbed his sore shoulder, acting as casual as possible while his brain skittered around the knowledge that Alexia was still at his place. He pictured her in his bed naked and then groaned. Embarrassed, he rubbed his shoulder harder.

Colin gave him a knowing grin. "Dude, you're so far gone, it's not even funny." But then he cocked his head. "I take that back. It is pretty damned funny to see you whipped like this."

"I'm not whipped."

"Right," he joked, but then sobered. "Things going okay with her, man?"

Jayden scraped his boot across the ground. "No, not at all."

Colin looked at him with a frown. "You coulda fooled me."

"She's holding something back and she won't open up," Jayden explained, but was surprised when Colin looked away as if he suddenly wanted to escape. "Wait, do you know something that I don't?" When Colin didn't immediately respond, Jayden persisted. "You do. What the hell is it? Something I did? Something that old bastard did to her?"

Colin shook his head and was about to respond when they spotted Brianna heading their way. "We'll table this for another time, bro."

"The hell we will."

"Jay, I really don't want to get into the middle of anything."

"The middle? Of what?"

Colin looked decidedly uncomfortable. "Look, whatever is in Alexia's past is up to her to tell." He held up both palms. "Leave me outta this. What goes down between you two is your business."

"You're skirting the issue. We'll talk later," Jayden said, and forced a smile when Brianna came up to them. He noticed with humor that Colin couldn't take his eyes off the little redhead.

"Hi, guys." Brianna gave Jayden a brief, friendly

smile, but she blushed when she turned her attention to Colin, who in turn shoved his hands into his jeans pockets and seemed equally flustered. For God's sake. They were both adults and were acting like love-struck teenagers.

"Hey there, Brianna," Colin said. "What's up?"

She held up her impressive-looking camera. "I thought I'd come out to take a few pictures. I want to do an introductory story before Alexia gets to the heart of things. Do you mind?"

"Not at all," Colin said eagerly. "Would you like me to show you around?" he asked quickly, as if he was worried that Jayden would beat him to the punch.

Hiding a grin, Jayden said, "I've got to get going." He flexed his shoulder. "I seem to have the knack for landing on the same damned injury."

"I saw your crash," Brianna said with wide eyes. "Are you okay?"

"It wasn't a *crash*," Jayden corrected, not wanting Brianna to give Alexia the wrong impression. "Just a minor lapse in judgment." He waved a dismissive hand through the air. "I'll be fine. I think I'll hit the hot tub for a long soak."

"You do that," Colin said with a you-can-leave-now nod, and then turned his full attention to Brianna. "Okay, where do you want to start?"

When Brianna turned her cute little pixie face up to Colin and nervously started chattering away, Jayden nodded to them and excused himself. The hot tub was calling his name, and if Alexia was still there he was going to do his damnedest to get her to join him. He hopped back on his bike and took a shortcut back through the woods, dodging trees and jumping creeks.

His shoulder throbbed in protest and his balls took a beating, but he was in a hurry so he gritted his teeth and pushed on until the A-frame came into view.

His heartbeat kicked it up when he spotted her SUV in the driveway. "Wow, she's still here," he said, wondering what that meant. After parking his bike in the garage, he took off his gear except for his jersey and pants and then entered the cabin through the front door. All was quiet with no sign of Alexia, but instead of calling her name he headed for the bedroom thinking she might be asleep.

He was right.

Jayden could hear the soft sound of her even breathing from where she lay curled up in the center of the bed. Her honey-colored hair fanned out over the pillowcase and one bare shoulder was exposed. Jayden glanced at the floor and when he saw her discarded clothing, his dick stirred in immediate reaction to the knowledge that she was naked. He wanted to crawl into bed with her, but he was mud splattered and sweaty so a shower was in order . . . first.

Then he was going to crawl into bed with her. The hot tub could wait.

Turning on his heel, he quietly hurried to the bathroom and turned on the shower. He peeled off his clothes in front of the mirror, and when he thought about her in his bed just a few feet away he decided to make the shower a quick one. When the hot spray hit his sore shoulder, he sighed, wishing Alexia was in the stall with him, wet and sleek with soap. When his dick stood at attention at the mere thought—not even the reality—of Alexia, he shook his head. Colin was right . . . He had it bad.

After finishing up, he quickly dried off and paused to brush his teeth. He slicked his hair away from his face and gazed at his reflection in the mirror, wondering what kind of reception he would get when he slid into bed with her. "Well, there's only one way to find out," he mumbled under his breath. Wearing nothing but a tented towel, he padded into the bedroom hoping that the sound of the shower hadn't stirred her awake. If she was gone, he would be sorely disappointed.

Jayden sighed with relief when he saw her sleeping form in his bed. For a moment he stood in the doorway and could only stare. The sheet was pooled near her waist, revealing not only her shoulder but also the delicate curve of her back. Her arm hid her breast until she shifted, sighed, and then rolled to her back. "My God . . ." He thought for the millionth time how beautiful a woman she had become. She had a softness about her now, a vulnerable quality that made him want to take her into his arms and simply hold her and chase away whatever fear she had that was causing her to keep her distance. Whatever it was that she thought she had to hide, to keep locked up inside was a moot point as far as he was concerned. He loved her and that's all that mattered.

As quietly as he could possibly manage, he joined her on the bed and then leaned over and took one dusky nipple into his mouth. She gasped but didn't push him away as he had feared. "Mmm," he sighed, loving the taste, the feel of her in his mouth. She was warm and smelled of floral perfume and musky woman. When Jayden licked in a circle she arched her back and moaned. Her eyelids fluttered and he knew she was awake, but instead of protesting she threaded her fingers through his wet hair and urged him on.

When her eyes remained closed, it bothered Jayden because he didn't want this to be a fantasy. He wanted this to be a real, lasting memory, but at this point he would take whatever he could get and work from there.

He spoke without words, cupping her breast in his hand, licking and sucking before pulling back to look at her wet, puckered nipple. He lightly blew and watched her shiver before leaning down to lick again. Then, longing to see more of her, he tugged the sheet down, exposing her luscious body. Her eyes remained closed, but when he caressed her breasts and then grazed her belly she inhaled sharply, as if anticipating where he would go next.

At first Alexia had thought she was still dreaming when she felt the shock of Jayden's mouth on her breast, but the reality of his smooth skin, soft lips, firm fingers was so much better than her sexy dream. He smelled of shampoo, soap, mint, and man. With her eyes closed she drank him in, let him seep through her senses. Her breasts felt full, her limbs heavy, and the sudden coolness of his wet hair trailing over her sleep-warmed skin made her breath catch. Goose bumps rose to the surface and she felt a tingle all the way to her toes. He teased her with featherlight caresses over her breasts, down her belly, but then instead of touching her mound with his fingers, he leaned down and nuzzled her there with his mouth.

She was wet, dripping with anticipation, and she arched up so that he could drink her in. With a low moan Jayden positioned his body between her legs, cupped her ass, and licked her with quick little flicks of his tongue. She was already so aroused that when he circled her clit and then sucked she climaxed hard and fast, arching against his mouth, but when she tried to pull away, he held her captive and continued to lick, kiss, and suck her slick, swollen flesh until she spiraled upward and then shattered with a mind-blowing second climax that left her trembling and weak. She gulped in shallow breaths, mindlessly riding out the aftershocks.

But he wasn't finished.

Jayden came up to his knees, lifted her ass up, and entered her with a long hard stroke. She moaned, clutched at the sheet while he began a slow and easy rhythm, bringing her back to heart-thumping arousal when she thought she couldn't take any more. She moved with him, arching up so he could go deeper. She felt him swell, throb, pulse within her. When his breath became ragged, Alexia opened her eyes to look at him.

He was gorgeous . . . tanned, muscled, and in the throes of passion.

His eyes were closed and his long lashes cast a shadow on his high cheekbones. With his dark hair slicked back, the planes and angles of his face were more pronounced, making him look fiercely masculine. His mouth was slightly parted and his chest rose and fell with each deep breath and every hard stroke. Corded muscles stood out on his neck and his biceps bulged and flexed with the effort of holding her up at an angle so he could go deeper, slapping against her flesh.

In this erotic position, Alexia could look down and watch with fascination where they were intimately connected. His dick, slick and shiny with her juices, pumped in and out with slippery ease. She knew he was holding back, waiting for her to come with him, but she wanted more . . . couldn't get enough. She was tender, almost bruised, but it only heightened the pleasure. Alexia grabbed hold of his hard, muscled thighs and matched his rhythm until she felt an orgasm start to build. Pushing her shoulders into the pillows, she went wild with him and as soon as she heard his hoarse, throaty cry, she let go and climaxed with him. He stopped, held her immobile while he shot hot and oh so deep within her. She held on to his legs, clutched at his dick while waves of pleasure washed over her and spread throughout her body.

For a long, heart-stopping moment he remained buried inside her wet heat while she milked every last drop from him. His eyes were closed, his Adam's apple bobbed, and his chest rose and fell as if he were trying to catch his breath. She tried to tell herself that this was just sex . . . hot, delicious, mind-blowing sex . . . but she knew better. Being with him was more, so *much* more.

As if reading her mind, Jayden suddenly opened his brown eyes and pinned her with a searing, intense look that seemed to see into her soul. She licked her lips, but when she would have looked away, he cupped her chin with a gentle but firm hold.

"I love you."

Joy and fear mingled at his unexpected declaration, making her speechless. Moisture gathered in her throat, but as if knowing she wasn't going to say it back, he drew her into his arms and rolled to his side, taking her with him while still buried deep within her.

"You don't have to say anything. Just breathe. Relax. Don't even think," he gently told her.

Unable to resist, Alexia rested her head against his

chest. He was warm and safe, and made her feel as if she were finally home. His heart thumped against her cheek . . . strong like a lifeline in a world tumbling out of control. God, how she needed this. Wanted this. A long, breathy sigh escaped her and if just for now she allowed herself the luxury of feeling loved, cherished. Melting with happiness.

Just for now.

Refusing to let reality intrude, she snuggled into his embrace and a contented sense of relaxation settled over her entire body from the inside out. For the first time in forever she felt at peace, and then she wondered if she should ever tell him about the baby and the accident. But she knew it would be the only way she could find complete peace and happiness with him, so she inhaled a deep breath and willed the words to come but they stuck in her throat. Still, she had to try. "Jayden," she began, but couldn't keep the tremble from her voice.

"Don't, Alexia," he said gently. "I know I've pushed for answers, but whatever is bothering you isn't important. You're here with me in my arms and that's all I want for now," he said, and she breathed a sigh of relief. Then his chuckle vibrated against her cheek. "Man, do I sound like a girl or what?"

Alexia smiled against his chest. "Yeah."

"You weren't supposed to agree."

"I call 'em like I see 'em," she teased and then lightly kissed his chest. She allowed herself to laugh, and it felt so damned good.

"What are you laughing at?" Jayden wanted to know.

Alexia didn't really have an answer. "Nothing . . . everything. Life, I guess."

Jayden rubbed her back. "We can't go back, Alexia, and change the past. But the future is out there waiting. The rest is up to us. But like I said, I don't want to put any pressure on you. Push. You set the pace."

When she nodded he hugged her close.

"And if there is something you need to talk about or tell me," he offered without hesitation, "you can do it without fear of judgment. Understand?"

"Yes," she answered softly, but a little niggling of doubt wiggled into her newfound peace.

"But for now, just chill. We can take this one day at a time."

"Okay," she agreed.

"Good." When he kissed the top of her head, she giggled. "What?" he asked.

"Nothing."

"Oh no, you don't." He lightly shook her shoulder.

"This . . . I don't know, kinder, gentler Jayden Michaels is going to take some getting used to."

"Are you making fun of me?"

She pushed up and rested her arm on his chest. "Not at all. You're just . . . different. Your appearance is, wow, so intense, but you've changed."

He put his index finger to his lips. "Shhh, don't tell. I have to keep my badass rep in place."

"Your secret is safe with me," she promised, but she was reminded of her own secret. *Forget the past; the future is waiting* echoed in her head. Words beautifully spoken, and she knew he meant what he said, but could she? And if he knew, would he?

"Stop," he said softly, and kissed the top of her head.

"Stop what?" she asked while drawing little circles

on his chest with her fingertips. She loved touching him. Kissing him.

"Stop thinking. Alexia, I can practically hear the wheels spinning in your head. Turn them off," he gently urged.

"Okay," she said, but they kept on rolling.

As if he knew this, he said, "Hey, how about a huge sandwich, a cold beer, and a long soak in the hot tub? Sound good?"

Alexia hesitated. Staying here with him meant opening herself up to a relationship instead of just sleeping with him. Part of her wanted to hightail and run like the wind . . . oh, but the other part, which she supposed was her heart because it was beating like a jackhammer, begged for her to stay . . .

And he had said that he loved her.

"Alexia?"

"Hmm?"

"Don't . . . *go.*"

Oh, how those simple words touched her heart, and when he hugged her tighter she knew he meant them. "What makes you think I'm going to leave?"

Jayden chuckled. "Well, for one thing your heart is beating like mine at the drop of the gate and I'm gunning for the hole shot."

"Jay . . . ," she began, deciding that she should just come clean, but he stopped her.

"Let's not make today complicated, okay?" He lifted her chin again so she had to look at him. "Not that I didn't mean everything I said, but let's lighten things up. Just have some relaxation and fun. Sound like a plan?"

"Yeah," she answered with a smile. If nothing else she would give herself this day. To prove her point, she leaned in and gave him a long, hot kiss. "Now go fix me that sandwich you were bragging about. I've got to pull myself together and then I'll join you."

"You got it," he said, and eased up from the bed. He paused at the doorway, not giving a fig that he was stark naked, and said, "By the way, clothes are optional."

"I'll keep that in mind," she teased, and let him wonder if she would have the nerve to waltz into the kitchen in the buff.

While shaking her head, she eased back down to the pillow and wondered what in the world she was doing. Having Jayden Michaels back in her life was so unexpected, so out of the blue that she felt as if she should pinch herself just to see if this was for real . . . But then with a deep sigh she wondered if this was going to be a dream come true or an extended version of the mess that she called her life.

God, she felt as if she were standing on the edge of a diving board, looking down at the water . . . knowing full well that it was safe to jump but so afraid to take the plunge. Alexia clutched the covers and swallowed while fear, excitement, and exhilaration twisted together in a big ball in her stomach. While she couldn't know how this would all play out, one thing was for sure. She felt more alive than she had felt in years, and it definitely beat standing on the sidelines watching the world pass her by.

With that in mind, she released the death grip on the covers and tossed them back with a determined fling of her arm. But for a long, heart-thumping moment she stared at the carpet as if it were a shimmering pool.

"Oh, come on, you *know* how to swim," she muttered, and after taking a deep breath she swung her legs over the side of the bed and jumped right in.

Chapter Eleven

"Oh my God," Alexia said as she walked into the kitchen.

"Look good?" Jayden grinned at her with pride.

"Well, yes, but I don't know how I'm going to get my mouth open that wide," she declared, and then blushed at the sexual innuendo as she stared at a giant sandwich that rivaled one from a New York deli.

"I don't cook much but I make a mean sandwich."

"Ya don't say."

"Just open wide and give it your best shot. It will be worth it, I promise."

"Okay, I'll give it the old college try," she promised. Even though Jayden was even more mouthwatering than the sandwich itself, she'd never let him know that her oh-my-God was meant more for him than the piled-high club sandwich. He had changed to faded jeans ripped here and there, but she knew it was from playing hard and not some fancy designer. A black turtleneck clung to his chest, showing off his defined pecs and baseball-sized biceps.

"Beer?"

"Sure," she answered, and even though it was too early in the day to start drinking, she thought that a little alcohol might loosen her up. When Jayden turned and bent over to grab the drinks from the fridge, she did what any red-blooded woman would do and ogled his butt. *Nice . . . ,* she thought while nodding, but when she noticed skin showing through a hole in the denim she realized with a hot shot of desire that he was going commando.

Holy crap, Alexia thought, and angled her head to get a better view. Of course he chose that exact moment to stand up and turn around. She straightened up so fast that the bar stool wobbled and she had to grab the edge of the counter to keep from toppling over.

"Whoa there."

"I'm fine." Alexia tried for an innocent smile and frowned at the floor as if there were a slippery spot, but he shot her a knowing grin while twisting the caps off the bottles. She would have been embarrassed except that the big bulge straining against his zipper made it quite clear that he was thinking along the same lines as she was . . . namely, that she wanted to gobble him up even more than she did her lunch. But a girl needed sustenance, after all, so she accepted the cold bottle and took a long swig before digging in. Well, she tried to anyway. Jayden laughed at her attempts to get the doggone thing into her mouth.

"Angle your head to the side, like this," he advised her, and then demonstrated.

"Okay." Alexia nodded and tried his method but could only manage to get the corners of wheat toast into her mouth. She giggled and tried again, getting a nibble of baby Swiss and a taste of turkey.

"That was weak," Jayden accused, and then crunched through a big bite with ease but almost choked on a swallow of beer while watching her dainty attempts to attack the sandwich. For the moment, anyway, she seemed relaxed and having fun. It hurt him to think of her in misery and he decided right then and there to make her laugh whenever possible. "Here, let me help," he offered, and came around to the other side of the breakfast bar to assist her.

"Now, just how are you going to help? Make my mouth bigger?"

"No, I'm going to make the sandwich smaller." He reached for her half and while squeezing the toast together he placed it up to her lips. "Now open wide," he urged. Mayonnaise oozed out the edges as he urged her to try. She crunched through the toast and managed to get a healthy bite into her mouth.

"Mmm," she said while chewing.

"Good, huh?"

"Mmm-hmm." Alexia nodded and then slowly licked excess mayo from her thumb.

When Jayden watched her tongue lick the white dab and then suck it into her mouth, his dick stirred with restless longing. While watching her take another bite, he wondered how eating a turkey club could be so damned sexy, but she somehow made it so.

"What? Do I have food smeared on my face?" she asked when she caught him staring at her like a dumb-struck fool.

"Yeah," he lied, "right there in the corner of your mouth."

"Oh . . . ," she said, but when she reached up with her napkin he stopped her hand. Instead, he leaned in and lightly licked the corner of her mouth and then slid the tip of his tongue across her bottom lip. "Got it," he said, but then frowned. "No, there's a bit more." He leaned in for another lick and nibble.

"There wasn't any mayo, was there?" she asked against his lips.

"Mmm . . . no," he confessed, but his tongue lingered on her mouth anyway. "I just wanted to taste *you*," he admitted, and then kissed her softly before pulling back. "Now I'm going to let you eat because you're going to need your strength." When Alexia's eyes widened at his comment Jayden sensed her fight-or-flight fear kicking in. She took a long swig of her beer and seemed to get herself under control. He really wished she would just open up to him and put it all out there, but he told himself to back off or she would definitely run like hell.

And running like hell wasn't the answer, as Jayden well knew. Even though he had ultimately hoped that she would follow him, what he had never told Alexia or anyone was that ten years ago he had roared out of town away from his small-town existence, and away from Alexia because she represented home, family, and the responsibility that he wasn't ready to face. Jayden's father, who had raced as a kid, had given up his career when Jayden had come along, and Jayden didn't want that to be his fate. Instead, he had chased his dream, not realizing the cost until he had gotten wind of Alexia's marriage and it had torn him apart. Now he had given it some serious consideration, and after this next season he was going to settle down and maybe even start a family. He smiled. The thought of Alexia having his baby was something that appealed instead of frightened him, and he was suddenly selfishly glad that she didn't have any children with her ex-husband. He wasn't running this time around, no matter what the hell was in her past that she was afraid to tell him.

Alexia watched Jayden dig into his own sandwich while she consumed hers. He seemed deep in thought, and while she was dying to know what was going on in his handsome head, she refrained from asking. Today she wouldn't allow the past to interfere or the future to matter. For today she was giving herself permission to live in the moment and was hell-bent on not letting anything get in her way.

"Dessert?" Jayden asked, jarring her out of her internal argument.

Alexia looked up from her empty plate, not realizing that she had eaten the entire giant sandwich. "Um . . . I'm not sure I have room," she admitted, but eyed the chocolate syrup he snagged from the refrigerator with interest. "Are you suggesting ice cream?"

"Sorry, I don't have any ice cream. I'll stock up, though, since I remember chocolate chip is one of your favorites."

"Yeah, ice cream and chocolate mixed together . . . whoever thought that one up was a genius." Alexia looked at the syrup bottle in question. "Oh, do you still put that stuff in your milk?"

Jayden grinned. "Yeah. I drink milk for the calcium to help avoid broken bones," he admitted, but then wanted to kick himself. Reminding her of the danger of motocross wasn't very smart.

"Right, I remember you doing one of those milk

mustache ads," she casually admitted, but recalled her reaction to seeing his photo in a magazine a few years ago. "Very impressive, I might add."

He shrugged. "It was to draw the attention of motocross fans. You know, the younger crowd. No big deal."

"Well, I thought it was cool." She had been waiting in line at the grocery store, just flipping through an issue of *People* magazine, when she spotted his full-page picture. His brown eyes had seemed to be looking right through her . . . seeing her sham of a marriage and knowing her misery. She had almost burst into emotional tears right in the grocery store. As if to torture herself she had bought the copy and tossed it on her coffee table. Every time she had passed the magazine, her heart had thudded, but she couldn't bring herself to look at it again and had eventually thrown it away.

"But I have to add chocolate to my milk unless I'm eating cereal," Jayden added, bringing Alexia back to the present.

Alexia forced a smile. "Cap'n Crunch?"

Jayden's eyebrows shot up. "You remember my favorite cereal?"

Alexia nodded her head. "I remember a lot about you too, Jay," she said softly. *I never stopped thinking about you,* she wanted to add but didn't. "So, are you going to drink a glass of milk?"

"No . . . ," he answered slowly, and gave her a hot look that had her heart beating wildly.

"Darn, I wanted to see you with a milk mustache," she said in a husky voice since she already suspected the answer. "What, then?"

"I want *you* for dessert, Alexia." He crooked his finger at her. "Come on over here and let me have a nibble." He leaned one hip against the countertop and looked so damned sexy that she couldn't have found the willpower to resist even if she wanted to . . .

And she didn't want to resist.

No, her whole body throbbed with anticipation as she slid from the stool and walked on shaky legs around the breakfast bar and into the galley kitchen. As soon as she was within reaching distance he snagged her around the waist and drew her in for a long, lingering kiss that had her clinging to his wide shoulders.

"Not here," his voice rumbled low and hot in her ear. "I want you on the rug in front of the fireplace where I can eat you from your blond head to your red-painted toes . . . and I don't plan on leaving anything out."

Alexia sucked in a breath when he grabbed the brown bottle and led her into the family room in front of the fieldstone fireplace. He flipped the switch to ignite the gas and then bent over to start the fire. When the seasoned wood started to crackle and pop, Jayden stoked the wood. After the fire took hold, he stood up and walked over to the entertainment center, and flipped through his selection of music. Alexia smiled when Michael Bublé singing "Fever" filled the room. "Sound good?"

"Oh yeah, I love his voice."

"But you're surprised that I listen to him," he said as if reading her thoughts.

"A little."

Jayden arched one eyebrow.

"Okay, a lot."

"I might still eat Cap'n Crunch and put chocolate in my milk, but I have changed in a lot of ways too. I want to show you that if you'll let me."

"Jay . . ." Alexia frowned. She didn't want this to take a serious turn.

"Okay, I'll quit the mushy crap," he promised, and Alexia had to smile. This was the kind of comment the younger Jayden would have made.

"Good idea," Alexia told him. When his grin faded and his eyes looked at her with such need, the air suddenly became so sexually charged that it took Alexia's breath away. The day had clouded over, leaving the cabin shrouded with muted light. Shadows danced on the wall and the flames flickered, sending smoke-scented heat curling into the room. The feeling of being with him like this was surreal; almost like a living, breathing dream.

Alexia eased up to her elbows on the soft rug and simply looked at him. "God, you're gorgeous." When Jayden looked at her in surprise Alexia decided that if she was going to enjoy this day she needed to park her inhibitions at the door. "Now . . . take your shirt off for me," she requested in a husky but firm voice.

"Oh, so you think you can order me around?" he asked with a wicked grin.

"Yeah, I do."

He shrugged and then put his hand up to his chin. "Hmm . . . okay, then, for the next . . . hour I'm your slave. Your wish is my command."

Alexia watched with heart-pounding fascination while Jayden crossed his arms and tugged the turtleneck over his head. "Okay, what next, princess?"

For a lingering moment she gazed up at him. The golden glow of the firelight made his bare chest appear bronzed and although she itched to order him to shuck his pants and join her on the rug, she wanted to draw this little scenario out and enjoy each and every minute of her hour of power. So instead she said, "A glass of wine would be nice."

"Coming right up. Red or white—and don't look so surprised that I have a selection of wine. I've evolved over the years from just cheap beer."

"Hmm," Alexia mused while tapping her cheek. "Whatever goes with chocolate syrup?" She then glanced over at the brown bottle, which appeared lonely and neglected, and she gave Jayden a pointed look. His eyes widened a fraction at the implications and Alexia had to hide a smile. This being-in-control thing was fun.

Fun . . . how long had it been since she had thought of herself as having fun? Well, it was about time!

While he went to retrieve the wine Alexia relaxed on the rug and let Michael Bublé's silky voice both soothe and excite her. She closed her eyes and inhaled deeply while imagining Jayden dripping cold chocolate syrup onto her warm skin . . . and then slowly licking it off. She shivered in anticipation of what was to come and told herself to just let herself go.

"Um . . . I know you're the boss but, princess, it would be very cool if you would undress for me."

Alexia's eyes opened wide when he interrupted her fantasy. He handed her a long-stemmed glass and then took a sip from his own. "Umm," she stuttered, suddenly a little nervous, but then arched an eyebrow. "You go first. Off with the pants," she ordered with a princesslike flip of her hand.

Jayden took a long sip of his wine and then carefully set the delicate glass down on the fieldstone hearth with a light clink. Then he oh so slowly unzipped his jeans, but instead of taking them off he let her get just a peek of what lay beneath. She swallowed a gulp instead of a sip of heady merlot and tried without success not to stare while he tugged his pants over his lean hips, revealing his penis inch by glorious inch. His penis stood proud and erect, jutting out of a silky-looking patch of dark hair. Alexia knew she was supposed to be in charge but she had the uncontrollable urge to please *him*.

"Come here," she ordered, and sucked in a breath when he stood mere inches from her. Rising to her knees, she then slid her hands up the back of his hair-roughened thighs to cup his ass. She palmed his smooth cheeks, kneading the hard muscle while drawing him closer and closer to her mouth.

"Alexia . . . ," Jayden said low and pleading. "Baby, what are you doing?"

"Having *you* for dessert," she explained just before running the tip of her tongue up the length of his shaft. She loved it when he moaned and threaded his fingers through her hair. She teased with light little licks up and down, pausing to lick his sacs before coming back up to swirl her tongue over his smooth head. She continued until he moaned, and then sucked him all the way into her mouth to the back of her throat. His hands tightened on her scalp, massaging, urging her on and on . . .

While loving him with her lips, her tongue, her hands, she inhaled his male scent . . . soap, musk, sex . . . and shivered with excitement. Alexia couldn't believe her boldness, but she took satisfaction in having him at her mercy like this, needing her, wanting her beyond all reason. This was going way beyond just fun and heading somewhere much deeper, but she couldn't stop herself.

When Jayden planted his feet firmly and held on to her head, bending his knees as needed, Alexia cupped his firm ass and took him in as far as he could go. She licked and sucked him slowly, as if savoring each taste, until his thigh muscles tensed and she knew he was close to coming. "Alexia . . . ," he warned, but instead of letting up she went faster, loving him until he angled his head to the side, breathing hard. Then Alexia went wild on him until he gave in to the pleasure with a loud, hoarse cry.

He shuddered, moaned, and then stood there for a long moment while running his fingers through her hair. "Holy . . . ," he began, but then chuckled weakly.

"What?" she asked softly while looking up, but staying on her knees. While it might appear that this was a submissive position, Alexia reveled in having the power to bring him to such a violent climax. When he seemed dazed, almost embarrassed at his intense reaction, Alexia gently caressed his ass while placing light, butterfly kisses on his inner thighs, his sacs, and then up his shaft. "It's okay, Jayden. Let's let everything else slip away and just give ourselves . . . *this*. No yesterday, no tomorrow, just here and now."

Jayden swallowed and shook his head, unable to come up with any coherent words. How could he? Her mouth was parted, swollen from pleasuring him, but it was her eyes that got to him . . . wide, *luminous*, full of emotion that he wished she would verbalize. The fact that she wanted to do this intimate act to him . . . *for him* screamed that she cared.

Didn't it?

Sure, this was sex at its most basic, but there was so much more here and they both knew it. God, but as much as he wanted to tell her that he wanted forever, not just today, he refrained. If they could spend a perfect day together, maybe, *then just maybe*, she would see that this could be reality for the rest of their lives. So he decided not to screw it up and just go with the moment. The rest, he hoped, would then fall into place.

"Your turn," he said gruffly, and then eased to the rug beside her. "Sip your wine while I undress you." He handed her the glass, wanting her mellow and relaxed, and then proceeded to slowly unzip her hoodie. He needed a few minutes to regroup after the mind-blowing orgasm that only reiterated that Alexia could bring him to heights that no other woman had ever come close to doing. Of course he knew the secret. Yes, she might be sexy as hell, but there were plenty of sexy women out there. No, it was because he loved her so much . . . felt a deep connection of mind, body, and soul. God, how he longed to tell her!

But instead he would just have to show her . . . speak with his body.

After he tugged off her shirt and bra, he paused to look at her. She might think she carried extra weight but he loved her curves. "You're beautiful, Alexia."

She turned her head to the side. "I'm overweight and out of shape."

Jayden gently guided her chin back to face him. "I don't want a teenager, Alexia. I want a woman." While palming her breasts he leaned in and kissed her, softly at first but then explored her mouth with unbridled passion. While clinging to his shoulders she kissed him back with equal fervor until Jayden was hot and hard and ready once again. But as much as he wanted to bury his dick deep, he wanted her wild with need . . . and with that in mind he turned and reached for the chocolate.

Chapter Twelve

When Michael Bublé's sexy, sultry voice began singing "How Deep Is Your Love," Alexia closed her eyes and let her chocolate fantasy become reality. Jayden gently pushed her down to the soft rug and then tugged off her shoes, followed by her pants. He paused to lean down and kiss her before whispering, "I'll replace them." Before she could comprehend his meaning he reached down and ripped her delicate panties off as if they were made of paper.

"Oh!" Alexia cried out in surprise and excitement. Her nipples tightened and she instantly became wet and ready. Then he straightened up to his knees and for a long, lingering moment caressed her with his eyes while holding the shredded silk and lace in his hand. Leaning over slightly, he let the panties trail over her skin, feather-light, until her skin tingled. She shivered, becoming both hot and cold at the same time.

The chocolate was momentarily forgotten until Jayden reached behind him and produced the bottle. He turned it over, and when a thin cold stream of chocolate hit her breasts, Alexia arched up from the rug. "God . . ." The chilled spray slid over her sensitive nipples, sending pure heat all the way to her toes. Without pausing Jayden leaned in and licked the sweetness away, flattening his warm tongue to lap it up. Then he rubbed his rough stubble over her puckered areolas until she squirmed and gasped at the contrast. While her eyes were closed she was surprised with another cool attack of syrup that started between her breasts and trickled down her torso. But instead of licking it off, Jayden swiped a bit onto his finger and slipped it into her mouth.

Alexia sucked his fingertip hard but then gasped again when Jayden squirted another thin line from her belly button to her mound. He licked and swirled his tongue and then played there with his fingers, dipping, smearing it onto her skin as if it were brown paint and she were the canvas. He followed the path with his mouth until he buried his face between her thighs. His tongue felt so sensual, so amazingly erotic that Alexia shamelessly let her knees drop to the side, giving him better access to work his magic. His lips were soft, his tongue slick, warm . . . sensual. He kissed her, licked her, and sucked her until she was mindless with the sheer beauty of it all.

"Oh . . ." Pleasure started to build, climb, and tighten like a spring ready to uncoil. Alexia tangled her fingers in his long hair, offering her body to him while she ached for release.

"Relax, let go . . ." Jayden slid his hands beneath her ass, lifting her up, and went wild, eating her up as if she were some sweet confection on a dessert platter . . .

And then she shattered like spun glass. "Jayden . . . ,"

she cried low in her throat. He held his mouth to her, riding out the orgasm with her until she fell back to the rug with a ragged sigh. With her eyes closed she lay there, breathing hard while her entire body throbbed with the aftermath of intense pleasure. She inhaled deeply, trying to make sense of her rocked world, and then he kissed her.

Alexia moaned. God, he tasted of sex, heat, and chocolate. She kissed him back, *deeply*, melting into him like butter on a hot biscuit. "I want you," she said into his ear, and instantly got her wish. He slid inside her wet, swollen sex with a powerful stoke. "Don't hold back. Jayden, make me go crazy."

"Okay," he said in a strained whisper. "Tell me if it's too much, okay?"

Alexia nodded. He went deep, hard, fast, almost roughly slapping against her skin, but she loved it. She grabbed on to his neck and wrapped her legs around his waist, pressing her shoulders into the rug, and let him love her with wild abandon. She opened her eyes and watched, thinking that he was so strong, so incredibly male. His skin glistened with a fine sheen of sweat from the heat of the fire, the intensity of their lovemaking. While he drove into her, Alexia held on, urging him to ride her hard. Letting go like this felt so freeing, so amazingly right to give herself to him without restraint. She panted, muttered random words of encouragement until she opened wide and climaxed.

When he eased her back down to the rug, Alexia clung to him and snuggled her face against his chest. He held her close, hugging her to his body, and she kissed his moist skin while he lightly rubbed her back. The music played softly in the background while the fire crackled and popped. And for the first time in such a long, long while Alexia felt a languid peacefulness settle over her that made her smile.

When Jayden kissed the top of her head as if somehow knowing, she sighed deeply and they simply lay there wrapped up in each other's arms. Oh, how Alexia wished that this bliss could last forever, but, knowing full well that it couldn't, she snuggled close and soaked up the moment.

With the warmth of Jayden's body, the golden glow of the crackling fire, and the sultry music, Alexia's sex-sated body became totally relaxed and she soon felt so bone-tired that she gave in and dozed. *I love you* swirled into her brain like misty fog and she sleepily wished that she could say it to him.

While Alexia slept, Jayden lay awake, not wanting to miss a minute of having her in his arms. He watched the flickering flames while listening to her breathe, wondering how he was going to keep her in his life for good. He knew he had to tread softly . . . and he also knew he somehow had to find out what she was keeping from him. Not that he could ever imagine it would change how he felt about her, but he wanted to *know* so that he could deal with it and dismiss it forever.

Colin knew the answer, Jayden was sure of it, and although he didn't want to put his friend in a tight spot, he was going to have to convince him to tell, to explain what in the hell had happened that Alexia was so afraid of him knowing.

Jayden sighed, wishing things between them were simpler, but then again he supposed that this was a pretty damned good start, all things considered. He held her close, kissed her bare shoulder, and then no longer able to fight it, he too fell asleep.

Jayden wasn't sure how long he slept, but judging by the glowing embers of the fire, quite a while. He smiled, thinking that he was on the doggone floor without a pillow or covers and he had snoozed like a baby when it was usual for him to be a light sleeper. The reason was suddenly crystal clear. Having Alexia wrapped in his arms chased away the restless longing that had plagued him so long. She calmed him down and yet revved him up too, much like the feeling he got while racing. She stirred in his arms, an unconscious sensual move that woke up his libido.

It suddenly occurred to him that since the fire had died down she might be snuggling for warmth. He should wake her, but hated to lose this sense of contentment. Jayden sighed. Oh how he wanted her to wake with a sleepy this-is-meant-to-be smile, minus the wary look in her eyes. She should feel safe and secure in his arms, he thought fiercely, and tightened his hold. She stirred again and sighed as if loath to wake up. Jayden hoped it was because she felt the same sense of peace snuggled in his embrace.

When her warm breath caressed his chest, peace dissolved into desire. Jayden had to swallow a groan when she moved her long leg to entwine with his. The moist heat between her thighs felt so damned good and then, heaven help him, her hand that was splayed on his chest slid downward, stopping just above his groin. Blood rushed south and his dick quickly stood at attention as if saying, *hey, here I am, Alexia.* Her hand moved a little lower and when she brushed against his shaft he about levitated off the rug.

Fully aroused now, Jayden had the incredible urge to roll her over and plunge inside the wet heat snuggled so innocently against his thigh. He supposed, though, that he should ask first . . .

When her back and butt started to chill, Alexia snuggled closer to the warmth. In the back of her head she remembered that she was naked on his floor, but she didn't want to face the reality that her day of free-dom with him was drawing to a close. She didn't know what she was thinking by staying with him anyway, since a future with Jayden meant revisiting the past . . . a painful past that she wanted to leave behind. But she sighed and moved languidly against his skin, refusing to open her eyes. This felt so damned good . . .

Oh my . . .

Alexia realized with a thudding heart that her hand had slid from his chest to his groin. Her fingertips rested in curly, silky hair and her knuckles brushed up against his . . . *penis*. She swallowed hard and wondered what to do. Pulling her hand away would most certainly mean a caress against his steely hard shaft.

But she couldn't just leave it there.

The devil on her shoulder whispered that wasting a perfectly good erection would be such a shame, but rea-son argued that she was getting herself in deeper and deeper when she should back off. Starting over with Jayden meant facing pain . . . risking her heart, which was already battered and bruised.

She wondered if he was awake or just had a case of morning wood. Wait, it wasn't morning, was it? Whatever—the man was as hard as a rock. And she was naked in his arms on a rug in front of the fire. *Why the hell not?* came from the devil, but then *don't you dare* shouted right back. Well, damn . . . , she thought, and then realized that his chest beneath her cheek was rising and falling with shallow breathing. Jayden was awake. He was aroused. And she supposed he was wondering just what to do about it as well.

Make a move, said the devil on her shoulder, and her body responded with a hot shot of desire to her mound that was—*good grief*—nestled against his thigh. She lay as still as a statue while her heart pounded wildly. Well, what the hell? Alexia thought. After what had gone down between them—*literally*, she mused with an inward sigh—what would be the harm? Especially if this was to be her last time with him?

That thought made her throat close up and she swallowed hard. She would not make a fool out of herself by crying. No, sleepy wake-up sex would be so much better than a crying jag. *You can cry later,* she thought, and gritted her teeth. With that in mind she opened her eyes a slit. Darkness. Okay, that meant it was late but she hadn't slept here all night. Which meant that she still had some freedom time left in the day she had allowed herself. So, with that thought in mind, she shifted ever so slightly, causing her knuckles to brush against his penis. He inhaled sharply but then went very still.

Alexia's heart thudded. She wished she was bold enough to just wrap her hand around him, but she decided it was easier to pretend that she was just moving in her sleep.

But then she got pissed at herself.

The old Alexia, the *real* Alexia would have cupped

his sacs and then curled her hand over his stiff shaft and let him know just what she wanted. And it was about damned time that she became herself again.

She was hit with an aha moment.

Enough, already!

She needed to face her doggone fears. Put her past behind her and move on! And if Jayden truly loved her still as he had proclaimed, then he would have to accept her . . . mistakes and all. Right? And if not? Well, then, it was his loss.

Alexia Spencer was back.

With a smile she reached up and softly cupped him as if weighing his sacs in her palm. When he moaned she curled her hand around his steely hard shaft and with a light but firm grip, moved her hand up and down a few strokes before rubbing her thumb in slow circles over the head of his penis. Jayden moved, shifted, moaned.

"Alexia . . ."

"Yeah, that's *me*," she softly proclaimed, and then chuckled at her own inside joke.

"What are you . . . ," he began, but she came to her knees, put a hand on his chest and a finger on his lips. "Just relax and let go," she said, mimicking *his* earlier suggestion to her. Then she leaned in and licked him up and down until he was wet enough to give her hand some help. Instead of going down on him she wanted to make love to him with her hand so she could watch him climax.

"Come up to your elbows," she said. She wanted him to watch too. When he obeyed, she repeated, "Now relax."

"Right . . . ," he said with a shake of his head, but

then moaned deep in his throat when she stroked him slowly. The silky soft skin contrasted with the hard, powerful length that pulsed and throbbed in her hand. When she swirled a French-tipped fingernail over the pearl of moisture his ab muscles tensed and then quivered when she ran a soothing hand over the hard ridges.

The fire, now merely embers, cast a red-gold glow over his skin, and with his long hair framing his face, dark stubble shadowing his jaw, and bold armband tattoo he looked so fiercely sexy that it took her breath away. She met his brown-eyed stare and held his intense gaze while stroking him a bit harder . . . faster. His breathing became shallow and a muscle jumped in his clenched jaw. "Alexia . . . ," he breathed, "God . . ."

Knowing what Jayden wanted . . . what *she* wanted . . . Alexia quickly straddled him. She came up to her knees and then came down hard, taking him inside her to the hilt. Loving the feeling of him buried deep like this, she paused. "Look at me," she said, and when he opened his eyes she cupped her own breasts, rolling her nipples until they were hard points. She moaned and then using his shoulders for leverage, she raised herself up, letting him slip out to the tip, slowing down the pace until she caught up. She rode him easy for a couple of strokes but then went harder, taking him deep and fast until his hips arched up from the rug and he called out her name.

Alexia went over the edge and gripped his shoulders hard while she rode out the waves of pleasure. Then with a sigh she leaned over and kissed him softly. It was on the tip of her tongue to say that she loved him . . . oh, how she wanted to, but couldn't go that far. But she kissed him deeply, almost desperately . . . wound her arms around his neck and wanted him to tell her it would be okay. She had made so many wrong choices, so many mistakes that the fear was so damned hard to shake. What if . . . what if? *what if?* echoed in her brain, making her shiver.

"Cold?" he asked in her ear, and wrapped his arms more firmly around her.

She shook her head against his neck.

And he understood. "Ahh, Alexia, have faith in me this time. I know I ran out on you but I promise I won't ever do that again. *Ever.*" He lifted her chin so that she had to look into his eyes. "And if you want me to retire, then, damn it, I will," he said fiercely.

Alexia shook her head. "I can't ask that of you," she said firmly, and saw such relief in his eyes that she knew how much it cost him to offer to quit his moto-cross career.

"You didn't ask. I offered."

"Oh, Jay . . ." she tilted her face up and kissed him. It blew her away that after all these years he would be willing to do this for her, and for the first time she allowed herself to hope.

... *Chapter Thirteen*

The nervous quaver in Alexia's voice gave Jayden pause. But just when she opened her mouth to reply, both of their cell phones rang. Since she finally seemed to be opening up, he wanted to continue the conversation, and considered not taking the call, but the fact that both phones rang at the same time was too coincidental to ignore. "I guess we should see who is calling us."

Alexia nodded. "I suppose you're right." She stood up and grabbed a throw blanket from a nearby chair and hurried to her purse on the kitchen counter and dug out her ringing phone.

Jayden reached for his jeans and reached into his pocket for his own phone. Glancing at the small screen, he saw that it was Colin. "Hey, dude, what's up?"

"Brianna and I are at Willow Creek Inn about to have a glass of wine. Why don't you and Alexia join us?" Colin asked in a rather hushed voice.

"A glass of wine? Since when do you drink wine?"

"Shut up. I enjoy a nice glass of merlot now and then. I did live in California, you know."

Jayden snorted.

"Okay, I started drinking wine since about ten minutes ago. Whatever. Brianna might be under the impression that I enjoyed wine country."

"Sure, to ride in."

"Yeah, yeah, a minor detail," Colin answered, but then laughed. "Dude, cut me some slack."

"Chill, Colin. I'm just bustin' your balls." He glanced over at Alexia, who was chatting away, and he wondered if it was with Brianna. "I have to wonder why you want company. Won't we cramp your style?"

"Jay, she's nervous as hell. I thought that maybe you two could, I don't know. Loosen her up or something."

"Right, and you're not nervous? Trying to impress her with a glass of wine when your sorry ass really wants a cold beer."

"Shut the hell up and get your ass over here so she doesn't bolt. She went to the bathroom and I swear she might not come back."

"Why?"

"Beats me. Damn, I'm as laid-back as they come."

"And just a little bit . . . uh, world famous."

"What? Come on, like you're not?"

Jayden scratched his chest. "I'm not an icon the way that you are, Colin."

"The hell you're not. You've surpassed most of my records and winning streaks. You jackass."

"Yeah, whatever," Jayden answered. Technically Colin was right. Jayden had more championship wins under his belt including two straight U.S. Open wins, but Colin McCord was instrumental in making moto-cross the popular sport that is was today. He was more than just an amazing racer—he had a personality to go along with it. He landed sponsors and television interviews and was once one of *People* magazine's hundred sexiest men. He even posed in *Playgirl*, something he hated to be reminded of, but of course Jayden did every chance he got. "Hey, has Bri ever seen your pic in *Playgirl*?"

"If you dare tell her, I'll pound you into the ground," he growled in a low, hushed voice.

"Okay, but it'll cost ya."

"Just shut the hell up and get your ass over here. Bring Alexia. Is she still with you?"

"Oh . . . yeah."

"You dog."

"Hey, watch it. I'm not playing with her, Colin."

"I know, or I'd kick your ass for that too."

Jayden turned away so that Alexia couldn't hear him. "Bro, you seem hell-bent on kicking my ass. I think you're the frustrated one who needs to get laid."

"You got that right. That little chick just does something to me . . . *damn*. Brianna's got this nerdy intellectual thing goin' on but there's just something so fucking sexy about her . . . Oh, shit, here she comes. Dude, get here fast!" Colin pleaded, and then hung up.

Jayden shook his head and smiled. Colin had dated supermodels and he was nervous with nerdy little Brianna? He was positively so into her that it wasn't even funny. Okay, it was funny. Colin was falling hard for a small-town, cute but nerdy newspaper editor, but Jayden actually thought it was cool because Brianna was the real deal, not some groupie or gold digger.

Jayden smiled, thinking that the two of them were polar opposites, but he sincerely hoped it worked out for them both. With that thought he glanced over at Alexia, who seemed busy checking messages on her phone. The fringed cover she had draped around her had slipped, revealing one sexy shoulder and enough cleavage to make him start to get hard *again*. Jayden glanced down and wondered how he could still get aroused after so much hot sex, but all it took was a glance her way.

Damn . . . she was really back in his life again. Unbelievable. A little embarrassed, he reached for his jeans and tugged them on, but had to zip them up very carefully or he could do some real damage. He only hoped that she felt the same way.

When Alexia looked up from her cell phone and over at Jayden, her mouth literally watered. His dark hair was bed-head . . . make that rug-head sexy, tumbling to his wide shoulders in a tangled want-to-run-her-fingers-through-it mess. The dark stubble on his jaw had thickened, making him look even more dangerously appealing. He had tugged his weathered jeans on, but if anything it was more enticing than being nude, especially since the top button remained unsnapped.

Today, Alexia thought, had been amazing, dangerously so because she was beginning to realize that she was never going to be able to walk away from a second chance with Jayden. The passion and the laughter that they had shared that afternoon only reiterated that her marriage had been a disastrous youthful mistake. Emotion welled up in her throat when she thought about those lost years, but when he caught her looking his way Jayden gave her a bone-melting, sexy smile and she swallowed her tears. He reached up to run his fingers through his tousled hair, causing a delicious ripple of muscle that had Alexia itching to walk over there and slide her hands up his chest, thinking that she could never get enough of simply touching him, kissing him.

Then, remembering that she was supposed to revert to her old Alexia kick-ass ways, she slowly walked over to him while maintaining eye contact. When she stood directly in front of him she ran her hands over his chest and encircled his neck. She looked up into his deep brown eyes hoping to somehow find her answers there, and then tangling her fingers in his long hair, she pulled his head down for a passionate kiss.

"My God, Alexia . . ." Words that were left unspoken hung heavy in the air.

"Mmm . . ." With a sigh, she leaned against him and rested her head on his chest, loving the steady beat of his heart against her cheek. "Brianna wants us to join her and Colin for a drink," she murmured. "Do you want to go?"

Jayden groaned and then threaded his fingers through her hair. "Is that a trick question?"

Alexia laughed deep in her throat. "We should join them. She's so nervous! It was totally cute."

"Okay . . . call and tell her we'll come," he said while nuzzling her neck.

"All right. We can leave after I freshen up a bit," she said. She rushed through touching up her makeup and a few minutes later they were on their way to Willow Creek Inn.

"I wish I was wearing something other than this jogging suit," Alexia complained as they pulled up to the quaint old farmhouse.

"You look fine."

She arched an eyebrow in old Alexia style and he grinned.

"No, make that amazing."

"I wasn't fishing."

"Well, I was serious. You always look amazing to me, Alexia."

"Right, spoken like a guy. You look stlyish in your black turtleneck." She turned the sun visor down and looked at her reflection in the lit mirror. "My hair is a total wreck." While wrinkling her nose she reached up and fluffed it.

"It's sexy as hell all messy like that. As a matter of fact I think we should just head right back home and—"

"Would you stop?" Alexia giggled as she put a fingertip to his lips, but her laugher became a moan when he sucked her finger into his mouth. The fact that Jayden had referred to his place as *home* shot like an arrow straight to Alexia's heart. "You're killing me," she said gruffly, and meant it in more ways than one.

"Killing you wasn't what I had in mind." He leaned across the bucket seat and gave her a hot, lingering kiss.

"Mmm, we have to go in," she said against his lips. "My God, we're like horny little rabbits. What's wrong with us?"

"We have a lot of lost time to make up for," Jayden said in a playful yet I-mean-it tone.

"Ahh, Jayden." Alexia hugged him close and hoped with all her heart that they could make this work. *I love you* bubbled up in her throat and would have spilled out this time but her cell phone rang. She pulled back and dug into her purse. "Hey, Bri." She grinned at

Jayden, who rolled his eyes. "We're here. We'll be right in." She winked at Jayden and then opened her door.

She was relieved that she hadn't dropped the L word. There was too much left unsaid before she went that far. But then Jayden took her hand and made her feel as if they were truly a couple, and God help her, she loved the feeling. A part of her thought that perhaps it would be best to leave the past buried, but then again that would be the coward's way out and the new Alexia was not a coward. No, she would tell him everything . . . when the time was right. For now she was looking forward to seeing her no-nonsense sister falling head over heels for hotshot Colin McCord.

The interior of the Willow Creek Inn was as quaint as the outside but with a touch of elegance. An elderly, mild-mannered hostess greeted them in the lobby.

"Two for dinner?"

"Actually, we're meeting another couple," Jayden explained. When he squeezed her hand Alexia wondered if he was feeling the warm fuzzies about being a couple. But then Alexia reminded herself not to get too used to the idea.

"Ah yes, right this way," the hostess said, and ushered them into the dining room. "They're seated in the corner."

"Thank you." Alexia followed the woman's slow pace across the room. Dimly lit, with fat flickering candles and lacy tablecloths, the inn smelled of cinnamon and freshly baked bread. On the far side of the room, a fire crackled and popped in a large stone hearth, lending both cozy warmth and golden light.

Brianna spotted them and eagerly waved. Alexia smiled at her sister while Jayden's hand remained possessively at the small of her back as they walked over to the secluded table near the rear of the restaurant.

"Hi there," Brianna said brightly, but appeared relieved to see them. Alexia noted that her sister had a cute, pink blush staining her cheeks and she didn't think it was from the warmth of the fire. Brianna had always been shy around guys and someone as charismatic as Colin was making her all a-flutter. Seeing her usual put-together sister come a little unglued amused Alexia.

"I'm glad you guys could make it," Colin told them while Jayden pulled out a chair for Alexia. "Brianna thought this was a good opportunity to conduct an interview for the paper."

"Oh, so this was your idea, Bri?" Alexia was careful to keep a straight face when Brianna's blush deepened.

Brianna nodded so hard that her curls bounced around her shoulders. "I wanted to do an article about Extreme Machines to pave the way for Alexia's series about Jayden."

"We were just about ready to order another glass of wine," Colin said.

"Sounds good," Jayden said. "What would you recommend, Colin? Is that a merlot you're drinking?"

"Yes, and it's quite . . . ah, tasty," Colin answered. He swirled the wine in his glass and arched a blond eyebrow at Jayden.

"Tasty?" Jayden mused, and then coughed as if hiding a laugh. Alexia wondered what the inside joke was as she watched the interaction between the two friends. When some of the wine almost sloshed over the rim, Alexia thought Jayden was going to lose it, and then it dawned on her that although Colin might dress and look like a California surfer, he was really a hometown boy at heart. The wine was his way of impressing her sister. It was so gag-me cute that Alexia couldn't hold back a smile. She bumped Jayden's knee with hers to let him know she was on to the joke.

"Well, then, let's order a bottle," Alexia suggested, and was met with nods all around. "And some food too."

"Yeah, I'm starving," Jayden agreed, and opened his menu.

"Hard workout today?" Colin asked innocently, but gave them an I-know-what-you've-been-up-to look. Jayden narrowed his eyes at his friend, but Alexia didn't mind the good-natured teasing. She knew that Colin was rooting for her and Jayden to get back together. He gave her a go-for-it look that she understood, then shot him one right back. Brianna could use a little walk on the wild side and she had a feeling that Colin was just the man to do it.

"Let's get down to business," Brianna announced after the wine arrived. Alexia noted that she seemed aware of but not quite sure what to make of the under-currents going on at the table.

"Good idea." Alexia nodded and retrieved a pen and notepad from her purse. Brianna, of course, had her laptop and opened it up for use. The conversation turned to Extreme Machines and motocross. While the wine flowed and food arrived, Alexia and Brianna took rapid notes. It was obvious that both Colin and Jayden were behind the project not only from a financial stand-point but that they wanted to make the motocross park a family-oriented outlet for outdoor physical activity.

"Keeping kids busy is key," Colin stated to Brianna. "Just ask my dad. I was going down the wrong path when he bought me my first two-stroke. Kids need physical activity, and not everyone is cut out for soccer or basketball."

Brianna nodded as she jotted down notes. "Yes, I agree, but how do you feel about your contribution to motocross video games? They're immensely popular and keep kids parked in front of the television. Both you and Jayden are in several of them."

Colin took a drink of wine. "I've wrestled with that question," he admitted, but then shrugged. "It has its downfalls but has increased the popularity of the sport as well."

"Motocross video games are fun, but nothing compares to the real thing," Jadyen interjected. "Having an outlet to do so is a step in that direction. We always had to travel to find motocross clubs. Either that or just tear through the woods without any safety built in."

"I agree," Colin said. "There just aren't enough practice tracks out there and we wanted to do this for the community and for the sport as well. We might not ever get as huge as Loretta Lynn's, but we want the kids of Braxton to know what racing safely is all about. Who knows? We might just discover the next James Stewart, Ricky Carmichael, or Jeremy McGrath. Or at least someone semitalented like Jayden."

Jayden pulled a face. "At least I'm not old and washed up like you."

Colin shook his head and took the jab with a good-natured grin. "Hey, you wanna go?"

"Anytime, man . . . anytime."

Alexia thought their banter was funny, but Brianna looked a bit peeved at Jayden.

"So," Brianna said while tapping her pen to her

cheek. "Who was your mentor in the sport, Jayden? You know, the best in the business?"

Jayden rolled his eyes. "You're gonna make me say it, aren't you?"

Brianna raised her strawberry blonde eyebrows innocently. "Well, yes. It's a legitimate question." She took another sip of wine and Alexia wondered if her sister was getting a little tipsy. When it came to drinking Brianna was a lightweight.

With a groan Jayden admitted, "Colin McCord is and will always be the best in my book. There. Happy?"

"Really?" Brianna asked while tapping her cheek again. "Now tell me, are you and Alexia back together?"

Alexia's eyes widened in surprise at her unexpected change of direction and she nudged Brianna with her toe beneath the table. "Um, I have to go to the ladies' room. Bri, why don't you come with me?"

"I don't—" Brianna began, but Alexia stood up and tugged her sister to her feet. "Um, sure, okay."

When they entered the bathroom Alexia whirled around and fisted her hands on her hips. "Just what the hell do you think you're doing?"

Brianna gave Alexia a sheepish look. "Sorry, I didn't mean to say that out loud."

"How much wine have you consumed?"

Brianna's brows furrowed. "Two glasses, I think. Not too much." She wet a towel and blotted her flushed face. "The question just popped into my head and right out of my mouth. I'm just so nervous!"

"Why?"

"Because he's Colin McCord!"

Alexia shook her head and then put her hands on her sister's shoulders. "He's just a guy, Brianna. He might be an MX champion but he was born and raised in Braxton just like you and me."

Brianna shrugged and averted her gaze.

"Wait, there's more, isn't there?"

While nibbling on her bottom lip, Brianna slowly nodded.

"Tell me."

"No!"

Alexia rolled her eyes.

"You promise not to laugh?"

"Yes."

"No, you don't. I know you better."

"Okay, not really, but come on. Tell me what has you so freaked out."

Brianna bent over to make sure there wasn't anyone in the stalls and then whispered, "When I'm around Colin, all I can think about is . . ."

"What?"

Brianna leaned closer. "What it would be like to . . . *sleep* with him," she finished in a high-pitched whisper, and then blinked at Alexia. "Is that normal?"

"Well, let me see, do you think about him all day long?"

Brianna bobbed her head. "I can't get my work done!"

"And when he touches you, even briefly, do you get a hot tingle all the way to your toes?"

Brianna looked down at her shoes. "Yes! So you're saying that's normal too?"

With one eyebrow arched, Alexia pinched Brianna's cheek. "Baby sister, you're falling in love."

Her eyes opened even wider. "You think so? I was afraid I was getting a little loony."

Alexia squeezed Brianna's shoulders. "It's all part of the process. And do you know what else?"

"What?"

"Remember when you said that you wished someone would look at you the way Jayden used to look at me?"

With a hand to her mouth, Brianna nodded.

"Well, Colin gazes at you like he wants to gobble you up."

"Really?" She picked up the wet towel and blotted her face again. "What should I do now?"

"That, baby sister, is up to you. But we'd better get back in there and finish the interview."

"Yeah, right. Hard to do when I keep picturing him *naked*."

"You're a pro. You can do this." Alexia tugged her toward the door.

Brianna groaned. "I just know I'm going to have some horrible slip of the tongue. If I do, you cover somehow, okay?"

Alexia laughed. "I'll do my best. Come on, you'll be fine."

Brianna tugged on Alexia's hand but then paused at the bathroom door. "Alexia, I'm so glad that you're back home where you belong."

"Me too," she admitted, and realized how much she meant it.

"And you know something? Jayden still looks at you that special way."

"I know," she answered softly.

"Does he still make you tingle, Alexia?"

She swallowed and then answered, "Yeah."

"Then what are we waiting for?"

"Good point," Alexia answered with a smile, but wished it were that simple.

"Then let's get back in there and picture them naked."

Alexia laughed as she followed Brianna out the door and into the dining room. It was fun seeing her serious little sister open up and blossom. Give her another glass of wine, Alexia thought with a grin, and who knew what might happen?

Chapter Fourteen

Colin couldn't keep his eyes off Brianna as she walked back over to their table. After the hot chocolate and whipped cream incident, Brianna had consumed his thoughts. He tried to remember when a woman had affected him so intensely and couldn't even think of one. Shy, but then again feisty, Colin was not only attracted but also intrigued by the sweet but sexy little redhead.

"Okay, let's get back to work, shall we?" Brianna said briskly, but Colin hoped that the flush in her cheeks wasn't due to the wine and instead meant that she was having similar steamy thoughts of him. "So, Jayden, tell me why you think that Colin is the best in the business."

Praise always made Colin squirm, but he thought it was sweet that Brianna had felt the need to come to his defense. While Jayden droned on and on about how he had inspired his motocross career, Colin took the opportunity to observe Brianna in her element. Her brow furrowed in concentration as her fingers clattered across the keyboard. Now, since when was typing on a computer sexy?

Colin smiled. Since right now.

Brianna Spencer was nowhere near the style of woman he usually went for, but perhaps that was why he was still single. Colin found Brianna to be smart, cute, and clever, yet down-to-earth in a grounded way that appealed on a deeper level than just physical attraction.

Not that he wasn't physically attracted to her . . . he was. Big-time. Luckily, he was getting the impression that the feeling was mutual, but he also seemed to make her so damned nervous. He could only hope that the wine relaxed her enough so that he could later pull her into his arms and steal a kiss. Colin chuckled at the thought. *Steal a kiss?* What was he . . . twelve? But then again, Colin knew that he should go slowly with Brianna. He also had the gut feeling that she would be a firecracker once she dropped her inhibitions.

"Colin, you shouldn't scoff at your accomplishments," Brianna commented sternly. "Motocross, Supercross, cross-county moto, X Games . . . is there anything you wouldn't do?"

Colin pursed his lips as if in thought, but what he really wanted to do was end this interview and show her everything he wanted to do with *her*.

"I think he's trying to think of something he hasn't done," Jayden answered. "Dude, remember when you did that monster truck thing?"

Colin laughed. "Hey, it was fun."

Jayden shook his head. "You are mental. The only guy I can think of who is crazier and who has done more stunts than you is Travis Pastrana."

Colin shook his head. "When Pastrana nailed the

double backflip in his run at the '06 summer X Games I was blown away. That's still one of the greatest moments in X history."

"That was tight," Jayden agreed.

"What about the danger?" Alexia asked.

Colin knew she was directing the question more to Jayden than to him but Colin answered. "If you wear the right equipment and service your bike, motocross is perfectly safe."

"Perfectly safe? Oh, come on," Alexia scoffed. "You're talking backflips, defying gravity, for goodness' sake."

Colin shrugged and flicked a glance at Jayden. "There's danger in every sport. We're just flashier about it. In a controlled environment we can keep injuries at a minimum. More wine, anyone?" He reached over and poured another glass of merlot for Brianna and Alexia in an effort to change the direction of the conversation. Colin knew that this was still a bone of contention between Alexia and Jayden. Damn, he hoped that she would just come clean and get the past off her chest. Colin was sure, well, relatively sure, that Jayden would understand.

As if tracking Colin's train of thought, Alexia reached for her wine and took a drink. He met her gaze but she quickly glanced away. Knowing that Jayden would pick up on the undercurrent, Colin said, "Drink up, ladies. The night is young."

"Oh, I've had enough," Brianna protested.

"I'm driving, so you enjoy," Colin encouraged her, and then popped a stuffed mushroom in his mouth.

When Brianna toyed with the stem of the glass

Alexia said, "Oh, go ahead, Bri. If it makes you feel better, I'll have another one with you."

Colin shot Alexia a grateful look while trying to convey that he wasn't trying to get Brianna drunk, just relaxed.

"Well . . . all right," Brianna relented, and took a baby sip and then nibbled at her plate of appetizers.

"Let's stop talking about motocross and just chill," Colin suggested, and Brianna reluctantly agreed. The conversation turned to movies and music, but when they started arguing about politics the hostess shuffled over to their table.

"We're closing up now, folks," she said, and Colin wondered if they were getting too rowdy for the Willow Creek Inn.

After they paid and were outside, Brianna surprised him by saying, "Would you guys like to come back to my house for a while? We can get as loud as we want to there," she added with a grin.

Colin gave Jayden a say-no look.

Jayden stretched, flexed his sore arm, and said, "Thanks, Bri, but I need to get back and soak this arm in the hot tub. I'm going to hit the sack early so I can head over to the track tomorrow morning."

Brianna looked at Alexia.

"I rode with Jayden." She gave her sister a hug. "This was fun but I'm going to work on putting my notes in my laptop. I wasn't smart enough to bring it with me like you." She hugged Colin and then they headed to Jayden's car.

"I wouldn't mind continuing our conversation," Colin offered hopefully.

Brianna hesitated but then nodded. "Okay," she answered so shyly that Colin wanted to drag her into his arms and tell her that she had nothing to be nervous about with him. He might be famous in some circles but he was just a hometown Braxton, Tennessee, boy at heart. And he was thinking that a hometown Braxton girl was just what the doctor ordered.

He walked over to his pickup truck and helped her up into the passenger side thinking that she had the cutest damned butt he had ever seen. Unlike curvy Alexia, Brianna was petite in every sense of the word and he just bet that she had no idea how sexy she was. Well, she was about to find out . . .

Brianna slid her laptop case to the floor of the truck and inhaled a deep breath. She wondered if Colin was going to kiss her before the night was over. A hot tingle slid down her spine at the thought. She had been thinking about him nonstop and now here she was sitting in his truck, about to have him all to herself in her house. Oh, wait . . . she thought while biting her bottom lip, had she left it a mess?

"Hey, don't look so scared," Colin said with a deep chuckle as he started the engine. "I don't bite."

"Unless I want you to?"

Colin laughed at her unexpected answer, thinking that there was so much he wanted to learn about her.

"I'm not scared of you, Colin. I was just worried about the condition of my house. I've been so busy with the paper that my domestic skills suffer." She blew on her hands and rubbed them together.

"Don't worry about your house. I tend to be a slob."

"Really?"

"No. I was trying to make you feel better."

"Oh," she said, and shivered. "I hate cold weather."

"Me too," he said as he pulled out into traffic.

"Then why did you leave California?"

"Because I'm a Tennessee boy in here," he said, and tapped his chest. "And by the way, I have a confession to make."

Her heart pounded. "What?"

"I'm not really a wine-drinking kinda guy."

Brianna frowned. "You're not?"

"No, I was trying to impress you."

"You're kidding, right?" Brianna said slowly. She couldn't believe that Colin McCord thought he needed to impress *her*. It was laughable but he seemed so sincere that it made her relax a bit . . . Of course three glasses of wine helped on that front as well.

"Yeah, I'm pretty much a beer drinker."

Brianna tilted her head and asked, "So did you enjoy the wine?"

He nodded his shaggy head. "Yeah, as a matter of fact, I did. You might be able to refine me if you work at it."

"What if I like you the way you are?" Brianna said, and then wanted to clamp a hand over her mouth. "I just said that out loud, right?"

Colin laughed. "Yeah, you did, but I feel the same way about you so we're even. You live on Cottonwood, right?"

"How'd you know?"

"I asked Alexia."

"You care about her, don't you?"

"As a friend," he said as if not wanting her to get the wrong idea. "As you know, she's had it rough. I'd love to see her and Jayden make it this time."

"Me too. It's obvious that they're crazy about each other. Wow, the way he looks at her . . . ," Brianna commented with a sigh, but then felt silly at her admission and looked out the window.

"Warm enough?" Colin asked when there was a stretch of silence.

"Yes, thanks, but I'm going to hate to step out into the cold," she admitted. "This is my house." She pointed to her little bungalow that was a fixer-upper, but she loved it. But then she remembered hearing that Colin just bought a huge house overlooking a lake. And he thought he needed to impress her by drinking wine? Even though he was retired Brianna knew that he still made tons of money doing personal appearances. He even had a line of moto-themed clothing that sold at malls nationwide. Inhaling a deep breath, she tried not to let that knowledge intimidate her.

"Cute house," Colin commented as they approached the front door.

"It's not much but it's mine." While she unlocked the door, she prayed it wasn't a mess. She breathed a sigh of relief when she flicked on the light and it was only a little bit of a mess. "Can I get you something to drink?" She smiled and said, "A glass of wine perhaps?"

He grinned as he shrugged out of his leather jacket. "Do I still need to impress you?"

"No. Surely you realize that you never did."

"Never did impress you?" he teased, and she rolled her eyes.

"Never needed to."

"Then a beer, please."

"Coming right up," she said, and he followed her into the small eat-in kitchen. When she flicked on the light she said, "The woman who owned this before me hadn't updated since the 1950s. Instead of replacing the cabinets and tile I decided to just go with the retro look and keep it."

Colin nodded after taking a long pull on his beer. "I think it's tight."

"Really?"

"Yeah."

"Well, since I couldn't afford to remodel anyway, it's a moot point." She looked down at her shoes.

"Hey," he said softly, and walked over to lean against the sink next to her. "I've been fortunate enough to have achieved some financial success, but I know where my roots are, Brianna. None of that really means much to me. I'm still happiest when I'm riding alone outdoors and not for the cheering crowd."

"You don't miss it?"

He shrugged. "Well, yeah, sometimes. But I was more than ready to come home."

Knowing she shouldn't, Brianna poured herself a glass of wine. "What about all the . . . you know . . ."

"Women?"

"Yes . . . no." She shook her head. "God, what am I saying to you?" When Colin put his beer down and gently took her glass from her and placed it on the counter, her heart started to pound. "What are you doing?"

"I'm going to do what I've wanted to do all night." He turned in her direction and tilted her head up. "I've wanted to kiss you."

"Then what are you waiting for?" She closed her eyes with anticipation. But instead of crushing her lips to his he stopped a hairbreadth away and paused while her heart pounded harder. Then he cupped her head with one big hand while drawing her close with the other one at her back.

Then he kissed her.

Softly, gently tangling his tongue with hers. "You tasted like I thought you would," he said gruffly into her ear.

"And how is that?"

"Sweet, honest . . ."

"I hear a but in there somewhere," she said breathlessly.

"But with a hint of hot . . . ," he began, but then stopped himself and shook his head.

"Say it," she demanded and looked up at him.

"Brianna, there's a sexiness about you that you're not even aware of and it just makes it all the more intense. God, it makes me want to just eat you right up."

"Then—"

"No." He put a finger to her lips. "Don't say it. Because I won't be able to stop myself. You've had some wine."

"I'm not intoxicated."

He let his finger glide back and forth over her bottom lip. "Yeah, but, Brianna, if we end up in bed I don't want any regrets. I'm not on the road anymore. I'm looking for something real . . . lasting. I don't want you to think I planned this." He smiled at her. "All I wanted tonight was to steal a kiss."

"That's so romantic."

Colin grinned while shaking his head. "I guess you bring it out in me."

"Don't look so embarrassed. I think it's adorable."

"Adorable?" He groaned. "This is getting out of hand. Is that the wine talking?"

"No, it's the sexy side that you bring out in me," she said with a low giggle. "Well, and a little bit of the wine."

Colin closed his eyes and breathed in deeply. "Okay, I'm officially crazy, but I'm leaving."

"What? Well, I'm not crazy, so I'm not about to let you go." Brianna wrapped her arms around his waist and gazed up at him. "Look, I'm not a kid anymore."

"So I've noticed."

"I'm not after a one-night fling either, but no matter what comes of this, I won't regret it, Colin. So if that's what's holding you back . . ."

He reached down and tucked a lock of red-gold hair behind her ear. "Sex complicates things, Brianna."

She pursed her lips. "You're right. We should wait. I mean, once you get to know me you might not even like me."

Colin threw his head back and laughed. "That's not gonna happen."

"Then just kiss me a little bit more . . ."

Colin's heart thumped in his chest because he wondered if he could stop at just kissing. He gazed down at her heart-shaped face, her lush mouth, but it was her eyes, her sincere gaze that had him dipping his head and capturing her lips.

Colin kissed her tenderly, exploring her sweet mouth thoroughly, deeply, on and on until he picked her up and cupped her ass. She wrapped her arms around his neck and her legs around his waist and without breaking the kiss he somehow found his way to her sofa. A small lamp illuminated the room that was sweet and feminine and yet neat and no-nonsense just like her personality. He gently placed her on the cushions and then looked down at her knowing that if he joined her he wouldn't be able to keep his mouth from hers or his hands off her body.

"You are insanely gorgeous," she said in that forthright manner that Colin found irresistible.

"Brianna." He shook his head.

"Don't you dare think about leaving," she said, and then her eyes widened as if she couldn't believe what she just said to him.

"Look," Colin began, and then raked his fingers through his hair. He didn't want this to be just physical, but he didn't know how to express his feelings without sounding girly or insulting. He glanced away while trying to find the right words.

"But you're so much more to me than eye candy."

Colin whipped his head around to face her. "Eye candy?" he tried to joke, but she hit way too close to home.

"You know what I mean," she said softly. The understanding in her eyes had him shaking his head in wonder.

"How is it that you're so perceptive?"

She shrugged. "I guess with all the interviews I've done, I've learned to read people."

"Mmm, maybe but I think you somehow get me, Brianna."

"I'm beginning to," she said, and patted the cushion

beside her. After he sat down she tucked one leg beneath her and turned to face him.

"This is an odd role reversal, isn't it?"

Brianna cupped his cheeks with her palms. "It just makes me want you even more," she said softly, and then leaned in to kiss him.

Colin moaned and then threaded his long fingers in her soft curls. Just another kiss, he told himself, but when she ran the tip of her tongue over his bottom lip desire unfurled in his gut and he knew he wasn't going anywhere. His heart thudded when she scooted back and then slowly unbuttoned her blouse to reveal a lacy white bra that pushed her small breasts up over the cups.

"I'm . . . not very curvy," she apologized as she struggled out of her sleeves.

"You're perfect," he said, and reached over to trace a fingertip over the delicate swell of her breasts. Her warm, soft skin felt amazing, making him want to have her naked so he could run his hands all over her delicious little body.

"Take your shirt off for me," she requested with a shy smile.

"Okay." When he complied, she put her small hands on his chest and leaned over and placed soft, moist kisses on his bare skin. He was so used to aggressive women but he found her gentle exploration, her tender touch to be achingly arousing. He needed to see more of her. "Brianna . . ."

As if reading his mind she lifted her butt so he could pull off her khaki slacks, revealing plain white panties that had one tiny pink bow in the waistband. They shouldn't have been sexy but on her they were.

"God, Brianna."

"I know," she said, and licked her lips. "I need a trip to Victoria's Secret."

"Hell no. You are the perfect combination of sex and innocence."

She shook her head. "I'm—"

"Sexy as sin. Driving me crazy," he assured her, and hot damn, she was. When he reached around her and unhooked her bra her small breasts tumbled free. Before he could do anything else he had to dip his head and capture a nipple in his mouth. With a quick intake of breath Brianna groaned and leaned back on her elbows. When Colin sucked one delectable breast and then the other she squirmed and giggled in such a free and uninhibited manner that he laughed along with her. At first he thought perhaps she was just nervous but then realized that she was enjoying herself in an honest and unpracticed way.

He loved that about her.

"God, your mouth feels so good," she said with a delightful laugh. "More, please!"

"You don't have to ask twice." Getting with the program, Colin playfully pushed her to her back. He nuzzled, licked, kissed, and caressed every inch of her body except for where she wanted him the most.

"Colin . . . ," she said with a deep giggle. "You are driving me stark, raving mad. Puh-lease!"

"Okay." He hooked his thumbs in her panties, tugged the white cotton to her ankles, and tossed them over his head. Then he eased up to his knees so he could simply look at her.

"Stop," she said, and for the first time seemed a little shy. She covered her breasts with her hands.

"Why?"

"I wish there was . . . more of me."

Colin gave her a soft smile. He gently pried one hand from her breasts and placed it on his erection. "This is what you do to me, Brianna. Your body is . . . exquisite."

She smiled. "Good word."

"Hey, I'm not just a dumb blond," he said with a goofy pout that made her laugh.

"Don't you think I know that?" She reached up and cupped his cheeks. "Colin, what you're doing for Braxton is amazing. This sleepy little town needed a shot in the arm. So much good will come from this because of your motocross club. Revenue, jobs, and not to mention outdoor fun for inactive kids."

Colin leaned in and kissed her. "Thank you," he said in her ear. "That means a lot to me." The fact that she took him seriously meant the world to Colin because no one had ever valued him for more than his racing. He had always been the daredevil, the goof-off, and she had just given him what he had always craved . . . *respect*.

"Now shut up and kiss me," she demanded softly.

"Okay, but I want you in bed," he said, and scooped her up into his arms.

"Down the hallway and to the left," she said, and then wrapped her arms around his neck.

When they reached her bedroom he let her slide slowly down his body. She reached over to turn on one small lamp and then turned around to pull back the covers. After sitting down on the bed she came to her knees, reached up, and unzipped his jeans. "Off with these," she said, and tugged the denim over his hips.

Colin stepped out of his jeans and kicked them away. When she seemed shy about removing his boxer briefs, he gently placed her hand over his erection, guiding her hand over the soft cotton. She sucked in a breath and then about made his knees buckle when she pulled his boxers off and put her cool hand over his hot skin.

"Okay, now kiss me, Colin."

Colin leaned down and granted her wish. Playfulness, though, turned to passion and as he suspected, Brianna was sensual and giving. She kissed him without holding back and opened her body to him in a somewhat shy and yet naturally sexy manner that blew Colin away. He moved his mouth from her lips to her breasts while grazing his hand over her mound. She shivered, moaned, and when he slipped a finger inside her he discovered that she was hot and more than ready. Pausing only to roll on a condom, Colin entered her heat with a happy groan. She was tight so he took it slow, letting her get used to his size.

"You okay?" he asked.

"Yes, oh yes," she answered, and rocked with him in a slow, easy rhythm.

"Wrap your legs around me, Brianna."

She nodded. "God," she cried when he held her up and went deeper.

Colin circled his hips, caressing her, hitting the spots he hoped would drive her crazy. He went deep but slow and easy since she was so small and he was a big guy, but she would have none of it. Arching her back, she wrapped her legs tighter, giving him everything and holding nothing back.

"Colin!" She kissed him deeply, drinking him in while he made love to her with heated passion until she climaxed, opening wide and then wringing a heart-stopping orgasm from Colin that had him holding her tightly while his body exploded with a hot rush of pleasure.

For a moment time seemed suspended while their hearts pounded. Finally, Colin kissed her tenderly and then rolled to the side with her in his arms. He thought she would be amazing, but this was even better than he had imagined. She was sweet honesty, hot sex . . . and he was completely taken with her. Although he had never been one to cuddle he pulled her closer so that her head rested on his chest. When she sighed he lifted her hand to his mouth and kissed her palm, a gesture that he didn't think he had ever done before but suddenly felt so right.

"Stay with me, Colin," she whispered.

He answered by tilting her head up and kissing her softly. Her lips were warm and pliant and she felt so good in his arms. It scared him a little because she was young, vulnerable, and could easily get hurt. This was too soon and yet felt so right. "There's nowhere else I'd rather be," he said, and then thought that it sounded too much like a cornball line and swallowed a groan. But her breathing was slow and deep and he realized with a grin that she was fast asleep. He made a mental note to back it down . . . not an easy task since slow just wasn't in his nature. But he'd have to try because this was too damned good to screw up.

Chapter Fifteen

"*D*ude, where the hell have you been?" Jayden asked when Colin showed up at the Extreme Machines office almost an hour late.

"I overslept," Colin admitted. He hung his leather jacket up with a sheepish grin.

"Right, like I believe that one." Jayden arched a skeptical eyebrow at his friend. "I had to do an interview with *Racer X* magazine, send the bulldozer over to the south woods, and talk to both Nate Adams and Brett Metcalfe about coming to the grand opening." He sighed. "Then your publicist called, DC Teamworks wants to design a shoe for you, Thor wanted you to test some gear, which by the way I volunteered for. Dude, the list goes on and on."

"Welcome to my world."

Jayden vacated Colin's seat behind his desk and gratefully let him take over the reins. "Yeah, but I'm the *silent* investor, remember?"

"Right, like you don't have to do all that same shit for your sponsors."

"Yeah, my shit, not yours. You're damned lucky I just happened to come in early to practice and thought I'd drop in and see how things went with you and Brianna. Obviously, good." He sat down on the edge of the desk and hoped for a full report.

"Hey, I'm not gonna kiss and tell."

"So you kissed." Jayden grinned while wiggling his eyebrows. "And spent the night."

"How'd you know?"

"I didn't."

"You jackass."

"Okay, I don't want to be all up in your business but give me something. Like how into her are you?"

"Totally." Colin leaned back in the desk chair and folded his hands behind his head. "She blows me away, man. She's not a hit-it-and-git-it kinda chick, Jayden. She's the real deal."

Jayden grinned. "The mighty Colin McCord has fallen."

"Don't be so fucking smug. You know, I thought at first that the age thing would come into play," Colin admitted.

"Dude, it's just a number."

Colin crossed his legs up on the desk and groaned. "I don't know . . . all those years of racing have given me aches and pains like I'm an old fart. Then I thought our personalities were so different, and we might not mesh, ya know? She's so reserved."

"And your ass is crazy."

Colin laughed. "You got that right, although I've toned it down a tad since retiring."

"Yeah, right." Jayden shook his head. "The buzz in town was that you did a backflip showing off the new ramp yesterday, landed sideways, and somehow muscled it back around and rode away without crashing. Then I heard you did a click flip with a no-handle lander. Yeah, you've sure toned it down, dude."

Colin shrugged him off. "I was showing off for the crowd. Trying to drum up publicity." He threaded his fingers through his hair, making it stand up on end. "It won't be an everyday thing, that's for damned sure," he commented while flexing his neck and shoulders. "I'm getting too old for that shit."

"Do you think that Brianna is cool with the danger or does she wig out like Alexia?"

"We haven't talked about it but she's totally behind Extreme Machines. I was glad to hear that from her since, as ya know, not everyone in Braxton is down with the idea." He smiled. "But, Jay, damn, she let down her guard last night. And she's got a sense of humor that I never expected and is just so open and honest. Nothin' fake or phony or put-on. After all those chicks on the road who just wanted a piece of me, I know that she's the real deal."

"So what are you gonna do about it?"

"Hope she doesn't come to her senses, I guess," he said with a grin, but then looked down at the floor.

Jayden frowned over at his friend. "Whoa-ho, wait a minute. Your ass isn't thinking something insane like you're somehow not good enough for Brianna, are you?"

"Naw . . . course not," Colin scoffed with a wave of his hand. "Screw that."

Jayden narrowed his eyes at his friend.

"Okay, maybe. Look, I started racing in junior high.

I dropped out of high school so I could compete and had to get my GED. Pissed my parents off so bad I don't think they'll ever get over it," he said with a chuckle, but then sobered. "Dude, Brianna's a smart little shit."

"Tell me that your ass is joking," Jayden sputtered as he pushed up from the desk. With a sweeping gesture he said, "Okay, all this is yours, you have a huge house on the hill and God knows what other property you own. You are a world-class, record-holding athlete and you're worried that you're not good enough for someone . . . anyone?"

Colin chuckled. "It sounds goofy when you say it out loud."

"That's because it's bullshit."

"Yeah, you're right," Colin replied, but there was something in his tone that had Jayden not completely buying it.

"Will ya look at us?" Jayden asked, and raised his palms in the air. "We're supposed to be badasses and we're a couple of love-struck fools."

"Damn, I know," Colin replied, but then grinned. "Coolness. It kinda gives me the same feeling as blazing speed across a tabletop," he said with such a dreamy expression that Jayden laughed. "Dude, if you tell anybody what I just said I'll kick your ass."

"Hey, I'm not one to talk. I've even been thinking of calling it quits so I can settle down and start a family. Can you see my wild ass as a dad?"

An odd expression passed over Colin's face that Jayden couldn't quite read, but then he said, "Screw this paperwork. Let's go catch some big air."

"You don't have to ask twice."

* * *

Lured by the rumbling whine of motorcycle engines, Alexia veered off the path through the woods and pushed through the winter brush to a clearing. While shading her eyes against the glare of the sun, she watched Colin and Jayden race over the winding motocross track from her perch on the hillside. The two-mile track now had two triples, about a dozen berms, four rhythm sections, some step-ups, step-downs, and tabletops. She knew from experience that the bumpy, choppy, uneven grade was an effort to simulate actual race conditions. She also knew that from wear and tear and weather the tracks never stayed the same.

"God!" Her heart leapt to her throat when Jayden popped up twenty feet or so in the air but then landed smoothly and veered into a left-hand turn as if it were nothing. It had been a long time since Alexia had watched him ride and she tried to shake that uneasy knot forming in her stomach. She reminded herself that Jayden was a seasoned pro and riding was like breathing to him, but after seeing him crash and burn, it was difficult not to worry. She had to smile, though, when he and Colin tried to outdo each other. "Show-offs," she mumbled with a shake of her head.

After Jayden had left the cabin earlier that morning she had worked on writing his story, but after a while had become restless and in need of a brisk walk. Luckily, the weather remained mild for November and she had already shed her hoodie and tied it around her waist. Alexia inhaled deeply, letting the woodsy scent of freshly turned earth and pine clear her head.

The entire time she had hiked her thoughts had been centered on Jayden. With the hushed peace of nature surrounding her as she walked, Alexia had been able to come to a couple of conclusions. One, she still loved Jayden beyond all reason and two, he could still make her explode with passion like no other.

Alexia closed her eyes and swallowed. No other man had ever come close to making her feel the way she felt while in his arms. After careful soul-searching she finally knew what she was going to do about it. Her heart thumped hard at the thought but she was going to tell him everything. Soon.

The high-pitched growl of the engines had her opening her eyes and watching again. From this vantage point it was easy to see why Jayden and Colin were world-class champions. Both rode as if the bike were an extension of their bodies. While Colin was more of a risk taker, Jayden rode closer to the ground in a more calculated way as they flew across the dirt. The track itself was still a work in progress and she knew that in the end Colin wanted three different courses, peewee, amateur, and advanced. Right now the track wasn't as hard-packed as it should have been, causing dirt to fly, but it didn't hold them back in the least. Alexia cringed when she watched Jayden zoom over the bumpy whoops, thinking that it must be jarring his sore shoulder. But if the pain bothered him he didn't let it show.

While she watched, it occurred to Alexia that if he was willing to practice through the pain, as much as she wanted to, she couldn't ask him to give up racing. Brianna was right. It was in his blood. This might well be his last year and she didn't want to take that away from him. And yet he had offered to give it all up for her. "Amazing," she whispered, and realized with heart-pounding clarity that he really did love her.

Accept it, embrace it, believe it seemed to come to her on the edge of the cool November breeze. With a slow smile followed by a soft laugh, Alexia turned back to the woods. It was about time that she forgave herself for her past mistakes and looked forward to a future that she deserved. With a lighter step she started walking back toward Jayden's cabin. With each step she took on the well-worn path, her resolve became stronger and by the time she reached the front door she had the entire day planned out. First, she intended to greet him in the hot tub . . . wearing nothing but a smile. Second, she would prepare a candlelight dinner that would knock his socks off.

Then . . . oh, then she was going to make love to him with such passion that he would never forget it.

"Wow, nothing to work with at all," she mused after taking inventory of his food situation. Typical bachelor, she thought, but then remembered that she too had existed on frozen dinners and canned soup. "Time to hit the grocery store," she said as she closed the refrigerator door, thinking that maybe she'd get lucky and that cute Aussie Take Home Chef would come to her rescue and prepare a kick-ass meal on her behalf. Okay, not likely that Curtis Stone would be hanging out in the Braxton, Tennessee, Piggly Wiggly, she thought with a grin.

But then Alexia began planning the menu in her head and actually got excited about cooking a meal. So it had been a while, but surely it was like riding a bike, right? She certainly hoped so and she was going to soon find out.

Chapter Sixteen

Jayden entered the cabin to the unfamiliar but oh-so-welcome aroma of food cooking. The closest he had come to preparing a meal had been milk poured on cereal. "Damn," he said when he peeked beneath a lid and discovered beef stew merrily bubbling in a big pot. "Holy crap," he said when he spotted a golden-crusted pie cooling on the kitchen counter. The delicious scent of apples and cinnamon mingled with the savory aroma of the beef and vegetables. His stomach rumbled in spite of the fact that he and Colin had devoured a pizza for lunch, but seriously, when was the last time he had eaten a home-cooked meal?

"Alexia?" he called out, but was met with silence. Her silver SUV was in the driveway, so he knew she was in the cabin somewhere. "Hello?" he tried again while hoping that she might be soaking in the hot tub. But when he got to the doorway of his bedroom he stopped in his tracks and smiled. Alexia was curled up in the middle of his bed, almost swallowed up in his white terry cloth robe. She snoozed on top of the covers as if she had lain down for a quick rest and then had fallen asleep. He must have made some noise, because she shifted and then sighed. The robe gaped open, revealing one long, shapely leg and making Jayden guess that she was nude beneath the robe. At that enticing thought an involuntary groan escaped Jayden and she opened her eyes.

"Jayden?" she mumbled with a frown, and then quickly sat up, looking a bit dazed and sleep-rumpled sexy. "Oh! What time is it?" She brushed back the hair from her eyes and blinked.

"Um, I'm not sure. Around five o'clock, I think." He noticed a dusting of flour on her cheek and smiled. "You've been busy."

She returned his smile with a sleepy one of her own. "I was supposed to be waiting in the hot tub, but I guess all that cooking and baking wore me out. I'm a bit rusty."

"Judging by the amazing smell coming from the kitchen, you've created a kick-ass meal."

"That was my intention. It's been a while. I hope you won't be disappointed."

"Impossible." He'd eat it if it tasted like cardboard just because she took the time to make it for him.

Her smile deepened, drawing him like a magnet to the bed.

"So, are you hungry?"

"Oh yeah," he said, and untied her belt. "God, Alexia," he said as he parted the robe, revealing her nude body. Her skin was warm, soft, and supple beneath his exploring hands. She moaned and stretched and then gasped when he dipped his fingers into her silky wetness and then into his own mouth. "I'm hungry for you." He kissed her then, needing to taste her everywhere.

"Jayden . . ." She tugged on his head.

"No, please. I've thought about you all day long. While I was riding."

"Mmm, dangerous."

"And I kept thinking of you while I was helping Colin design the next moto track." He chuckled. "Don't blame me if the course is shaped like you. Lots of hills," he said, and licked his way over her breasts. "Peaks," he said, and sucked on her nipples. "Mmm, and valleys," he continued as he licked his way down her belly to her mound.

Alexia laughed. "Jayden, you're a crazy man."

"That's a given. I'm also a horny man. You are the only cure."

Alexia laughed harder. "Did you mean horny or corny?"

"Shut up. I mean what I say and I say what I mean. Or something like that," he joked, but then raised his head and looked at her. "Seriously. I know we kid around but, Alexia . . ."

"I know," she said, and pulled his head down for a long, hot kiss. He tasted like sex and man and desire. "I've been thinking about you all day long too. Now let's eat."

"Mmm, okay." He dipped his head and kissed her again.

"I mean food," she insisted against his mouth.

"It will keep," he protested, but then frowned. "What?"

"I'm a dusty mess from the track. I need a shower . . . or better yet, let's soak in the hot tub."

Alexia nodded. "Okay, I'll turn the stew down to simmer. We can start with some appetizers and wine. You heat up the tub while I gather the food together."

"Sounds like a plan," Jayden answered. "Oh, and, Alexia?"

"Hmm?"

"Thank you for cooking dinner," he said, and then leaned over and kissed her tenderly. "The pie smelled amazing."

Alexia gave him a pleased but almost shy smile that tugged at his heart. "I just hope the crust turned out. I haven't made a dessert from scratch in years."

"It's going to be delicious," he assured her as he reluctantly pushed up from the bed, but he was a dusty, dirty mess. He sensed a shift in her attitude and she seemed more relaxed and at ease with him. He wasn't sure what brought on this sudden change of heart, but it gave him renewed hope that their relationship was headed in the right direction. Jayden hated thinking about all the years they had lost, and he didn't want one more day to go by without Alexia back in his life.

While Jayden turned on the heat in the hot tub, he had the weird sensation that he was being watched, but then shook it off. Who would be out here in the woods? It was too late for hiking. But then he heard some rustling in the dry leaves and turned to peer into the semi-darkness. "Probably just a raccoon," he muttered beneath his breath as he headed back inside.

After taking off his dusty clothes, Jayden tugged on a pair of sweats and joined Alexia in the kitchen. An offer to help was on the tip of his tongue, but watching her was so enjoyable that he stood a few feet away and observed. Wow, she looked so cute in the oversized robe, no, make that damned sexy, Jayden thought when she reached up into the upper cabinet for wineglasses. The terry cloth molded to her ass, making Jayden want to walk over and cup her cheeks in his hands.

Thinking *why the hell not?* he came up behind her in three long-legged strides and did just that. She jumped as if startled but then sighed and leaned back against him. "You look much better in that robe than me," he commented in her ear, and then let his hands roam over the soft, nubby material.

"Hmm, I don't think I would be of the same opinion," she replied in her husky voice that was an immediate turn-on. Of course anything to do with her caused an instant erection.

"Yeah, but I don't have these," he said, and moved his hands to her breasts.

With a low chuckle Alexia rubbed her ass against his groin. "But you have . . . *that*."

"True . . ." Jayden sucked in a breath and then decided to get even by sliding one hand inside her robe and onto her warm skin. When he caressed her breast while nuzzling her neck, she moaned and wiggled her ass back and forth. "God, Alexia." He loosened her belt and let the robe slide to her waist. While cupping the weight of her breasts in his hands he circled her nipples with the smooth pads of his thumbs and then went one step further and flicked back and forth with his thumbnails.

Alexia gasped and leaned her head back on his shoulder. "Ahhh, baby," he said hot and breathy in her ear. "You feel so good in my hands," he said, and then tilted his head down for a long intense kiss. He continued to caress her breast with one hand while he untied the knot with his other, allowing her robe to part and then slip to the floor. When he slid his palm over her belly her stomach muscles quivered in response. Then he teased her mound, parting her folds before slipping his middle finger inside her slick heat. With a groan he used the silky wetness to lubricate her and then lightly rubbed in small circles. Jayden kissed her deeply while he continued to caress her. He increased the pressure while rubbing faster and then rolled her nipple between his finger and thumb.

"Bend over for me, Alexia," he said, and when she did he yanked his sweatpants down, freeing his dick. "Hold on to the counter," he told her, and then entered her from behind.

"Ahhh," she moaned, raising her head and arching her ass. From this position he could go so deep that his groin was flush against her smooth ass. Jayden grasped her waist with one hand while he continued to finger her with the other. "Mmm," she breathed, and gripped the counter harder. Jayden continued to thrust deep but slowly, watching the intensely erotic sight of his dick moving in and out of her. The delicate curve of her back and smooth, rounded flair of her ass was enticingly feminine and even now, when he was almost mindless with passion, it occurred to Jayden how much he cared for her. "Jay . . . ," she said, and when she turned her head to the side he could see her closed eyes and pink parted lips, and when she cried out he thrust in as far as he could go. While splaying his hand over her stomach he spilled into her with a long hot rush that seemed to come from his toes and go on forever.

Alexia put her palms on the smooth countertop and

then rested her forehead there as well. Her nipples, still hard and pointed, grazed the cool surface, making her shiver. From behind her Jayden's breathing sounded labored, ragged, and she smiled thinking that he was as affected as she. With a groan he pulled out and then turned her around and wrapped her in his arms.

"You drive me insane," he said before kissing her softly.

"Mmm, same here," Alexia admitted with a low chuckle. She kissed both cheeks, his nose, and then licked his stubble-roughened chin. "I want to eat you right up." When she boldly cupped his package he sucked in a breath and his ab muscles tightened. "Sensitive?"

"Yeah." He nodded and then rested his forehead against hers. "Let's soak in the hot tub, drink some wine, and then eat. We need an intermission."

"Intermission?"

Jayden pulled back and looked down at her. "Hey, as they say, the night is young."

"Yeah, but we aren't—young, that is."

Jayden laughed. "You make me feel like a teenager, Alexia. God, you're good for me." His smile faded and his expression became serious. "For a long time I was focused on my career. I was scared shitless that once I retired, I would be lost . . . unhappy. But you came along when I needed you most. I needed to be reminded of the importance of love, friends, and family. Thank you, sweetheart, for bringing that back into my life."

Alexia's throat closed with sudden emotion. She reached up and put her palms on his cheeks. "It feels wonderful to be needed, desired, loved. The amazing sex is a product of how we feel. I've opened myself up in ways I didn't dream were still possible." She squeezed his cheeks. "Jayden, after what I've been through, I'm still afraid, but I want this to work."

Jayden frowned. "Alexia, there's no reason I can think of for it not to."

Alexia looked down at the floor and then back up at Jayden. She wished that the past could remain buried, but because it could affect their future as a couple, Jayden had the right to know.

After she shrugged back into the robe and he into his sweatpants, Jayden took her hand. "Let's hit the hot tub."

"Okay," she agreed while feeling both relief and a measure of anxiety. "I guess we can talk later."

Jayden gave her a quick kiss and then searched in the drawer for the corkscrew. "Aha, here it is," he declared, and then popped the cork with ease.

"Thank you." Alexia reached for a glass and after Jayden poured the Shiraz she followed him through the small cabin. As they passed the furry rug and fireplace, memories of their lovemaking flooded her brain. Pretty soon they would have utilized every nook and cranny of the rustic A-frame. After so many years of unhappiness this joy felt surreal, almost too good to be true, and she found herself waiting for the other shoe to drop. But then Jayden turned and gave her one of his bone-melting smiles and she latched on to the fact that they were in love. Inhaling a deep breath, she smiled back and told herself that surely with feelings this strong everything would be all right.

Armed with that thought, she stepped out into the cool night breeze. She draped her robe over the fence and then watched as Jayden removed his pants. The tub was secluded, so there wasn't any chance of being watched and she didn't have a swimsuit anyway. Jayden politely held her hand and assisted her into the steaming, gurgling water. "Ahh," Alexia breathed as she settled onto the slippery seat. "This feels wonderful," she commented as she leaned her shoulders against the edge of the tub and took a sip of wine.

Jayden sat down across from her and rolled his head from one shoulder to the other. "Mmm, you got that right."

"How's your shoulder doing?"

"Better," he admitted, and then grinned. "It would be healed if I would stop riding for a few days."

"Like that's going to happen."

He shrugged and then slicked his long hair back away from his face. "Probably not."

Alexia arched an eyebrow. "Probably?"

"Okay, just not." He leaned back and looked over at her for a long moment.

"What?"

"Nothing."

"Oh, don't give me that." She extended her leg and nudged him with her foot.

"Okay, I was just thinking how amazing it is to have you here with me like this." He shook his head and then looked up at the stars that were coming to life in the inky night sky. "The mush that keeps coming outta my mouth sounds so damned corny." He shook his head but then continued. "But I mean it, Alexia. When you stop and think, it's amazing that after all this time we're back together."

Alexia stared down at her wine and then took a sip. "Life sure isn't what I expected. You have to roll with the punches."

He shifted on the seat to find a jet. "Yeah, but then again, here we are."

She smiled and said softly, "Yeah, here we are."

Jayden looked at her for a moment that seemed suspended in time. But then he suddenly swallowed hard and his eyes rounded. But when Alexia opened her mouth to ask what was wrong he put his finger to his lips. Her heart pounded at the strange expression on his face, but she remained silent. Was it something she said? Did she have something hanging from her nose? She reached up and swiped at her face but found nothing out of place. He slowly placed his wineglass on the ledge and then sat there blinking at something behind her, but when her shoulder twitched as she started to turn around to look Jayden shook his head and mouthed, "Don't move."

As if on cue the timer on the hot tub ceased. Eerie silence followed but Jayden's finger went back to his lips. Really alarmed now, Alexia mouthed, "What?"

Jayden's mouth moved in what looked like *abracadabra*. Alexia frowned wondering if this was some kind of joke. He used to be pretty good at practical jokes, but she hoped he remembered that she was better. "What?" she mouthed again, but he did the same abracadabra thing, only slower as if that would help. Alexia was getting frustrated, but if this was a practical joke the look on his face was some darned good acting. A cold shot of fear cut through the hot water. She blinked over at him and waited.

Chapter Seventeen

Jayden narrowed his eyes in the waning light and tried to telepathically send a message for the doggone bear to head back to the woods, but the big animal just chilled there on the deck as if waiting to be invited to dinner. Jayden's heart about pounded out of his chest when the bear started lumbering around sniffing as if searching for food. While not really predatory, black bears could do some damage if threatened, he knew, so he sat very still and hoped that he would leave.

Jayden wanted to shout, "Shouldn't you be sleeping in a cave somewhere?" But then he remembered reading a recent article in the *Braxton Times* that the unseasonably warm weather could lure the normally hibernating bears out into the open and they would be searching for food.

If Jayden were here alone he would do something to try and startle the bear away, but the thought of harm coming to Alexia set his heart pumping. The bear was actually pretty cool looking, but the fact that he could swipe at them with his big paws was a bit unnerving.

Oh, shit. It came closer to the tub. Okay, make that a lot unnerving. Jayden pulled his gaze away from the animal and slowly shook his head at Alexia in case she thought about moving or breathing too loudly. He mouthed "A bear" again, but she just frowned at him as though he were one wrench short of a toolbox. "Smokey," he mouthed, hoping that clue might help but she just shook her head. God, he wished he knew sign language, but the best he could do was to keep his finger to his lips.

Jayden watched as the bear lumbered over to the glass sliding door and peered inside as if knowing stew was simmering on the stove and cold beer was in the fridge. Jayden felt a little sorry for it, thinking it must suck to have to go scrounging around for your dinner. Finally, the poor thing seemed to give up and sadly lumbered off into the night.

Jayden waited a few minutes to make sure that Smokey was indeed gone before releasing the breath that he had been holding. "Okay, don't panic," he said softly to Alexia, whose eyes rounded in fear.

"I wish you hadn't said that," she whispered.

"Just get up quietly."

"Okay."

"Then hurry like hell into the cabin."

"Why?" she fervently whispered.

"Just do it," he pleaded, afraid that she might scream if she knew the reason and somehow, like in a horror movie, cause the bear to go crazy and come back to eat them for dinner before heading inside for the stew, a beer, and the entire apple pie. "Don't go too fast or you might get an ass full of splinters. I don't recommend it," he added with a grin to try and ease her wide-eyed fear.

Failing to find humor in the situation, Alexia nodded solemnly. She slowly eased up from the water and
even under these conditions Jayden noticed how amazing her body looked bathed in moonlight. She shivered
but didn't stop for her robe. Instead, she did as instructed and hurried her cute, bare ass into the cabin.
Once inside she turned to him dripping wet and full of
questions. "What was that all about? Who was out
there? Were we being spied on? Paparazzi? My God,
we're naked!" She fisted her hands on her hips and
seemed too fired up to care about her state of undress.
"And why in the world were you saying abracadabra?"

Now that they were safe, for the moment all Jayden
could think about was how sexy she was when she got
her panties in a wad except she wasn't wearing any
panties. "Wait a minute . . . what?" Jayden had to
laugh.

She narrowed her eyes. "Jayden Michaels, if you're
messing with me so help me I'll kick your ass."

It must have been the nervous aftermath of the incident, but this made him laugh harder, which was a
mistake.

"Jayden!" She stomped her foot so hard that her
boobs jiggled.

"It . . . it was . . . a . . ." He laughed so much that he
couldn't speak.

"A *what*?"

"Bear."

Alexia blinked at him and her anger deflated like
a popped balloon. "Ohmigod, on the deck? Like,
with us?"

Jayden nodded.

She put her hand over her mouth and then pointed

at him. "The one from the other day! See, I told you that I saw a bear!" She started to laugh with him. "I thought you were s-saying abracadabra. Wait, what were you saying?"

"I was saying, *a bear is out there.*" He laughed harder. "I wish I could have said abracadabra and made the damned thing disappear," he admitted. "I was so freaked that I was trying to send the bear a telepathic message."

Alexia snorted.

"Pretend I didn't just admit that to you."

"Okay, but I'm surprised you didn't do something Jayden-like and try to scare it off or something."

He sobered. "Not with you there."

"Why?"

"Because I didn't want you to get hurt. Scared the hell outta me sitting there thinking of that bear taking a swipe at you. Not that I wouldn't have wrestled it or whatever but damn, Alexia." He drew her into his arms. "If anything happened to you . . . shit."

Alexia shook her head at him. "You would have wrestled the bear?"

He shrugged and then gave her a sheepish grin. "I'd have done something heroic before getting my ass whupped."

"Oh, let's stop talking about it." She shivered and hugged her arms around him.

"Hey, you're naked."

She grinned at him. "It's naked day in Braxton. Guess we both got the memo this time."

Jayden laughed and kissed the top of her head. This was so much like the Alexia he remembered . . . and loved. "You're freezing."

"Ya think?"

"Luckily we have some hot stew bubbling up a storm. Oh, and did I mention apple pie?" He glanced over at the stove.

"Hmm, you must have slaved away all day," Alexia joked.

Jayden laughed and then tilted her head up to kiss her. "Let's get you into some clothes. I'll go get your robe."

Her eyes widened. "Oh no, you don't. You're not going back out there."

"Alexia, we'll probably never see him again. Seriously, it was a fluke."

"No, the first time was a fluke. You have a stalker bear." She wrapped her arms around his waist and looked up at him. "You are seriously *not* going out there."

"Okay. But someday we have to leave this cabin."

"Mmm." She hugged him close. "But not for now." She giggled when his stomach growled. "I'll go get some clothes on and then we'll eat."

"Hey, did you forget that it's naked day?"

Alexia arched an eyebrow at him. "Do you seriously think we'll make it through dinner if we remain naked?"

"Point taken," he said with a funny pout. "Okay, I'll put on some clothes, but not for long," he promised.

With a laugh Alexia hurried to the bedroom but instead of putting on her clothes she opted for one of Jayden's flannel shirts and nothing else, just to tease him unmercifully. She had to roll back the sleeves and the shirttail came to her knees but she didn't care. "Mmm," she inhaled deeply, and closed her eyes. Heaven

help her, the soft fabric smelled like him. Drawing the
sleeve to her nose, Alexia felt a hot wave of desire while
thinking that she had become a love-crazed sex fiend.

And it was fun.

With that thought in mind she laughed again for no
real reason as she headed back to the kitchen. Her own
stomach rumbled as she stirred the stew and after taking a taste she smiled. "Yum," she mumbled with relief.
After locating a sharp knife she sliced a round crusty
loaf of sourdough bread, found the tub of whipped butter in the fridge, and set the table. The domestic feeling
of fixing a meal for Jayden felt so cozy that she laughed
softly. *I could get used to this,* she thought, and then
turned around. "Oh!"

Jayden, who was casually leaning one shoulder
against the door frame, smiled. "What?"

Alexia put a hand to her chest. "I was so lost in
thought that you startled me."

"Well, get used to me being around."

"How is it that you can suddenly read my mind?"
she mused out loud. She looked over at him and their
eyes met.

"I can't, Alexia. You have to tell me what you're
thinking."

Alexia looked down and toyed with a napkin. Part
of her wanted to totally open up and tell him that she
loved him, but the words wouldn't come.

"Hey . . ." He came over and tucked a lock of hair
behind her ear before tilting her face up so he could
softly kiss both cheeks. When his tender gesture made
her mouth tremble, he kissed her lips. "When you're
ready to talk to me, I'll be here for you. I can't read
your mind, Alexia, but it's obvious that we've recon-

nected. I might not know what the hell it is that contin-
ues to hold you back, but," he said, and gently tapped
her chest, "all I really need to know is what is in here."

Alexia looked up and searched his face. She wanted
to believe that what was in her heart was truly enough.
"Jayden . . . I," she began, and then her voice cracked.

"Alexia. Do you love me?"

She nodded.

"No, say it."

"I love you," she said in a low but firm tone.

His eyes were stormy. "Listen, that's all I need to
know. Nothing else matters. Not me leaving you. Not
you marrying someone else. Not the danger of motocross or me giving it up. Our life together begins here
and now."

"You promise?" Alexia knew she shouldn't say that
to him given the facts, but she desperately wanted to believe it.

"Yes."

Alexia, you have to tell him, screamed in her head.
"Yes, but—"

He put a finger to her lips and shook his head.
"Deal?"

Her heart beat fast. She shouldn't. Couldn't.

He cupped her face in his hands. "Alexia, please."

"Deal," she quietly agreed, hoping that she was
making the right decision. Deep down she knew that
she wasn't, but the thought of losing him was enough
to make her nod and then stick her hand out.

Jayden took her hand, shook it, and then put her
palm up to his mouth for a kiss. "Good, don't forget
it," he reiterated before drawing her into his arms for a
fierce hug. Alexia melted into his embrace and allowed

herself to feel warm, safe, and loved. "Now you sit down, and let me dish up the dinner," he offered.

"I won't argue with that," she said, and was glad that although he might look all male, he was willing to share in the domestic chores. While they consumed the stew the conversation turned to motocross and Extreme Machines. After her extensive research Alexia found herself able to fire questions at Jayden.

"I was fascinated at how the sport has evolved over the years," she commented. "Motosports seem to be taking over the X Games."

"You're right." Jayden nodded while sopping up gravy with a crust of bread. "It won't be long before ESPN's summer X Games are basically an all-motosports affair. I know that skateboarding and BMX events probably will stay alive with amazing athletes like Tony Hawk, Shaun White, and Ryan Sheckler pushing the limits on boards. Plus, dudes like Dave Mirra, Ryan Nyquist, and Jamie Bestwick will step things up on twenty-inch bicycles."

"Those popular guys are keeping those sports going strong," Alexia agreed as she took a sip of wine.

Jayden reached for his own wineglass. "Still, there is a definite trend of adding engines to what is pretty much becoming the Olympic Games of the younger generation. That's what makes practice clubs like Extreme Machines so important. Like any sport you have to learn the right way first or like me have to unlearn a lot of stuff. Trust me, unlearning poor techniques is way harder than getting the right instruction initially."

"You love this sport, don't you?"

"Yeah, Alexia, I do."

"I missed so much, didn't I?" she said more to herself than to him as she rubbed her finger over the rim of her wineglass.

"I always wanted you there. When I would have a podium finish, I would sometimes scan the crowd and hope that I would see you there."

She looked across the table at him. "Oh, Jayden . . ."

"I have a year left," he reminded her hopefully. "I swear, I'd quit for you but it would mean so much to look out in the fans and see you there, if only just once."

"I will. I promise."

"Thank you." Jayden gave her a slow smile that lit up his whole face. "Now let's start a fire and put on some music."

Alexia nodded. "Excellent idea. I'll clean up and then bring in the dessert."

"Make my piece a big one," he requested.

Alexia laughed. "You got it," she promised, and then started clearing the table. She hummed softly to the Rascal Flatts CD he turned on. As she entered the family room, the song "Broken Road" came on, and before she could stop herself a tear slid down her cheek. She placed the pie on the coffee table and said, "I think we have a song."

"Come here," Jayden said gruffly, and pulled her into his arms. They swayed to the music while letting the words sink in. After the last note Jayden tilted her face up and kissed her as if there were no tomorrow . . .

But there *was* tomorrow . . . and the next day and the next.

"Make love to me, Jayden."

"Now you're reading my mind," he said before kissing her. "Even though you suck at reading my lips."

Alexia laughed when he sat down and playfully pulled her onto his lap, straddling his legs and facing him. "Ready for dessert?" she asked.

"Mmm, yeah," he said, and closed his eyes for a kiss, but Alexia reached for the apple pie and placed a warm bite into his mouth. He opened his eyes in surprise and after savoring the bite said, "Wow, that was good."

"Want another bite?"

"After I have you," he said, and gave her an apple-and-cinnamon-flavored kiss.

"You taste yummy," she lazily told him, but then her breath caught when he slid his big warm hands beneath the flannel shirt and caressed her back.

"So do you," he said, and kissed her again.

Alexia threaded her fingers through his long hair, pulling him in for a deep, hot exploration of his mouth. Her tongue curled around his and then she pulled back to lick his bottom lip before sucking it into her mouth. As if knowing she wanted control, Jayden leaned back on his hands and watched as she slowly unbuttoned the shirt.

"Ah, Alexia."

With Rascal Flatts singing a love song in the background and the fire casting a soft glow, she let the shirt slide from her shoulders to the rug. His eyes, half-lidded and full of desire, caressed her body, making her feel needed, wanted . . . sexy. She let Jayden look his fill before reaching over and tugging his shirt over his head. Then she leaned over and kissed his neck, his chest, while letting the silky skin slide over her tongue. She licked one nipple and then the other, slowly kissing downward. When he sucked in a breath and his ab muscles tightened she knew that her hair tickled and teased his skin.

As if knowing where she was heading, Jayden lifted his ass up from the rug so she could remove his sweatpants. She tugged them off with a whoosh and tossed them over her head with a low giggle. Her smile faded, however, when she looked down at his penis jutting upward in invitation. "Jayden . . ." His name was on her lips when she gripped his shoulders, rose to her knees, and sank down until he filled her completely. "God . . ." He felt so good that she took a moment to enjoy him buried deep like this. Their eyes met and she leaned in and kissed him deeply until she felt his dick swell and stir inside her. Then, while holding on to his shoulders, she leaned forward, letting her breasts graze his chest while she began to ease up and down. She continued kissing him while sheathing him with her slick heat.

Jayden leaned back on his elbows, letting her set the pace. She angled her body to get delicious friction against her clit, slowly, until her orgasm began to build, climb, reaching higher and higher. With a little cry she rode him hard, coming up to her knees and slamming back down, loving it as he sank deep within her slick folds. Her flesh was so tender that she had to bite her bottom lip, and yet it only seemed to enhance the growing pleasure. Her thigh muscles protested but she ignored the burn, going faster.

The golden flames of the fire were so hot that they both began to perspire. A bead of sweat rolled between her breasts, cool against her heated skin that slid against Jayden. Instead of closing her eyes, she watched him, reveling in the sight of his sweat-drenched chest, his corded neck muscles as he leaned back and pumped upward from the rug.

Heat, friction, sweat, skin . . . Alexia panted and dug her fingers into his shoulders when her orgasm burst upon her. "Jayden . . ." God, she felt as if she were opening up from the inside out. Waves of ecstasy had her arching her back, her neck while he thrust upward hard. His hips rose from the rug and he climaxed deep within her in a pulsing gush of sheer pleasure.

For a few moments they remained silent, panting, chests rising and falling. Finally, with a weak laugh, she collapsed against him. He wrapped his arms around her and kissed her over and over while running his hands up and down her sweat-slicked back.

Finally he said, "Let's got to bed. I want you in my arms all night long."

Physically and emotionally depleted, Alexia could only manage a nod. They both slowly got up and pretty much stumbled on shaky legs into the bedroom. But instead of falling asleep they talked for a long time, ending with the crazy bear incident.

With a smile on her face Alexia was finally unable to hold her eyes open. With a sigh she snuggled against Jayden's chest and fell into a deep, contented sleep.

$\mathcal{B}$rianna looked up when the bell over the door warned her that someone entered the office, jarring her from the sexy daydream she was having about Colin. She felt a warm blush stain her cheeks when none other than the man of her daydreams himself entered the office. Of course, it didn't help matters that she was wearing a thong for the first time in her life, just for him. After their heated lovemaking she had felt the need for lacy lingerie. He couldn't possibly know she was wearing the doggone thong, which made her butt feel very free and exposed, but still, she suddenly felt tongue-tied when their eyes met.

"Hey," Colin said with a smile that lit up the room. "I was in town to run some errands and I thought you might like to go grab a bite to eat."

"Oh . . ." Brianna had been thinking of Colin non-stop, so much so that she was extremely behind in her work, yet she snatched the Snickers wrapper from her desk that had been her hasty lunch and sneaked it into her top drawer. Why she felt guilty eating candy, she didn't quite know, but she licked her lips just to make sure there wasn't any chocolate in the corners of her mouth. "Sure, I could eat."

"Great," he said, but looked at her messy desk in question. "Unless you're too busy."

"Oh no, not at all," she answered with a breezy wave of her hand even though she was swamped. "I'd love to." She scooted back from the antique desk and snatched her coat from the old-fashioned hook on the wall.

"Here, let me." When Colin assisted her with the blue trench coat his fingers brushed the back of her neck, causing a hot tingle to zing down her back and land somewhere in the region of her thong. When she turned around and secured the belt, Colin eyed her coat and grinned.

"What?" Brianna asked, wondering if something was out of place or she was wearing something inside out. When she worked long hours she sometimes became scatterbrained, although lately it was more due to having Colin on the brain than work issues that scattered her thoughts like leaves in the wind. "Really, what's wrong?"

"Nothing," he insisted, and reached up to run his fingers through his shaggy hair that she found incredibly sexy.

"Come on." Brianna angled her head at him. The reporter in her had to get an answer. "I don't believe you."

"Really?" He jammed his hands in his slouchy jeans pockets and rocked back on his heels. "Now, why is that?"

She tapped the side of her cheek. "Hmm, maybe the look in your eye?" she tried to tease, wishing her flirting skills were better. It didn't help that instead of sensible work attire as she wore, he looked like an ad for Abercrombie & Fitch. A green-striped polo peeked from beneath a white Catamount jacket, making Brianna feel dowdy in her blue dress pants and crisp white blouse . . . and to top if off she was wearing a trench coat! The saving grace was her sexy undies, she thought with a hot little shiver. But he didn't know about them, well, not *yet* anyway, she mused, and then almost clamped a hand over her mouth for the direction of her thoughts. But this falling-in-love thing was making her act a little crazy . . . but crazy, she decided, could be fun.

"Okay, I'll confess," he began, but then shook his head. "No, I can't."

"Oh, come on. What?" Brianna repeated, and then spontaneously stomped one sensible loafer on the floor like a child. Thankfully, the rubber sole didn't make much noise. She made a mental note to go shopping with Alexia so they could work on sexing up her outer wardrobe and not just her underwear.

Colin ran a hand down his face and then cleared his throat. "It's just that your coat . . ." he began, and then trailed off.

"Yes?" Brianna prompted, and tugged the belt tighter. She glanced down at the coat and decided she needed something leather. Black . . . no, *red*. She looked back at Colin and waited.

Finally, he cleared his throat again and said, "I've always had a thing for trench coats."

"Really? You don't look like a trench-coat-wearing kind of guy."

"I mean on women." He hesitated but then leaned closer and whispered in her ear, "It makes me imagine you nude beneath it."

What? Brianna looked up at him to see if he was serious or making fun of her no-nonsense coat that was lined for winter but repelled the rain on account of you-just-never-know . . . but the heat in his light blue eyes made her swallow hard. "Oh," was all she could manage. He was taking flirting to a whole new level.

"I have another confession."

Still speechless, she could only nod.

"I wasn't really running errands. I should be working but all I could think about was seeing you."

"Is that so?" she asked breathlessly.

He nodded. "For real, and now I feel like an idiot for admitting all this stuff to you."

She gave him a slow smile. His admission made his comments cute and sexy instead of smarmy. "Well, you shouldn't."

"Shouldn't what? I have to warn you that when I'm told I shouldn't do something, I usually . . . *do* it."

Brianna laughed. "The nature of a motocross racer."

He took a step closer to her. "So now, why shouldn't I feel like an idiot? I know that you're not naked beneath that coat."

"Because I have a confession too." She took a deep breath but her lips twitched and she lost her nerve.

Colin shook his head. "Oh no, you don't. I confessed." He jammed a thumb at his chest. "Your turn."

"No, forget it."

"Right, like that's gonna happen."

"Okay." She drew out the word but blinked at him for a moment before blurting out in a heated whisper,

"I'm wearing a thong." With a little squeak she clamped a hand over her mouth. "Tell me I didn't just say that."

"Oh, you said it." Colin stared back at her, letting her secret sink in. The vivid image of her in nothing but a thong made him instantly hard. But then he had to know . . . "What color?"

Her cheeks flushed a becoming shade of pink. She glanced left and right and then whispered, "Black."

"Hot damn. Black." He grinned and let his imagination run wild.

Brianna put her hands to her cheeks. "I can't believe that I just told you that."

"Brianna Spencer," Colin said in her ear. "Did I mention lately that you are sweet innocence and hot sex all wrapped up together in one gorgeous package? You drive me crazy."

"I don't mean to," she said in such an apologetic tone that he laughed.

"That's the cool part." Colin tilted her face up and very slowly leaned toward her lips. He hovered there for a moment, loving the anticipation of finally getting to do what he had thought about all morning . . . okay, and all night long as well. To his surprise, when he waited a fraction too long, shy little Brianna rose on tiptoe and pulled his head down to hers. Their mouths met . . . and passion exploded.

While kissing her like a starving man, Colin stumbled backward into a nearby hallway, where it was semidark and secluded from the front window. He pushed her up against the wall, lifted her hands above her head, and trapped her there but she shook her head. "No."

"Okay." Disappointed, Colin backed away. "Brianna . . ."

She placed a finger to his lips. "Shhh, I'll be right back," she whispered as she ducked beneath his arms. Before Colin could stop her she scurried past him but then paused and turned around. "Oh, and, Colin. Lock the front door," she added before she disappeared behind a closed door that Colin surmised was a small bathroom.

For a moment he stood there confused and a little stunned, but then he rushed over to the door and flipped the dead bolt. One of those be-back-in-so-many-minutes signs dangled from a suction cup. With a grin Colin pushed the arms on the clock to thirty minutes . . . but then on second thought, turned it back around and made it forty-five for good measure. He had no idea what scheme was formulating in Brianna's head, but he wasn't about to miss a minute of it.

Brianna closed the bathroom door and leaned against it. What had seemed like an amazing idea a minute ago suddenly terrified her. She flipped on the light and looked at her refection in the mirror. Her eyes seemed bigger than usual, her cheeks were flushed, and her mouth was swollen and rosy from kissing. God, what was she doing? She put her hand to her chest and took a deep breath.

"Just go for it," she demanded to her reflection. For a long moment she licked her lips and stared back at herself while trying to muster up the courage. She groaned, stomped her foot. "Come on, Brianna, you big chickenshit. Alexia would do this in a heartbeat." She shook her head, about to throw in the towel, but then narrowed her eyes. With a determined glare at her scared self, she shed her coat, removed her clothes except for her thong, and then put the trench coat back on. *Wow.*

But then of course, she was too timid to open the door. After a few heart-pounding what-was-I-thinking? minutes Colin knocked sharply, making her jump.

"You okay in there?"

Brianna nodded but then realized that she had to verbalize her answer. "Um, yeah. I'll be out in a minute . . . or two." Or never.

"Listen," he said in a worried voice, "I shouldn't have, you know, confessed all that stuff. Come on so strong. I didn't mean to freak you out."

What? Brianna's eyes rounded. Oh, crap, he was getting the wrong idea.

"I'm sorry, Brianna. I'll just leave so you can come out and not have me pounce on you."

Wait, no! She wanted him to pounce on her. Brianna swung open the door and came face-to-face with Colin.

"Hey, I didn't—" he began, but then seemed to notice that her legs were bare. He looked down and then back up and when his eyes widened Brianna knew he got it. "Holy crap." He gave her a slow smile.

"Why did you think I asked you to lock the door?"

"I . . . uh," he stammered, and Brianna felt a certain sense of power that she could render him speechless.

"Pouncing is okay . . . Feel free." Brianna felt the familiar heat creep up her neck and she caught her bottom lip between her teeth. "I can't believe I'm saying this, doing this," she said, and looked down at the floor. "I should have my head examined. Colin, I—" she began, but before she could finish Colin gently pushed her back up against the wall where the interlude had begun.

"Kiss me, Brianna," he growled, after placing his hands on the wall on either side of her. She could smell the spice of his cologne, feel the heat of his body, and her heart beat wildly in response. When she reached up and slid her hands around his neck his skin felt warm against her cool hands. She threaded her fingers through his hair and pulled his head down for a long, lingering kiss.

"Mmm." He pulled back and then brushing her hair to the side leaned and nuzzled her neck before sucking her earlobe into his mouth. A hot tingle began a slow downward slide and intensified when Colin parted the collar of her coat and kissed the soft swell of her nearly exposed breasts. "You smell amazing, taste sweet," he murmured while untying the belt. When the coat gaped open he raised her hands over her head and pinned her against the wall with one of his own hands and caressed her bare skin with the other. While cupping one small breast, he dipped his head down and took a nipple into his mouth. He licked in circles and then flattened his tongue to lick up and down.

Unable not to, Brianna moaned and squirmed against the wall. Colin didn't let up. He laved and then sucked hard while his fingers toyed with the lace sides of her thong. Then, moving the barely-there patch of silk aside, he dipped his middle finger between her folds, sliding back and forth before suddenly dipping deep inside her. Brianna gasped when he moved his mouth to her other breast and continued fingering her. Brianna bucked her hips and strained at his hold. It was too much . . . she was so aroused, so slick and wet that she was going to come and she wanted him inside her when she climaxed. She gritted her teeth and tried to hold back, but, *God*, when he applied the slightest pressure, she cried out and exploded with an orgasm.

"I want to be inside you," he whispered in her ear.

"I . . . I didn't mean to . . ."

"Shh, I'm not nearly finished."

While she stood there, panting and dazed, Colin took off his jacket, and then tugged his shirt over his head. Brianna gazed at his chiseled chest lightly dusted with dark blond hair. She swallowed, reached out, and with trembling fingers touched his warm skin. He sucked in a breath and then unbuckled his belt. But before he unsnapped his jeans he placed her hand over the bulge in his pants. "Oh . . ." She caressed the hard ridge while he fumbled in his wallet for a condom.

While he tore open the wrapper she undid his pants and unzipped the fly. With a soft sigh she pulled his jeans and boxers over his lean hips and wrapped her hand over his penis. He felt like satin wrapped in steel, pulsing and full of power. "Mmm, wow." While she caressed him his stomach muscles clenched, showing off his six-pack.

"Damn," he murmured, and then closed his eyes. "Brianna . . ." He inhaled a deep breath as if trying to get himself under control but then a pearly drop of pre-come appeared and she just had to lean in and lick it off. "God!" He fumbled with the condom and an instant later had her back up against the wall. She was short so he had to lift her up, but Brianna helped by wrapping her legs around his waist. He pressed her back to the wall and thrust his hips up, burying his dick deep in her heat.

Brianna locked her legs around his waist and held on while he pumped in and out. With her eyes closed her mouth found his and she kissed him wildly while he pinned her to the wall. She whimpered, moaned . . . he was so big, so strong that she had to brace herself to take him all the way in.

"Baby, are you okay?"

"Mmm, yeah," she managed to reply breathlessly. He filled her, stretched her, hitting that magic place that drove her crazy. With a throaty cry she roughly pulled his hair back so that she could find his mouth once again. She thrust her tongue deep, licking, tangling, tasting. He cupped her ass, lifting her higher while putting pressure on her groin, friction on her clit. Her heart pounded harder, pleasure climbed higher until she was bucking wildly with his upward thrusts. Then, when he took her breast into his hot mouth, she pushed her back against the cool wall, took him in so deep that he filled every inch of her . . . and then she climaxed.

Colin continued to pump into her until he found his own release, causing Brianna to come once again. With a whimper she put her face in the crook of his neck, kissing, nibbling while little aftershocks of pleasure pulsed and throbbed in tandem with her heartbeat. This was insane; this was amazing . . .

And then she heard a knock at the door.

"Holy crap," Brianna breathed. "No one can see us, can they?" she whispered.

Colin shook his head. "No, not as long as you're up against the wall. So don't move, okay?"

"Sorry you have to hold me up."

He grinned. "Yeah, like you're really heavy."

When the knock got louder, Brianna felt a thrilling

fear come on and had to bite her bottom lip. She looked at the amusement in Colin's eyes and had to bite harder. As if sensing that she was going to burst into a fit of laughter, Colin leaned in and kissed her.

Her giggles dissolved into lazy lingering desire until the knocking was forgotten and all that mattered was kissing Colin.

Colin licked her bottom lip as if savoring the taste of her mouth. "You still up for some lunch?"

Brianna opened her eyes and looked into his smiling face. "Sure. I'm swamped but I'm suddenly starving."

"Worked up an appetite, huh?"

"Yes," she admitted. "But, um, Colin . . . just so you know, I mean, um—"

"Hey," Colin interrupted, and kissed her lightly. "I think you're trying to say that you don't usually do things like this. I already had that figured out. And if you think I'm going to tell anyone, you're dead wrong."

"Thank you," she said softly. "But you know what?" she asked with an impish grin.

"What?"

"It was fun." Her whisper in his ear was followed by low laughter. "So I have a naughty side. Who knew?"

"You got that right." He let her slide to the floor, but when she turned to leave he grabbed her for another quick kiss. "I'm glad that I was the guy who discovered it."

"Me too," she admitted, and felt a surge of joy that he was as blown away as she had been. "I guess you must bring it out in me."

"You can thank me later."

"That's a promise." Brianna giggled again even though she wasn't a giggling kind of girl. Of course she wasn't the kind of girl to get naked in her office and have hot sex up against the wall in her trench coat, either.

Until now.

"I'll hold you to it," he warned her, and then kissed her on the tip of her nose.

"I'll be right back," she told him, and then hurried into the bathroom to put on her clothes. After flicking on the light she put her hands to her cheeks. "Holy cow," she murmured, but then smiled at her reflection. She arched one strawberry blond eyebrow and whispered, "Colin McCord, you ain't seen nothin' yet."

Chapter Nineteen

"Hey, where were you earlier?" Alexia asked Brianna after she entered the *Braxton Times* office. "I knocked on the door around noon but no one answered.

"Really? Around noon?" Brianna asked casually . . . too casually. "Hmm, I must have been at lunch." She glanced at Alexia but then averted her gaze. "Sorry, I keep forgetting to give you a key."

"Yeah, a key would be nice." Alexia sat down at her desk and opened her laptop. "You know, though, the lights were on and I thought I heard voices."

Brianna's eyes rounded. "That is odd," she commented, but a telltale blush stained her cheeks.

"Bri, why are you blushing?"

"It's the curse of being a redhead," she answered in a bit of an annoyed tone. "Well, you know and being me, I always blush."

"Okay," Alexia said briskly, but then tapped the side of her cheek. "But I could have sworn I saw Colin's street bike parked out front. I wonder where he was?"

"I told you we had lunch. We walked down to

Dorma's Diner and had a bite to eat. Her cheeseburgers are still the best on the planet."

Alexia gave her sister a deadpan stare.

"Oh, okay! We were in here," she said in a stage whisper.

"Where? I looked in the window," Alexia said, but then let her jaw drop. "You did it in the bathroom! A nooner! Ha! High five!" she said, and put her palm up in the air even though they were too far apart to slap hands.

"Shut up. We didn't do anything in the bathroom."

"Fibber," Alexia accused. She waited expectantly but got nothing. "All right, I won't pry." She started clicking away at the keyboard but snuck a peek at her little sister and then smiled. Brianna glowed.

"Stop staring at me."

"I'm not.

"Are too."

"Are you going to say nanny-nanny-boo-boo?"

"Shut up!"

"Close enough." Alexia inhaled a deep breath. She had forgotten how much fun it was to torment her sibling. She typed for a few minutes to let Bri think she was giving up. But Alexia almost grinned when, through her eyelashes, she noticed Bri glancing her way as if disappointed that she had given up so easily. Which meant one thing. Whatever had happened between Bri and Colin was juicy and Alexia was damned well going to get it out of her sister one way or another. She decided to try the unexpected direct approach. "So, just where did you have your afternoon delight?"

"I'm not telling!" Brianna hissed, and then put a hand over her mouth and glared at Alexia.

"Gotcha."

"I made Colin promise not to say anything, so I can't tell you!"

"I'm your sister. You can tell me *anything*." She folded her hands on her desk and waited.

Brianna chewed on her bottom lip. "I want you to take me shopping."

"You're changing the subject," she accused. "Wait, shopping for what?"

"For some . . ." She paused and whispered, "Sexy clothes. Cool stuff like you wear. I mean, I know my boobs aren't big and I'm, you know, petite and stuff, but I can still be sexy, right?"

Alexia looked over at her cute little sister and shook her head.

"So you think I'm a hopeless cause?" Brianna gasped, totally mistaking Alexia's intent.

"Of course not."

Brianna looked at her closely. "Promise?"

"Oh, come on! This sounds a little awkward coming from me but you *are* totally sexy, Brianna."

"Oh yeah, sure I am. I'm a . . . a pip-squeak! I have itty-bittys," she complained, and cupped her hands beneath her breasts. "I blush like a doggone schoolgirl. There is nothing remotely sexy about me."

"Then why do you have Colin McCord, voted one of *People* magazine's hundred most sexy guys, I might add, falling all over you?"

Brianna's eyes widened. "I had forgotten about that!" She put her hands on her cheeks. "Ohmigod, I am so out of my league it isn't even funny." She narrowed her eyes. "So don't laugh."

"My God." With her palms up in the air, Alexia

looked up at the ceiling and then back at her sister. "You're a natural beauty, sweetie."

"You really think so?" Brianna asked while wringing her hands. "You don't think that Colin is just toying with me, you know, for a change of pace?"

Alexia angled her head at her sister and then shook her head slowly. "Look, I realize that Colin is a hometown hero and a motocross superstar."

"Not to mention gorgeous."

"Okay, I won't," Alexia said with a grin, but then sobered. "Look, I've known him for a long time and believe me, he's a straight shooter."

"Alexia, I'm just so scared. I know it sounds trite but I've never felt this way about a guy before."

"I'm happy for you."

"What if I get my heart broken?"

After taking in a deep breath and blowing it out, Alexia said, "Well, then you pick yourself up, dust yourself off, and start all over again. I'm an expert, remember?"

Brianna put the heel of her hand to her forehead. "I'm sorry. I'm so insensitive sometimes."

"Oh, bull. You're one of the kindest people I know, Brianna. That alone has its own sex appeal. You might not have that high-maintenance, in-your-face sexpot thing going on, but—" Alexia stopped short when she saw the expression on her sister's face. "Or then again, maybe not. Correct me if I'm wrong, but I think I might have been mistaken about the sexpot part. Ohmigod, you have to tell me what you did with Colin."

"I can't!"

"Bri, you don't have to go into detail, but just what happened between you two? Did you do, you know, do the deed in here?" She nibbled on the inside of her cheek while looking around trying to decide where.

Brianna turned beet red but then suddenly nodded and said, "Yes!"

"What did you do?"

Brianna rolled her eyes.

"Okay, I know that part . . . but where?"

"You promise not to tell?"

Alexia nodded rapidly. "Cross my heart." She did an X over her chest for good measure just like when they were kids.

"You're not gonna believe this . . . Oh, I can't . . ."

"I won't tell!"

She pressed her lips together for an indecisive moment and then said, "We were going to lunch." She swallowed and then went on. "And he mentioned how he had this thing for . . ." She leaned in close while Alexia held her breath. All sorts of things went through her mind.

"Brianna!"

"Trench coats."

She blinked at her sister. "Trench coats?"

After a choppy little nod Brianna pointed to her blue coat hanging innocently on the hook. "Yes."

Alexia's eyes widened when it dawned on her where this was going. "Shut up! You didn't."

She pressed her lips together again while nodding and then yelled, "Yes!"

If her sister's face got any redder Alexia feared it would burst into flames, but Brianna grinned and even forgot to whisper. "I went into the bathroom, took off my clothes . . ." She paused for drama, pointed to her butt, and continued. "Except for my thong."

Alexia's mouth formed an O.

"I know, I know, I bought some kick-ass undies."

"Kick-ass?"

"Shut up, your language is rubbing off on me. You're a bad influence," Brianna accused, but then grinned. "Or then again, maybe a good one."

"You're getting off the subject."

Brianna glanced at the small hallway and then admitted, "We did . . . stuff in there."

"Stuff?"

"Yes. Lots of stuff."

"You mean you came out of the bathroom, in nothing but your trench coat—"

"Don't forget the thong."

"Forgive me, in the trench coat and thong, and then let me guess, did the wild thing up against the wall."

Brianna nodded. "Don't breathe a word of this to anyone. Especially Jayden."

"I crossed my heart, Bri."

"Okay, then. Yes! My God, I thought my heart was going to beat right out of my chest!" She put her hands to her cheeks. "I can't believe I did that! Oh no, do you think Colin thinks I'm . . ." She closed her eyes and moaned.

"Easy?" Alexia asked, and tried to keep a straight face.

"Yes!" she whispered. "Oh, I shouldn't have behaved so . . ."

"Like you're falling in love? Bri, open your damned eyes and look at me. Love, *passion* will make you do crazy things. It's just the way the brain works." She walked over and leaned against the big desk. "Just go with it. Open up your heart and don't hold back."

Brianna looked at Alexia with soulful eyes. "But what if it ends badly? That thought already terrifies me. My God, how did you cope?"

"Poorly." Alexia picked up a pen and toyed with it. "Made huge mistakes."

"Oh, Alexia, I wish I had been there for you."

"Sweetie, you were a kid."

She nodded sadly. "So that's why you married Mitchell?"

Alexia nodded at her sister, wishing she could spill her guts and tell the whole story. "Yeah," she finally answered gruffly. "I was young and stupid." She left out heartbroken and devastated and forced a smile instead. "But that, as they say, is water under the bridge."

Brianna nodded brightly. "Now you have a second chance with Jayden." She placed her palms on the desk and leaned forward. "He loves you. I'm telling you, Alexia, it's still in the way he looks at you with such— wow, I can't even explain it. With such passion, but then again with this little, like, twinkle in his eye as if you just flat-out make him happy."

Alexia looked at her sister, who was such a combination of innocent youth and yet incredible insight. It suddenly hit her hard that she held Jayden's happiness in the palm of her hand. Which also meant that she simply had to tell him the truth before taking their relationship one step further.

"Alexia, why do you have such a stricken look on your face? After all these years it's clear that Jayden still cares, still wants you in his life. You've done the dusting-off thing. Now it's time to start all over."

"You're right." She stood up and went back to her desk to gather up her things.

"What are you doing?"

"Taking your advice." As she shrugged into her coat she looked over at Brianna. "I'll be back after I do what I should have done a long time ago," she explained, and hurried over to give her sister a quick hug before heading out the door.

Once she was in her SUV she started the engine but then had to sit there for a few minutes while her heart pounded wildly in her chest. "You have to do this," she whispered to herself, and gripped the steering wheel like a lifeline. Glancing at the digital clock, she knew that Jayden would most likely be headed back from Extreme Machines to the cabin. After a deep cleansing breath she pulled out from the curb and headed back to his place while feeling both relief that she was finally going to do this and anxiety that it could end their relationship forever.

Knowing how difficult it was going to be to relive that horrible night, she felt her eyes filling with tears. But it had to be done. Then, and only then, could her life truly begin again.

When she pulled into the driveway she felt relief that Jayden's car wasn't there yet so she had time to compose herself before he arrived. "God, give me the strength to get through this," she prayed beneath her breath. But after she entered the cabin, memories of their recent lovemaking came flooding back and she started to tremble.

"Oh, stop it," she grumbled at her shaking hands. "You're made of stronger stuff than this!" She took a deep breath and then about jumped out of her skin when her cell phone beeped loudly, letting her know that she had a text message. She laughed nervously at her startled reaction and then dug into her purse for her phone. After she opened the message, she smiled as she read the text from Brianna out loud. "Whatever you have to do, just know that I'm here for you. I love you."

Alexia swiped at a hot tear that rolled down her cheek as she texted back, "Thank you. I love you too." Then she poured herself a glass of wine, sat down on the sofa, and waited for Jayden to arrive.

Chapter Twenty

"Hey, how'd you like the vented helmet?" Colin asked when Jayden entered the office.

"A lot," Jayden said, and placed the red and white sleek HJC SPX on the desk. "The moisture-wicking interior helped soak up sweat. It was a little big but comfortable. I give it a thumbs-up."

"Cool," Colin replied. "Thanks for staying late to try it out for me. I got a little tied up this afternoon," he said casually, but then ruined his attempt to keep his date with Brianna on the down low when he couldn't keep the silly smile off his face.

"So you were, uh, taking care of business?" Jayden asked with such a tongue-in-cheek tone that let Colin know he was busted.

"Okay, I had lunch with Brianna."

"Just lunch?"

"Dude, come on . . ."

Jayden raised his hands in the air, palms up. "Hey, I'll back off. Ya don't have to answer anyway since you've got that just-laid look on your face."

"Don't be talking' smack about her that way."

"Aw, Colin, chill. I didn't mean anything. I'm just sayin' that you look . . . happy. Am I right?"

Colin rubbed a hand down his face. "I didn't mean to jump your shit. She just blows me away."

Jayden arched an eyebrow. "Really?"

"Stop, before I jack your jaw," Colin warned, but laced his hands behind his head with a grin. "Yeah, she makes me happy."

"Hey, man, good for you. I gotta admit you two are an unlikely pair but I say go for it. Even as a little kid Brianna was smart, sensitive, and cute as hell. She's grown into quite a woman."

"Damn, Jayden, don't remind me how young she is."

He laughed. "She's mature and you're immature so that closed the gap real quick."

"Jackass."

Jayden grinned back at his best friend. "I can't argue with that. Listen, I'm cutting out of here."

"Going to hang out with Alexia?"

"Not right away. I'm heading to the mall," he said.

"Going to Victoria's Secret?"

Jayden should have just nodded but he had to tell someone and Colin seemed the best person to confide in. "No, the jewelry store."

Colin's blue eyes widened and he unlaced his fingers from the back of his head and leaned forward. "Dude . . ."

Jayden nodded. "Yeah, I'm going ring shopping."

"As in engagement ring?"

While raking his fingers through his hair he nodded. "Yeah. I figured that if I'm going to be leaving town here shortly I wanted to seal the deal, ya know?"

"Yeah, but, Jay . . ."

"What? I thought you'd be on board with this."

"I am."

Jayden raised his eyebrows. "I hear a but," he said, and got a weird feeling in his gut when Colin looked away. "Hey, is there something I need to know?"

"Have you and Alexia talked about marriage?"

"No, I'm just going to pop the question. Why? Look, I'm asking you as a friend to tell me if there is something I need to know."

Colin chewed on his bottom lip for a few seconds. "Have you talked about . . ."

"What?"

"Kids?"

"No." Jayden shrugged. "Hey, I never thought I'd say it but I want a family. Kids. Is that what you're worried about? That I don't want kids and she does? Hey, I know I'm a crazy ass, but I think I'd make a pretty good dad." He grinned. "Well, I'd try anyway." He waved a hand at Colin. "Hey, that's a ways off. First she has to say yes," he joked, but Colin failed to laugh and remained quiet. "Hey, if it puts your mind at ease I'll tell her straight up that I want kids."

"Jayden, no, man, don't do that," he pleaded.

Colin looked so shaken that icy fingers of fear slid down Jayden's spine. He drew in a deep breath. "I'm not going anywhere until you tell me what the hell is going on, here. Damn it, Colin, help me out. This is my life we're talking about. I fucked up before and I have a chance to make it right. Is there a reason I shouldn't ask Alexia to marry me?"

"No. She's amazing. Deserves happiness."

"Then what the hell is the problem?"

"Aw, damn, Jay . . ."

"Whatever it is I'd tell you," he said quietly.

Colin looked at him with tortured eyes. "She . . . aw, fuck!" He swallowed and a muscle ticked in his jaw. "The night you left town, Alexia followed you. A nasty storm kicked up. And, aw, shit, she had an accident."

Jayden shook his head, confused. "I remember calling her but she didn't pick up." He shook his head harder. "I remember getting pissed off that she ignored my call and it was the last time I tried. I was so fucking stupid." He inhaled deeply. "So she had a wreck?" He turned questioning eyes to Colin and his blood ran cold at his friend's expression.

"Ran off the road. Hit a tree." When he paused Jayden's heart hammered in his chest. "Oh God, Jay . . . she"—he cleared his throat—"lost the baby."

"Baby?" His heart skittered in his chest.

Colin nodded. "That's why she flipped out when you had that motocross accident. She already knew she was pregnant."

"Oh God." Jayden sank down into a chair. "Why didn't she tell me?"

"She didn't want you to stay because of the baby. She wanted you to quit for her. But I convinced her that you should know. Jayden, you had a right to know." He closed his eyes and a tear leaked out of the corner of one. "If I hadn't told her that, maybe she wouldn't have gone after you in the rain."

"If she had told me before, then I wouldn't have left." He paused when a thought occurred to him. "Colin, did my call to her come before or after she ran off the road?" When Colin failed to reply he had his answer.

"Jayden, she blames herself for driving under those circumstances."

He looked closely at his friend and said quietly, "There's more, isn't there?"

Colin nodded. "She . . . miscarried, but then hemorrhaged."

"God."

"Jayden, this isn't my place to tell you."

"Please, I have to know."

He frowned. "She was told that there was very little chance of her having more children."

Jayden's heart beat so loudly that it seemed to echo in the room. "Wh-what? You mean she can't have kids?" He blinked as it started to sink in. "Ever?"

"Very little chance." Colin nodded. "But that was a long time ago. Maybe there's something that could be done. I don't know."

Unexpected anger hit him like a sucker punch. "If she had let me know right away, none of this would have happened. And she shouldn't have been driving under those dangerous conditions."

"Jayden, she was a kid. Scared. No one else knows but me. Not even Brianna."

"Why did she call you?" He jumped to his feet. "Huh?" He jammed his thumb toward his chest. "She should have called me."

"You were gone. Her parents were in Florida and Brianna was a kid. She had no one close to home but me. Believe me, it's an experience that still gives me nightmares."

"Ohmigod." He suddenly remembered Alexia's nightmare and knew. He was flooded with guilt but he slid into unreasonable anger. He pounded his fist into his hand. "She should have told me from the moment she found out she was pregnant!"

"Jay, she was a kid!"

"She was my girlfriend! I loved her. I had a damned right to know." He jumped up and started pacing the room.

"If you still love her, and I know you do, you have to put the past to rest and forgive her."

"But she can't have kids . . . ," he said as much to himself as to Colin.

"Probably not, but you could deal with that, Jayden. If you want a family, there are options."

"Yeah, but, Colin. Damn." He turned his face to the ceiling and shook his head.

Colin stood up from his desk. "I know she wanted to tell you."

"Really? Well, she didn't. But once again confided in you."

"She's a friend. That's all."

"Ah, shit. I know that."

"Jayden, I made a promise to her never to tell. I feel horrible that I did."

"Don't. I forced your hand. I'll take the rap for that."

"What are you going to do?"

Jayden shook his head. "Man, I don't know."

"Jay, get the ring. You love her!"

"I gotta get past this." He closed his eyes and inhaled a shaky breath. "I think I'll go get plastered."

"Not alone. I'll come with you."

Jayden shook his head hard. "No, man. I gotta sort this out for myself."

"Keep a cool head. Drinking isn't a good idea when

you're messed up like this. Jayden, just go to her. Talk it out."

"I'll go for a ride on my street bike first to clear my head. Colin, I hate to put you in the middle of this. I won't divulge the fact that you told me. Don't let her know that you did, okay?"

"Fuck, I hate this! Hate it! Damn it, Jayden, be careful. Dude, just go home and think this through."

He nodded. "After I ride."

Colin hesitated but then as if knowing he needed to give Jayden some space, he nodded. "All right, but do me a favor and call me later."

"Gotcha," he said, and headed out the door. He hopped on his Suzuki and hit the road. He rode hard, taking to the winding roads aggressively so that he had to concentrate on riding and not on Alexia, his lost child, the heartbreaking knowledge that they would never have a child together . . . again. When the thought hit him hard that her pain drove her into the arms of that bastard he took a turn too hot and almost lost it. He pulled off on the shoulder of the road and waited to calm down before heading back out at a slower pace. But instead of turning toward home, he headed into Braxton to the local pub and decided that getting drunk was the perfect escape.

After peering out the window for the hundredth time, Alexia decided to head home. When her phone calls and text messages to Jayden went unanswered, she had a gut feeling that something was terribly wrong. First she was pissed but then became increasingly worried. Finally, after she was inside her own cabin, she tossed her purse on the kitchen table and called Colin.

She breathed a sigh of relief when he picked up after several previous tries. "Hey, have you heard from Jayden? I've been trying for a couple of hours to get a hold of him."

"Um, sorry, I don't know where he is, Alexia."

"Really? When was the last time you saw him? I'm getting worried. He could have been in an accident."

"I'm sure he's okay."

"How can you be sure if you don't know where he is?" Alexia asked with a bit of irritation, but something in his tone was off. "You are a terrible liar, Colin. What's going on?" she asked, and the silence at the other end of the phone screamed that there was something terribly wrong. She put her hand to her chest. "Oh God, he isn't hurt, is he?"

"No," Colin answered quickly, but again, something in the tone of his voice gave her pause.

"He knows," she stated flatly, and his silence shouted back the answer. "Colin, how could you? I was going to tell him tonight."

"I'm so sorry. I didn't mean for this to happen. We were having this odd conversation and . . . shit."

"He didn't take it well, did he?" Her voice cracked and she felt everything closing in on her.

The other shoe had dropped.

"Don't go anywhere. I'm coming over."

"No. Don't. I'm not blaming you, Colin, but I don't want to see you or anyone right now. Just let me deal with this."

"No! You've dealt with way too much on your own. I'm coming over."

"Then I'm leaving."

He inhaled sharply. "Not in the state you're in.

Look, okay, I'll give you your space too. But know that I'll be watching for you to call and I can be there in minutes. Or if you just need to talk, Alexia, I'm here."

"I know."

"God, I'm so sorry."

"It had to come out anyway." Part of her wanted to know exactly how Jayden had reacted, but she suddenly felt bone tired. "I should have told him before now."

"Alexia, that horrible night played out because of a lot of things leading up to it. Do *not* blame yourself for a freak accident. Jayden will understand. He needs to adjust to this."

"I know," she said with firm resolve that she was nowhere close to feeling. "I'll call you later," she added calmly even though she was shattering inside. When she ended the call Alexia dropped to her knees on the cold, hard tile, but the sharp physical pain didn't even register. She held her head in her hands wanting to cry, but the release of tears wouldn't come. Instead, she scooted over and leaned against the cabinet doors for fifteen minutes, an hour or who knows how long? After a while she lost track of space and time.

Darkness fell and the chill of the night seeped into her bones but she didn't care. She simply sat there, dry eyed and full of sorrow. Regret surrounded her like a dense fog, making it difficult to breathe, impossible to move. What-ifs and should-haves filtered into her brain making her heart ache with the pain of it all. She put her palm over her flat stomach, thinking that their child would be in grade school now . . . playing soccer or learning to ride with Jayden? Of course she didn't even know if the baby had been a boy or a girl.

When a sob finally bubbled up in her throat she

hugged her knees to her chest and rocked back and forth. After the sense of fullness she had experienced with Jayden she suddenly felt so empty. Lost. She wanted him, needed him with her right now, hugging her close and telling her everything would be all right.

Alexia rested her head in her hands and wondered if Colin would tell Brianna. She wanted to call and ask him not to and that she would tell her sister in her own way, her own time, but she couldn't muster up the energy to get up from the floor. She was just so tired . . .

Finally, she found the strength to get up and stumble to her bedroom. Without bothering to shed her clothes she crawled beneath the covers and closed her dry, burning eyes. She huddled in a tight ball and prayed for blessed sleep to come . . .

Chapter Twenty-one

When his cell phone rang, Colin pounced on it like a cat on a mouse, hoping it was either Jayden or Alexia calling. A glance at the screen let him know it was Brianna on the other end. "Damn," he muttered, remembering that he had promised to call her earlier, before all hell broke loose. "Hey there," he answered, trying to put some cheer in his voice but failing miserably.

"What's wrong?" she asked in a concerned voice that Colin smiled at in spite of his mood. She was such a sweetheart.

Although *nothing* was on the tip of his tongue he knew that she would see right through him, so he said, "I'm just a little stressed."

"Oh, I thought you must have been busy when you didn't call, so I took it upon myself to buy a pizza and, well, I thought you might like a little company. Now, you're under no obligation at all, but if you want a slice of supreme extra cheese, I can deliver. No tip required," she said, and then added, "Okay, I talk way too much when I get nervous."

"Brianna, don't be nervous around me."

"I'm not used to calling guys."

"Well, I hope you get used to calling me whenever you feel like it. I like hearing from you."

"So I'm not bugging you?" she asked, and Colin could hear the smile in her voice.

"Of course not. You wouldn't be bugging me even if you were bugging me. Wait, that made sense in my head."

She laughed on the other end. "Yes, in a weird way it did. But then again, I'm kinda weird."

"Normal is boring and overrated."

"Thank goodness."

Colin grinned again, thinking she was the only person he knew who used phrases like thank goodness, but instead of dorky he found it cute. And somehow, sexy.

"Really, Colin, if it's a bad time, just say so. I won't be offended."

Colin hesitated but then went with honesty. "Yeah, it's a bad time but all the more reason why I wanna see you. Meet me here and I'll drive you up to my house."

"Okay," she answered. "I'll be there in about ten minutes."

"That's tight." Colin ended the call and leaned back in his desk chair. He had been working for hours in an effort to keep his mind off the situation with Alexia and Jayden. He hoped that right now the two of them were together talking things out. He also hoped that he could keep from telling Brianna, but sooner or later this would come out in the open and he wondered if he shouldn't let her know what was going on with her sister.

Colin inhaled a deep breath and decided he *would* tell her, thinking that Alexia needed her sister to be there for her. If he had gone to her family all those years ago, perhaps Alexia's life would have turned out differently. He wanted to respect her privacy but not if it risked her well-being. Right or wrong, he was going to do it. With a groan, Colin closed out of the spreadsheet he had been working on and tidied up his desk. Then as he had been doing all night, he looked at his phone but this time picked it up and sent a text message for Alexia to call and let him know that she was okay. And, damn it, if he didn't hear back from her he was going to head over to her cabin with Brianna.

Colin held the small phone in his hand as if that might somehow make her text back quicker. When his hand vibrated a few minutes later he anxiously opened the message that, thank God, was from Alexia. It read simply "I'm okay." With a heavy sigh, Colin flipped his phone shut. He wasn't totally buying the message but at least she replied and for now that would have to be enough.

The rumble of a car engine followed by the crunch of gravel prompted Colin to peer out the window into the darkness. He smiled when he spotted Brianna's sensible sedan sliding into a parking space. Not wanting to waste a minute, he grabbed his leather jacket and headed out the door.

"Hey there." Colin greeted Brianna with a quick kiss that would have lasted longer if the pizza box hadn't been between them. "You're an angel. I'm starving."

"Me too . . . starving, that is." She gave him a shy smile that tugged at every major part of his body. It blew him away how happy it made him to simply see her.

"Well, then, let's hurry up to my place and dig in."

"Sounds like a plan," she agreed, and followed him over to his four-wheel-drive truck. Holding the pizza in one hand, he helped her up the big step into the truck, trying not to ogle her cute ass. Instead of her work clothes she was casually dressed in jeans, a blue hooded sweatshirt, and tennis shoes. Her hair was pulled up in a loose ponytail, slightly askew, with curly tendrils of golden copper hair escaping. Her makeup was minimal but she was wearing some glossy stuff on her lips that made him want to kiss her senseless.

Colin found this dressed-down version of Brianna Spencer sexy as hell. Although he kept a steady stream of casual conversation going as he drove up the winding road to his house, all he could think about was making love to her. His desire for her, however, went beyond wanting her in his bed. He needed Brianna. For perhaps the first time in his life he recognized the difference.

"Wow," Brianna said when they arrived at Colin's house. Even though it was dark outside she could tell that the log and stone house was magnificent. She felt a little out-of-her-league pang of nervousness but shook it off. "Your house is amazing."

"Thanks," he answered in an understated way but also with a measure of pride. "I loved my motocross career but it feels good to have a permanent home and not be on the road all the time. I always knew I wanted to overlook the water. The lake is what drew me to this property."

"I wish it was light out so I could see it better."

"I hope you'll be here when it gets light," he answered, and then shook his head. "I was supposed to keep that thought to myself."

She reached up and cupped his chin. "Of course I'll stay."

He gave her a kiss and then came around to the passenger side of the truck to help her down. Spanning her waist, he lifted her to the ground with ease, taking his time about letting her go. Brianna felt a heavy pull of desire that had her almost forgetting about the pizza on the seat. She grabbed the box, but as they entered the house she had other things on her mind than eating.

When Colin flicked on the lights Brianna drew in a breath. "Your house is gorgeous." She looked around at the furnishings, thinking that it looked like pages in *Southern Living* magazine. "Rustic, but . . . wow, somehow elegant."

"Elegant?" He wrinkled his nose.

"Okay, um, rustic but sophisticated?" She raised her eyebrows and smiled.

"Well, some snooty chick came here and decorated," he admitted with a grin. "It's not exactly me . . . you know, MX posters, beanbag chairs and beer signs, but I like it."

Brianna shook her head at him, knowing he was trying to play down his amazing house. It didn't really hit her until now just how much money he must have made over the years through both racing and endorsements. She followed him into a huge gourmet kitchen and when he flicked on the overhead recessed lighting it took her breath away.

"Wow." Brianna put the pizza box on the tiered center island and took in the endless cabinets, the suspended copper pots, and the stainless steel appliances. Thinking of her own outdated kitchen, she swallowed hard, trying not to feel out of her element.

"What?" he asked with a frown.

"Everything . . . gleams."

Colin nodded. "Because it never gets used."

"If I had a kitchen like this I'd . . ."

"Cook?"

"Yeah."

"Feel free to whip something up any time the spirit moves you."

She pointed at the pizza box. "I think it's embarrassed to be in here."

Colin laughed. "Yeah, well, I'm not embarrassed to eat it. Let's heat it up and dig in." He walked over and put his hands on her shoulders. "Hey," he said softly, and sliced one hand through the air. "This is all . . . stuff. I'm a beer and pizza kind of dude, Brianna. This is fun to have, don't get me wrong, but it's also meaningless."

"Okay," she said, but didn't sound convincing to her own ears.

He cupped her chin in his palm. "I didn't bring you up here to impress you. I just wanted to be with you."

Brianna looked up into his eyes and saw nothing but sincerity. She wrapped her arms around his waist and realized with a sense of wonder that she was falling harder for him by the minute.

"Of course, if you wanna be impressed, that's cool too," he joked. Tilting her head up, he licked his tongue across her bottom lip and then captured her mouth in a tender yet heated kiss. "Mmm, damn, if I wasn't so hungry I'd say skip the pizza and move on to . . . other things."

With her arms around his waist she looked up at him. "Well, then, I'll warm up the pizza while you handle drinks."

He nodded. "Red wine?"

She nodded.

"I bought it just for you."

"Thanks," Brianna said, and was pleased that he thought of her throughout the day. She wondered if she was on his mind as much as he was on hers. She watched as he bent his blond head over the bottle and deftly uncorked it with a sharp pop. Although his mood was playful and sweet she sensed that there was something else on his mind. He mentioned stress and she considered asking but then decided getting his mind off whatever was bothering him was probably the best scenario.

Brianna sipped her wine and then sank her teeth into a warm slice of pizza. The cheese stretched and curled around her tongue, but as much as she was enjoying the soft crust she hurried through her dinner so that she could be in his arms. After two quick slices Colin tossed the remains in the fridge and then pulled her into his embrace.

"I've been thinking about kissing you all day long," he confessed.

"Stop thinking and start doing," she teased, and then let out a throaty little laugh when Colin scooped her up in his arms.

"You don't have to ask twice."

She wrapped her arms around his neck and said,

"You're sweeping me off my feet, Colin McCord." Her tone was light, but when Colin looked down at her Brianna realized that she had spoken the truth. When his blue eyes searched her face, her heart pounded. For a moment she thought that he might drop the L-word, and while she knew it was too soon to say it, Brianna was beginning to feel it.

Instead, he cleared his throat and smiled that sexy, playful had-her-eating-out-of-his-hand smile and carried her into his bedroom. With a flick of a switch or two, he had a gas fire going, jazzy music in the background, and a paddle fan turning in a lazy circle. Cathedral ceilings made the room appear open and airy, but the deep maroon walls lent a cozy, warm feel to the huge space. A massive four-poster bed constructed of rough-hewn logs had the same continuing rustic appeal that contrasted with the jewel-toned, down-feather comforter that must have cost the earth.

"Rough around the edges and yet gorgeous," Brianna commented.

"You talkin' about me?" Colin asked as he tugged his shirt over his head.

Brianna chuckled, knowing that he knew her comment referred to the furnishings. "Yeah, I was," she kidded, and then swallowed a groan when she let her gaze roam over his body. The firelight gleamed off his light hair and bronzed his skin.

"Hey, I'll be right back," he said, leaving her to wonder what he was going after. "Oh, and if you want to, ah, take your clothes off, there's a robe on a hook in the bathroom."

Brianna nodded while trying to keep her usual blush

under control. "Okay, thanks." She scooted from the bed and headed into the bathroom that seemed as big as her entire house. An enormous garden bath with tiered steps with a huge mosaic window above it filled one corner. The floor appeared to be marble and an open, two-headed shower stall took up the other side of the room. A double sink coupled with a giant mirror lined the far wall. A separate door led to the actual toilet.

"Dang, I could live in here," Brianna mused with a shake of her head. After locating the robe hanging on a hook, she began with trembling anticipation to take off her clothes. Brianna paused to look in the mirror at her body and for the first time felt a sense of sexual power. Angling her head, she cupped her small breasts and grinned, deciding that although there might not be much of her, she made up for it in enthusiasm. Plus, when Colin looked at her with such heat in his eyes she felt beautiful and it brought out a sensual side of her personality that she never knew existed until now.

Brianna slid her arms into the black robe that was miles too big. When she inhaled Colin's spicy scent on the collar she brought the soft material to her nose. A hot tingle of desire slid down her spine and splashed into her tummy. Taking a deep breath, she padded on bare feet to the door and walked into the bedroom. Colin had turned down the covers and fluffed up the pillows. A long-stemmed glass of wine sat on the nightstand along with a bottle of massage oil.

Colin gave her a rather shy smile when she looked at the oil and then back at him. "I thought you might like a back rub."

She arched one eyebrow.

"Okay, I thought *I* might like a back rub."

Brianna smiled and walked over toward the night-stand for the wine but tripped on the long robe. Colin reached out and saved her from falling. "I meant to do that," she joked.

"Okay, I'm going to the mall to get you a robe that fits," he said with a shake of his head. "But I have to admit that you look sexy and cute in my robe even though it swallows you up." He parted the folds and kissed the skin he revealed before handing her the wine.

Brianna took a sip and then placed the glass on the nightstand with a soft clink. She boldly reached for his jeans, and unzipped the fly. While looking up at his face, she reached in and ran her hand over the impressive length of his shaft encased in the soft cotton of his underwear. He felt hot and hard and she longed to have him inside her.

"Colin . . . ," she said, and let her robe slide to the floor. With a moan he picked her up and placed her on the crisp, smooth sheet. Then he shucked his jeans and briefs before sliding next to her.

"Turn over on your stomach," he requested, and then reached for the oil.

"Will it be cold?"

"I warmed it up for you," he said, and then drizzled some onto her back.

"Mmm," Brianna moaned when his big hands began massaging the warm, slippery oil into her skin. The spicy vanilla scent aroused and soothed at the same time. "It smells heavenly."

"I'm glad you like it. It took me forever to pick it out." He rubbed lightly at first and then with more pressure down her spine and then to her ass. He kneaded her cheeks and then straddled her body while working his way downward. "Feel good?" he asked while working on her thighs.

"Heavens, yes," she answered with a groan, a moan followed by a lingering sigh. "If you ever change careers, put me on this list."

Colin laughed as he used the heel of his hand to turn her muscles to jelly. Brianna didn't think it was ever possible to get this relaxed. The wine and the sultry music combined with the heat radiating from the fireplace were working magic on her body. She felt as if she were melting into the mattress like a pat of butter in a skillet . . .

And then he turned her over.

While propped up slightly on the pillows she watched through half-lidded eyes as he dripped oil onto her breasts and down her tummy. The warm oil felt erotic, so sensual, and when he massaged her small breasts with his big hands she closed her eyes and moaned in pure pleasure.

"God, do you even have a clue as to how amazingly hot you are?"

Brianna opened her eyes and shook her head.

"The oil makes your skin glisten." He drizzled more onto her body and then rubbed his fingers over the slick, slippery trail. Tilting the bottle, he let three warm drops hit her mound before massaging it in with featherlight strokes. Brianna sucked in a breath when he circled his fingertip over her clit. He parted her folds and inhaled a sharp breath. "You are so pretty there, Brianna. I have to taste you . . ."

He dipped his head between her thighs and lightly licked her labia before looking up at her. "Mmm, you taste like vanilla spice and hot sex." He bent his head back to his task and at this point Brianna was so aroused that the mere touch of his tongue made her climax immediately.

"Colin!" She threaded her fingers in his hair and arched her hips up from the bed. "God!" she cried when Colin slid his hands beneath her ass cheeks and pressed his hot mouth to her pulsing body while she rode out the orgasm. He sucked even more pleasure from her until she pushed her shoulders into the pillows and somehow managed to raise her melted-muscle body from the bed.

When Colin eased her back down to the sheets Brianna felt unbelievably relaxed and tingling with awareness at the same time. She tried to form words but could only manage sounds like *umm* and *ahh*.

Colin smiled and leaned in for a kiss, and even though she felt heavy limbed and languid she still needed him inside, connected to her body. His erection brushed up against her thigh and she moaned. "Colin . . . I want to massage you too, but my body feels like it's made of putty." She gave him a groggy giggle. "Now I know what Gumby feels like. You could probably twist and bend me in all kinds of weird ways."

Colin laughed, thinking that her candor was so damned refreshing. There was no pretense, no games, just pure and honest Brianna. In that moment he knew that no one else would ever measure up to her tiny but exquisite body or her sharp mind and playful personality. "There's only one place I want to be and that's deep inside you, Bri." He paused to sheath his dick in a condom and then came back to the bed.

"Make love to me, Colin." When he smiled she finished for him, "I know. I don't have to ask twice."

Colin loved that she was getting to know him so well. She seemed to understand him and he instinctively knew that she sensed an undercurrent that something was bothering him and she was trying to make him forget. She was his soft place to land . . . someone who knew and understood . . . and he wanted to be the same thing for her.

When he knelt on the bed and sank his dick deep within her, it was a connection that went well beyond sex. The emotion of this knowledge had him making sweet love to her on a level that entwined love with desire like a vine encircling a sturdy tree. She was slick and ready, open and giving. He wanted her so badly but then he realized that desire had become need.

Colin needed Brianna.

With that in mind he thrust into her over and over but holding back his release until he felt her tighten and grip, wringing an orgasm from him that started slow and then exploded. Colin wrapped his arms around her and held her close, wanting so much to tell her the depth of his feelings. But even though it was too soon for a declaration of love, surely she tasted it in his kiss, felt it in his touch.

Damn, he was a goner.

When Brianna laid her head on his chest, he smiled, curled his body around hers, and then kissed the top of her head. Colin loved the fact that she would be in his arms when the sun came up. He could get used to this, he thought, and smiled into the night.

His smile faded a bit when his thoughts drifted to Alexia and Jayden. He hoped that Jayden ended up at her house and that they talked things out. He truly believed that those two belonged together despite the pain of the past, and he could only hope that they had the sense to realize it.

Chapter Twenty-two

*I*t wasn't long before Jayden decided that drinking in the little pub held very little appeal. He didn't feel like being social and then realized that he didn't want to cloud his thoughts with alcohol. After tossing down some cash for his beer he left the bar feeling restless and wired. Then, in spite of the cold breeze, he knew what he had to do. He needed to ride.

Jayden strapped on his helmet and roared out of town. He rode his street bike hard, fast, and long into the night until his muscles screamed in protest and his body felt frozen stiff. At one point he drove near Alexia's cabin and almost turned up her driveway but then rumbled on past. He knew she must be hurting and it killed him to stay away, but he needed time to think this through. He hit the throttle and drove way too fast over a long, straight stretch of road, pushing his mind and body to the limit. Finally, when he knew it was too dangerous to drive one mile farther, he headed back to his cabin.

After stiffly dismounting his bike, he made a beeline

for the bathroom and turned on the shower. With a moan deep in his throat Jayden slicked his long hair back and raised his face to the hot spray. His body was so cold and bone-weary that the hot water pelting his body almost hurt, but it was the mental exhaustion that made him feel as if he could simply slide right down the drain. "Why?" he growled, becoming so frustrated that he barely refrained from punching the wall. Just when he thought that everything was falling into place this had to happen!

Grief for his unborn child washed over him and seeped into his soul. "She should have told me," he mumbled in a sad, broken tone. If he had only known about her pregnancy, that horrible night would never have happened, he thought, and then slapped his hands against the wet tile. Anger slammed head-to-head with his grief, sending Jayden into a tailspin that he wasn't sure he could ever bounce back from . . .

But then with his eyes closed, memories of the past few days with Alexia played in his brain like a slide show. He could see her smile, hear her soft laughter, and God, almost taste the passion that they had shared. Looking back, he realized now that on several occasions she had tried to tell him and he had shut her down . . . declared his undying love no matter what was in the past.

But he couldn't have anticipated this heartbreaking news. "God!" It wasn't just the lost child but also the knowledge that she probably couldn't conceive again. Jayden shook his head. Until recently he hadn't even thought about children, and now . . . *this*. He let anger and grief battle it out.

"Shit!"

Guilt slammed into his gut like a sucker punch, stealing his breath and sending unbelievable pain coursing through his body. He should never have left her. Her fucked-up life was in so many ways his fault and there wasn't a damned thing he could do about it.

Except to love her.

The past was over.

That thought echoed in his brain and seemed to bounce off the shower stall walls. *Love her, Jayden. She needs it, deserves it . . .*

But after stepping out of the shower stall and toweling off, he couldn't immediately bring himself to dial her number. Instead, he crawled into bed and stared into the darkness for a long time with his cell phone clutched in his hand. He thought about what he should say when he called her and finally decided that a simple *I love you* would be the right thing, not only because she needed to hear it but because no matter what, it would always be true. But before he made the call, mental and physical exhaustion overtook him and in an instant Jayden fell into a deep, dark slumber.

When Alexia awoke before the crack of dawn, the first thing she did was reach for her cell phone on the nightstand. With trembling fingers she checked her phone log to see if Jayden had called. She let out a disappointed sigh when the hope that she had been wearing like a warm coat suddenly felt like a heavy burden. So much for *I'll love you no matter what*, she thought as she sadly snapped the phone shut. But then again, she should have at some point had the courage to tell him everything. There's no room for secrets in forever. Tears welled up in her eyes and she tugged the covers to her chin thinking she would curl up on the bed and pray for sleep, but then something inside her snapped.

"No!"

Alexia sat up in bed and punched both fists into the mattress. Jayden knew her dark secret, her mistake of tearing out after him in a rainstorm and the devastating results. She had paid—oh, how she had punished herself for years—but Alexia wrapped her arms around herself and while rocking back and forth she said in a trembling, but loud voice, "I forgive God for the rain. I forgive Jayden for the call." She rocked harder. "Oh God . . . oh God, *oh God*, and the baby for dying." She swallowed hard and would not allow tears to overcome her resolve. "Most of all . . . ," she began softly, and then said loud and clear without a hint of tremor in her voice, "Most of all, I forgive *myself*."

Her chest heaved as she sat there in the dark, quiet room but she slowly calmed her breathing. A sense of peace washed over her. She stopped rocking and instead, embraced the feeling. Looking up, she said, "Thank you. I am finally healed."

She inhaled sharply and wondered what she should do next. She thought about calling Jayden but then decided that she needed some time alone. While she realized that he was processing the news in his own way, the lack of communication from him hurt. Leaving town would give him time as well to make some decisions. Alexia didn't doubt his love for her, but sometimes love wasn't enough. So she sat there for a few minutes and then she knew where she would go . . .

South. To the beach. A sudden need for sand between her toes and warm waves washing over her feet hit her like a craving for dark chocolate. Alexia scrambled from the bed and in less than an hour she had her suit-case packed and she was in her SUV heading south. She hit the interstate just as the sun stretched golden fingers from behind gray clouds and welcomed in a new day.

Alexia put her sunglasses on and slid Rascal Flatts in her CD player. She skipped tracks until she found the song she was looking for and then cranked it up when Gary LeVox's unique voice belted out "Feels Like Today," and for the next several hundred miles the lyr-ics became her anthem. She repeated the song, belted the words out right along with him and meant every single one.

When she stopped for gas Alexia took the opportu-nity to send a text message to everyone who would get worried about her. It read simply "I'm fine but I need some time away. Don't worry." She hit the SEND but-ton, turned her phone on silent, and armed with junk food and caffeine she munched on empty calories while her SUV gobbled up the miles.

Alexia was on her last bag of Doritos when she crossed the Florida state line. She rolled down her win-dow and shouted, "Whoo-hoo!" and popped another triangle of cool ranch flavor into her mouth followed by a big gulp of sweet, fizzy Mountain Dew. Her mood re-mained a weird combination of exhilarating freedom while missing Jayden, but if he couldn't accept her past, then they had no future. That much, she knew for sure.

Alexia headed in the direction of the Florida pan-handle toward a little slice of heaven called 30-A, which was nineteen miles of scenic roadway hugging the Em-erald Coast, so named because of the sugar white sand that butts up to glistening, green water. Her final desti-nation was Seagrove Beach, a tiny resort town nestled between the more commercially populated Destin and Panama City. She had discovered Seagrove by taking a wrong turn, something she was prone to do, and had visited the area whenever she needed to escape from reality.

She had come here often when her ex-husband had been doing . . . other things.

Just about dusk, Alexia pulled her SUV into One Seagrove Place, a high-rise where she had stayed before, and rented a condo with a spectacular view of the gulf. Alexia knew that this northern part of Florida would be all but deserted, except for snowbirds and locals and that was just fine with her. She planned on walking the beach, reading, and renting her favorite movies for an entire week or maybe even a month if the spirit moved her. She already had enough material that she could work on Jayden's story as promised to Brianna and e-mail it to her when completed. She, of course, would let them know that she was safe and relatively sane but not disclose her destination.

After unpacking her few belongings she ordered pizza and was about to uncork a bottle of wine but decided it would put her to sleep and she wanted to enjoy the remainder of the evening. So she opted for water until she could make a trek to the grocery store in the morning.

After the pizza arrived she settled onto the sofa with the intention of eating while watching a movie. She refused to feel lonely, to think about Jayden, or to miss her sister. But of course she did all those things and her sense of freedom became edged with sadness. She looked over at her phone and thought about calling home but then with determination took a big bite of warm and gooey pizza and turned her attention to the Lifetime movie. She smiled when she realized that she could hear the sound of waves slapping against the shore and looked forward to a sunrise walk on the beach. She would let the sand and the sun heal her wounds before returning to Braxton and facing her future.

Chapter Twenty-three

"Colin, if you know where the hell Alexia is, you have to tell me."

Colin looked up from his desk and cringed at the ragged condition his best friend was in. "Dude, I don't know."

"Then ask Brianna."

Colin shook his head and sighed. "I did, Jayden, the first dozen times you asked me to. She doesn't know either. We all got the same text message, so at least we know that she's safe."

Jayden raked his fingers through his hair and growled in frustration. "I should have called her, but my stupid ass fell asleep."

"Maybe she needs this time away. To sort things out." Colin paused and then said, "Maybe you do too."

"No! I don't!" He paced back and forth. "I thought I did," he admitted, and then stopped short. "But, Colin, I can't lose her again."

"Jayden, man, I'm so sorry. I should have kept my

mouth shut. It wasn't my place to tell you anything, much less something I had promised not to ever disclose. I feel like shit over it."

"Oh, just stop, both of you," Brianna demanded as she breezed into the room. Colin looked over at her in surprise and Jayden turned around to face her. Brianna fisted her hands on her slim hips and continued. "No one, and I mean *no one*, is responsible for what happened that damned stormy night." She pointed at Jayden. "Not you!" And then pointed at Colin. "Or you!"

"She knows?" Jayden asked.

"I thought I should tell her. Damn, I wish I had let you know all those years ago."

Brianna inhaled a deep breath and blew it out. "Colin, we've been over this. What happened that night was no one's fault. Right or wrong, choices were made." She frowned and then shrugged. "We could argue that it was fate or, in some way we don't understand, meant to be, but the bottom line is that we can't go back. Only forward." She turned her focus to Jayden and said, "Do you love my sister?"

"Yes," he answered without hesitation. "It kills me what we lost." He swallowed and then continued. "And never will have, don't want to . . . no, make that I can't live without her, Brianna. Nothing else, at this point, matters more than that. I wish Alexia knew how I felt."

"Well, then, you have to tell her."

Jayden jammed his hands in his pockets. "She won't answer my calls. And we don't know where the hell she is."

Colin looked over at Brianna. "Do you know something we don't?"

Brianna nibbled on the inside of her lip. "I'm trying to track her down. After all, I am a reporter. I have some phone calls in and some feelers out there." She looked at Jayden and said, "I can't promise anything and I might have to break a few laws like pretending to be my sister. If we're lucky she used her credit card and I'll figure out her location. I have an inkling anyway."

"You do?" Jayden asked hopefully.

Brianna nodded.

"When do you think you might know for sure?" Colin asked.

"Soon, I hope," she answered, and when her cell phone rang she looked at the screen and grinned. "Keep your fingers crossed."

Colin listened to Brianna talk in a brisk, professional tone. With each passing day he was becoming more and more impressed and he realized that he was falling for her on a deeper level that included admiration and respect and not just physical attraction. Intelligence, he decided, was damned sexy and instead of being intimidated as he was at first, he felt she was driving him to recognize his own attributes other than just racing, and in fact, making him a more confident, better man.

"Well?" Jayden asked as soon as Brianna snapped her phone shut.

"Bingo!" she shouted in a voice so different from her professional tone that Colin had to smile. She put her fist in the air and said, "Seagrove Beach, just as I had suspected. For someone who didn't want to be found, she sure left a trail of bread crumbs." Brianna arched an eyebrow at Jayden. "Which leads me to believe that she wants to be located."

Colin shook his head. "Not everyone is as savvy as you, Brianna. I'm not so sure she really wants anyone to intrude on her privacy. She's probably sorting things out for herself."

"Too bad," Jayden said. "I'll just have to help her sort things out." He went over and hugged Brianna. "Thank you. I owe you one."

"You owe me a kick-ass story."

Jayden pulled back and grinned. "You'll get it. Now get me directions and then I'm outta here."

"Coming right up. If she gets ticked at me, that's too bad too. All of you needed some sense knocked into you." A few minutes later she had MapQuest directions in Jayden's hands but then said, "No offense, but you look like crap. Get some rest before you hit the road."

When Jayden looked ready to protest Colin jumped on the bandwagon. "Dude, she has a valid point."

After inhaling a deep breath Jayden reluctantly nodded. "I rode too hard last night. I fell asleep but it was restless and shitty with weird-ass dreams. I'll rest up before I hit the road. I should probably fly anyway, but it's such a pain that I think I'll just drive. Brianna, I hate to ask this but don't let Alexia know I'm on my way, okay? I don't want her to skip outta there before I even get a chance to see her."

Brianna nodded. "I understand." She gave him a hug. "You two belong together. Don't lose sight of that, okay?"

"Not a problem," Jayden answered. "I'll call and let you know when I arrive." He gave them a tired but hopeful smile. "I'm outta here."

After Jayden left, Colin got up from his desk and

came around to tug Brianna into his arms. "You are amazing. Have I told you that lately?"

Brianna laughed and hugged him around the waist. "Um, last night and again this morning," she reminded him, and then blushed. "But you can tell me again."

"You're amazing," he said in a somewhat teasing tone, but then added more seriously, "In more ways than one."

"Thank you," she said, and then slid her hands up his chest. "You've brought me out of my shell, Colin, and made me feel so alive. Who would ever have thought that . . . ," she began but then trailed off.

"What? Finish your thought."

She toyed with his collar and then said, "I shouldn't make assumptions."

"Then, let me. I think you were going to say, who would have thought that we would end up together? Am I right?"

Brianna nodded. "Yes."

"Hey, I already think of you as my girlfriend, Brianna. Unlikely couple or not, I'm serious about you. I hope you know that."

"I do."

"Good." He smiled at her. "I have a lot of work to do but will you have dinner with me? I'll even cook."

She raised her eyebrows. "You cook?"

"No, but I can assist. You can order me around the kitchen."

Brianna giggled. "You're on. How about around seven? I have some catching up to do, especially with Alexia gone."

"Okay," he said, but then frowned.

"What?"

"That's too long to wait."

"To eat?"

"No, for this . . ." He shook his head and then captured her mouth in a hot kiss. Then he walked over and locked the door.

"Colin, what are you doing?" she asked breathlessly. "I have to—"

He cut her protest off with another kiss. "Colin, we can't . . . ," she began, but when he kissed her neck she sighed. "Okay, we can. But where?"

"In my chair."

"Your chair?"

He nodded, not quite sure how it would transpire, but the floor was out and his desk was piled high with paperwork. Acting as though he had a plan, he grabbed her hand and led her behind the desk. After sitting down in the chair he said, "Sweetie, take your clothes off for me."

"Colin, maybe this isn't such a good idea," she said, but started unbuttoning her prim little shirt, revealing a cream-colored bra that pushed her breasts up to where they almost spilled out of the satin cups.

"God, you're sexy."

"In this?" she asked, and he nodded.

"Because I know how hot your little body is beneath your clothing," he added, and kissed the soft swell of her breasts. "Your underwear rocks."

"I told Alexia she needs to take me shopping for sexier clothes."

"Mmm, whatever, but I like the contrast between your plain clothing and the hot underwear," he admitted while unzipping her pants to find lacy little panties.

"It's like a secret that only I know," he said while pulling her close to kiss her belly.

She tilted her head to the side and laughed. "The lingerie is a recent addition to my wardrobe," she told him as she threaded her fingers through his hair, but then pushed his chin up for him to look at her. "For you. Only for you, Colin."

"I want to keep it that way," he said, but then shook his head. "Sorry, I don't mean to sound like a caveman."

"Don't be sorry. I love it that you're being possessive." She cupped his cheeks with her palms and then leaned down to kiss him softly. "If you're asking me not to date anyone else, you have nothing to worry about."

"That's what I was hoping you'd say."

She gave him another heated kiss followed by a slow, sultry smile. "Now, just how are we going to make love in this chair?" she asked as she shimmied out of her khaki slacks and stood there in nothing but sexy bikini panties. Colin arched one eyebrow. "Damned if I know, but let's give it a shot." He sat down in the chair and pulled her close. "These are pretty." He slid his fingers over the patch of silk and lace until she became hot and moist beneath his hand. Then with a groan he slipped one finger underneath the silk, where she was wet for him. "You feel so good." He sank his finger deep and then swirled it over her clit, lubricating her, teasing, until she reached down and tugged her panties off.

"God, you're gorgeous," he said, and replaced his fingers with his mouth, giving her a hot, intimate kiss. He palmed her ass while he licked and sucked, sinking his tongue deep before pulling out and giving his full attention to her clit. He made his tongue rigid and increased the pressure.

"Oh . . . ," she said breathlessly, gripping his shoulders hard. Colin flicked his tongue faster and then sucked hard until she climaxed against his mouth. He caressed her smooth ass and kissed her there tenderly, licking her swollen flesh until she laughed weakly and then moaned, "My God . . ."

Colin wrapped his arms around her, letting her recover for a minute or two, and then stood up to tug his jeans down to the floor. "Let me help." Brianna peeled off his tight boxer briefs with trembling hands. He sucked in a breath when her cool fingers curled around his hot, hard dick. When she lightly pumped her hand up and down, Colin sat back down in the chair and said, "Ah, Brianna, sweetie, get a condom from my jeans pocket."

"Here," she said, and ripped it open with her teeth.

"Thanks." He quickly rolled it on and then put his hands around her waist, helping her on top of him. She knelt on either side of his thighs and then, using his shoulders as leverage, reached down and guided his dick to her wet heat and then eased down until he was buried inside her. He cupped her ass and took a pebbled nipple into his mouth, licking and sucking while holding her in place.

"God . . . Colin, let me move," she pleaded, but he shook his head, wanting her wild for him. He pulled her head down for a long, intense kiss while moving his hips slightly to give her a taste of what was to come. She pulled her mouth away and licked his earlobe, gently sucking and nipping until he was squirming in the chair.

"Ahh, Bri." Colin let go and gave her the freedom she craved. She pushed up, using his shoulders, and came to her knees in the chair and then sank back down. Her nipples grazed his chest and she licked his bottom lip back and forth until he groaned and crushed his mouth to hers.

"Faster," he said, spanning her waist, guiding, helping, and pumping up into her while his tongue explored her sweet mouth. The chair squeaked and bounced when they picked up the pace. At one point Colin accidentally pushed his foot against the desk, and the chair sailed backward and bumped into the wall. Brianna giggled but Colin didn't miss a beat and pumped harder, guided her faster until they were both panting.

"Colin!" she cried out, arching her back. He felt her grip his dick with an intense orgasm that brought him over the edge. Holding her waist, he braced his feet on the floor and thrust upward hard, going deep while he climaxed with a rush of hot pleasure.

"Ah, Brianna," he said softly, and then pulled her mouth to his for a light, tender kiss. "That was one wild ride," he said with a laugh, and then hugged her tightly to his body.

"Mmm," she said into his ear, "are we insane or what?"

"You know it, but damn, it rocks," he told her with a grin.

Brianna smiled back and while brushing his hair away from his forehead said, "Do you think it will always be this way between us?"

Colin arched one eyebrow. "I was a crazy motocross racer, remember? I love a challenge and have lots of stamina."

"So your answer is yes."

He nodded. "Oh . . . yeah."

Brianna laughed but then said, "We have to get to work, don't we?"

"I'm afraid so. But I'll catch up with you later and we'll have some fun in that big-ass kitchen of mine."

"Excellent idea," she said in her Brianna business voice that was in direct contrast to her sweet, little naked body. He was learning that she had many facets to her personality and he planned on learning each and every one.

"I hope that all goes well with Jayden and Alexia," she said with such concern that Colin fell for her even harder. She was a loving, caring person and he made a vow to himself right then and there to treat her like gold.

"I'm sure it will. If I know Jayden, he won't rest long before hitting the road."

She frowned. "That worries me."

Colin shrugged as he pulled on his pants. "He's a seasoned athlete, Brianna. He's in good shape. He'll be fine." He came over and pulled her into his arms. "I'm sure they'll work everything out. They deserve happiness after all they've been through."

"Yeah, they do." Brianna hugged him back. "I just hope we hear from them and don't have to wonder and worry."

"I'm sure we'll hear." He kissed her on top of her cute head. "I'll see you tonight."

She nodded and squeezed him around the waist hard. "You have a good day, okay?"

"You too." Bending his head, he gave her another lingering kiss, knowing it would have to last him all day, but then reluctantly he let her slide from his arms. He watched her walk out of the office and then went to the window to watch her walk to her car, thinking that he finally knew what real, honest-to-goodness love felt like.

And it felt great.

Chapter Twenty-four

Alexia placed the takeout box on the kitchen counter, anxious to sink her teeth into the grouper sandwich from the deli across the street. Although she had eaten a huge breakfast, her stomach growled in anticipation. When she opened the refrigerator and snagged a bottle of juice she shook her head. "I sure must have been hungry when I went to the grocery store," she mumbled as she took inventory of the contents. From the moment she embarked on her vacation she seemed to be eating all the time . . . and craving weird stuff that usually didn't appeal to her palate.

She supposed it was the endless beach walks, the sun, and the sea-scented air that stimulated her appetite. But when she popped open the box, the aroma of fish suddenly made her stomach lurch. "What was that all about?" she wondered, and with her hand to her tummy snapped the lid shut. After taking a deep breath Alexia was about to try again when she heard a knock at the front door. She hurried through the living room to the entrance but then stopped short before opening the door. *Who could it be?* She certainly didn't know anyone here and had made a point of keeping to herself so she put her eye to the peephole and gasped when Jayden's face came into view.

"Ohmigod." Alexia turned and leaned her back against the door wondering how in the world he found her. Her heart pounded rapidly while several emotions, surprise, joy and then anger, all tangled together. With a groan she looked down at her baggy sweats, her bare feet, and reached up to her sloppy ponytail but then became annoyed at herself for caring how she looked. He wasn't supposed to be here! She considered telling him to go away, but when she looked through the peephole again he frowned and swiped a hand down his face as if worried and perhaps tired. With a pang of guilt Alexia realized that these past couple of days had to be emotional for him and she made her decision. Just when he raised his fist to knock again she twisted the dead bolt and opened the door.

For a long, awkward moment Alexia didn't know what to say, but the fact that he looked road-weary tugged at her heart. "Can I come in?" Jayden finally broke the silence and the sound of his raspy, tired voice got to her as well.

"I . . . ," she began, but then another wave of nausea rolled over her and she put her hand to her mouth and ran to the bathroom, barely making it before she became sick to her stomach. She finally pushed up from her knees and with trembling fingers splashed cool water on her face while wondering if she had food poisoning or had perhaps picked up a bug. She inhaled a deep cleansing breath and then swished some mouthwash around while trying to muster up the courage to open the door and face Jayden again.

"Hey, you okay in there?" Jayden asked with concern lacing his voice.

Alexia cleared her throat. "Yes, I'll be out in a couple of minutes," she responded weakly.

"Okay," Jayden answered, but wasn't convinced. "Can I get you anything?"

"No," she croaked.

"Let me know if you need something. I'll be right out here," he assured her in a tone that let her know that he wasn't going anywhere. Ever. But they could address that when she felt better. He also wondered whether she had the flu or he had caused her distress, but he really couldn't wish for either one. With a weary sigh born of driving straight through from Braxton on very little sleep he headed to the small kitchen and grabbed a soft drink from the fridge. After popping the top he walked over to the sliding glass doors and admired the view of the gulf. The sun sparkled off the white, frothy spray, contrasting with the emerald green water lapping against the snow-white sand.

"Beautiful, isn't it?"

Jayden turned at the sound of Alexia's soft voice and nodded. "Yeah. I always did like this area of Florida."

Alexia joined him at the glass doors. "I've been coming here for years mostly by myself when life would get to be too much. It's like my happy place to regroup and unwind."

"I guess you're mad at me for intruding."

She turned to look up at him and felt her eyes well

up with tears. "I don't know what I am, Jayden, but I do know this," she began, but then had to pause for composure. Jayden wanted to take her into his arms, but he knew he needed to let her finish. She cleared her throat and continued. "I regret driving in that horrible storm, and you had a right to know what had happened. I'm sorry."

"Alexia . . . ," Jayden began, but she shook her head.

"Let me finish, please. For a long time I blamed you for the call, blamed God for the rain . . . the baby for"— she swiped at a tear—"dying." She shook her head and sighed deeply. "I was to blame."

"Alexia, no—"

"Yes, Jayden, I was. I got into that car knowing the nasty conditions. No one forced me."

"You were little more than a kid."

"I know. But I had to take responsibility for that night so that I could finally forgive myself. Jayden, that burden has been lifted." She tapped her chest. "I forgive myself for my mistake." Then she looked at him with tearful eyes and said, "But do you forgive me?"

Jayden wanted to tell her that she didn't need his forgiveness for something that was an accident, but she seemed to need him to say that he did, so he nodded. "I forgive you, Alexia."

She closed her eyes and exhaled a ragged sigh.

"But listen to me. It was a series of events that led up to you getting into that car. If I hadn't left, you wouldn't have gone after me. If Colin had let me know what happened, I would have come to you and you wouldn't have married that son of a bitch. You know Colin blames himself for that."

Her eyes rounded. "He shouldn't! I made him promise."

Jayden took a step closer and put his hands on her shoulders. "No more what-ifs or should-have-beens. It's done!"

"But, Jayden, you know the rest. It's unlikely that . . . ," she began, but then stopped and put a hand over her mouth.

"Alexia, I'll be honest. I hate that we can't have children together. It seems so damned unfair. But I love you. Nowadays there are options. Maybe some medical procedure or something . . . who knows? The accident happened a long time ago. But the bottom line is that I want you in my life no matter what." He waited for her to say something but she just blinked at him with a frown. "Alexia, what's wrong? Don't you believe me?"

"I . . . ," she began, but then shook her head mutely.

"What? Are you still not feeling well?" he asked when she suddenly appeared shaken and pale.

"Jayden," she whispered, swallowed, and then said, "I hadn't thought about it with all that's been happening, but . . . ohmigod. I'm late."

He looked at his watch. "For what?" he asked, and then his heart skittered around in his chest. "Wait, you mean . . ."

She nodded slowly and then put a hand to her belly.

"But I thought . . ."

"Me too," she said in a breathless voice, and seemed a little dazed. "I blocked out most of that horrific night. Mitchell made it clear that he didn't want children, so it never became an issue." She tucked a loose tendril of hair behind her ear and looked at him with big eyes. "The doctors let me know that there was very little chance of me conceiving ever again . . . too much scar tissue and other things that I'm sure they explained but I was so out of it at the time that I never completely comprehended."

"They could be wrong, or then again, we might have just beaten the odds."

"Of course, I'm just late. I don't know . . . I'm probably *not*," she said, and then whispered, "Pregnant." She looked at him and licked her lips. "Jayden, what if I am?"

Jayden pulled her into his arms and hugged her. "I'd be overjoyed." He pulled back and tilted her head up. "But if you're not or can never be, I'm okay with that too. Got that?"

"I love you," she whispered, and then pulled his head down for a sweet, soulful kiss. "I always have and I always will."

Jayden nodded while holding her cheeks in his palms. "We're lucky, you know, to have come back together like this after all these years. No matter what the outcome, we belong together, Alexia."

She nodded.

"Okay let's go."

"Where?"

"To the drugstore for one of those test kits."

Alexia put her hand to her chest and nodded. "Okay."

Jayden took her hand in his and tugged her toward the door. His fatigue had vanished and his heart pumped in his chest like a jackhammer. He tried not to get excited at the thought of her carrying his child, because he didn't want to show bitter disappointment if she wasn't, but he couldn't help but be hopeful. The fact that he wanted this so much reiterated how much he loved her.

"We'll have to use your SUV. I'm on empty," he admitted, and then pulled her into his arms. "I was in a hurry to get here and didn't stop to fill up."

She smiled as she grabbed her purse. "I shouldn't have left like I did."

"No, you needed this," he said, and returned her smile. "You just forgot to take me with you."

They hurried to the elevator and then all but ran to her silver SUV. Too nervous to drive, she tossed him the keys. "There's a drugstore about ten minutes down the road," she said when he pulled onto 30-A and headed in the direction of Destin. "So, I guess Brianna tracked me down," Alexia added.

Jayden nodded. "Don't be mad at her. I begged."

Alexia shrugged. "You know, I think in the back of my mind I knew she would and I hoped you'd follow me here. I'm glad that everything is out in the open. I just didn't expect to be doing *this* . . ."

When she closed her eyes and inhaled a shaky breath Jayden reached over and took her hand in his. When he squeezed her hand she realized how happy she felt having him there with her. "Whatever happens, we're in this together."

"Thanks," she said as they pulled into the parking lot. She had been so lonely for far too long and in that moment she knew that everything was finally going to be all right no matter what the outcome of the pregnancy test was.

From that point forward everything seemed to happen in a blur. They located the aisle and then stood hand in hand blinking in confusion at the dozens of choices. Finally, Jayden picked up the most expensive kit and for some reason decided they needed two. Alexia didn't protest but followed him in a nervous daze.

The ten-minute drive back to the high-rise seemed to take an eternity. Once inside the condo she opened the box with trembling hands. When Jayden followed her to the small bathroom she said, "You read the instructions."

"Okay." He cleared his throat and began, "Take the test stick from the wrapper and remove the cap."

"Okay."

"Insert test stick into holder."

"God . . . okay, right."

"Place absorbent tip in urine stream for five seconds."

"This wasn't supposed to be done in the morning, was it?"

Jayden shook his head. "Nope. This says any time of day from the first day of your missed period. It will read either pregnant or not pregnant. Easy enough, huh?"

She inhaled a deep breath. "So I can't really mess this up?"

Jayden shook his head. "Don't think so. It says here that it's ninety-nine percent accurate."

"How long will it take for the results?"

"As long as three minutes but as little as one."

"God."

"Hold the stick by the thumb grip and remember to keep it pointed downward, okay?"

She nodded.

"And it says not to lift it while the hourglass symbol is flashing. Pee for five seconds only."

"Ohmigod, I *am* going to mess this up."

"No, you won't." Jayden hugged her tightly. "Go on in and do this. I'll be right outside this door."

"Okay." Her legs felt wobbly and her stomach was doing flip-flops, but she made it into the bathroom and quietly closed the door. She was so nervous that it took her a few minutes before she could even pee and then her hand holding the stick shook so violently that she almost missed it completely. "One, two, three, four, five," she counted, making sure that she saturated the tip and that it pointed toward the floor. Her heart was pounding so hard that she looked down thinking it would appear as if it were rising out of her chest like a cartoon character. With her other hand she pulled up her sweatpants and then opened the door.

"Well?" Jayden asked. He looked as nervous as she felt.

"I'm still waiting. I wanted you with me."

"No problem." They huddled together in the bathroom and stared at the little window for what seemed like an eternity. Jayden held her free hand in a viselike grip but she didn't mind.

Then the answer popped onto the small screen.

"Ohmigod," Alexia whispered, and she wondered if any moment she might wake up. She raised her gaze to Jayden and then burst into tears. "I can't believe it."

Jayden gathered her in his arms and said, "We're going to have a baby, Alexia."

She buried her face against his neck and cried happy tears but then pulled back to look at the screen, terrified that it might suddenly read "just kidding," and then she would wake up.

Jayden laughed. "Sweetie, it isn't going to change," he assured her. "You're pregnant."

"Are you happy?"

He nodded and then said, "Shit."

"What?"

He bit his bottom lip and then his brown eyes filled with tears. "I'm . . ." He sniffed and then said, "Damn . . . going to cry." He wrapped his arms around her and his big, strong body shook with emotion. They held each other tight for a long, long time and then he captured her mouth with a sweet, tender kiss.

"I'm so happy. I want to be cuddled in your arms in bed."

"Me too. Ahh, God, I want to make love to you," he said, but then pulled back. "We can do that, right?"

"Yes, we can," she assured him, and then took his hand in hers. She led him to the bedroom and pulled back the vertical blinds to reveal an amazing gulf view. Then she opened the sliding glass door. "I want to hear the gulf in the background and smell the tang of the sea."

Jayden smiled. "Come here," he said, and when she stood before him he splayed his hand over her tummy. "I can't believe it." He shook his head in wonder. With a sigh he cupped her head and leaned in for a kiss that Alexia knew came directly from his heart. She could feel the warmth, the tenderness in his touch and she ached with the sweetness.

"I think that after all we've been through we'll never take this for granted. I know I won't."

"Alexia," he said, "I only wish—"

"No." She put a finger to his lips. "We're beginning again from this moment forward. Okay?"

Jayden nodded. "And this is the perfect way to start . . . ," he agreed before dipping his head to kiss her again. Then he tugged her sweatshirt over her head and unclipped her bra, stopping to cup her breasts while untying the string of her sweatpants. He dropped to his knees and placed a series of butterfly kisses on her belly.

"Jayden . . . ," she said with a happy sigh, and sank her fingers into his long hair. He looked up at her so fiercely masculine but his brown eyes were full of emotion. Alexia thought of Brianna's comment. She laughed softly.

"What?"

She smiled. "Brianna told me not long ago that she wished someone would look at her the way you used to look at me."

"Used to?"

"The way you *look* at me."

"That's better," he said, and squeezed her butt. "Well, if you ask me Colin is totally into your little sister. He's definitely a goner."

"They are so cute together."

"Damn, I can't wait to tell Colin you said that . . . cute?" He laughed. "Not good for his badass rep."

"What about your badass rep?"

"I gotta back it down for my baby," he said, and kissed her belly again. "When do we get to tell?"

"When we get back."

"Do you seriously think you can hold it in that long? What about your mom and dad?"

"You've got a point." She reached over and cupped

his chin. "But let's keep the news to ourselves for a few days. Just you and me."

"Okay. I plan on keeping you occupied anyway."

"You mean swimming, right?" She angled her head toward the window.

"Yeah, right," he said, and gently pushed her back onto the bed. "Swimming is what I always have on my mind when I think of you."

Alexia laughed, glad that he appeared so happy with the unexpected news. The depth of his emotion touched her deeply, but this playful, teasing side of Jayden made Alexia feel lighthearted and younger than she had felt for years. She watched as he tugged his T-shirt over his head and made quick work of his worn jeans and then joined her in bed.

"For six hundred miles I've thought about making love to you." With a half moan, half growl he pressed his mouth to hers. The kiss was gentle, loving, but the heat of desire shot up from Alexia's toes and she opened her mouth for more. His tongue slid against hers, teasing and tangling, until Alexia moaned and pressed her body against his in sensual longing. She loved the feel of his smooth, warm skin and the ripple of muscle beneath her fingers. She rubbed her palms over his back and kneaded his shoulders, then slid to his arms thinking she could never get tired of touching him. His mouth moved from her lips to her neck, making a hot shiver shimmy down her spine. Then he pulled back to nuzzle his face between her breasts before coming up to one elbow to watch her face while he lightly caressed her body.

"You make me feel beautiful."

"Because you are," he said, and then trailed his

fingers to the tender inside of her thighs. Alexia shivered and her breath caught when he slid his fingers inside her body, gently caressing until she was slick and ready for him.

"God, Alexia," he said, and then entered her slowly with the utmost of care. He moved in a sensual circle, making love to her as if savoring each stroke, the touch of her skin, and the taste of her mouth. Alexia held him close, entwining her legs with his while matching his slow, easy rhythm. Her pleasure accelerated slowly, climbing higher and higher . . . heated desire mixed with pure love. Jayden slid his hands up her arms and threaded his fingers with hers. He whispered words of love and passion in her ear until she held his hands tight, arched her back, and climaxed. She immediately felt the hot rush of his release and then he kissed her . . . a deep delicious kiss that went on and on.

Finally, with a contented little growl, Jayden rolled over and pulled her into his arms, holding her close. The cool breeze filtered into the room, cooling their heated skin until she shivered and he tugged the cover up over their bodies. The only sound in the room was their breathing and the gentle swish of waves licking up against the shore.

Jayden spooned her to his body, holding her as close as possible. With a smile she hugged his arms to her and said, "I'm so happy, Jayden. I hope you are too."

"You know it," he said, and kissed her shoulder. "Very, very happy."

"I want you to know that I want you to finish out your career. Writing about it has made me realize how much you've accomplished. I want you to break more records and be ready for the Supercross circuit."

"I don't want to be away from you, especially now."

"I'll come to as many races as I can. I want you to look out and finally see me in the crowd."

"But, Alexia, what about the danger? Considering your accident the first time, I fully understand where you're coming from. I don't want to risk anything."

She shook her head. "This is who you are, Jayden. Even if you aren't racing you'll be riding. The danger will always be there. But so will I."

"I love you," he said softly in her ear.

"Mmm, I love you too." She snuggled to him and then yawned. "Let's sleep for just a little while and then do this all over again . . . after we eat."

He chuckled tiredly into her ear and then sighed. "Sounds like a plan."

Alexia smiled when just moments later his breathing became slow and even. She closed her eyes but remained awake for a long time basking in a happy glow. She felt so peaceful and content and yet stronger than ever before. A smile crossed her face when she thought about telling her parents and Brianna and Colin. Her sister would be ecstatic, and Alexia wondered if she could wait even a few days to tell her and Colin the unbelievable news. Alexia was still trying to process the fact that she was having Jayden's baby and that he was lying right there in bed with her. She snuggled close to him, thinking that although she might never have life figured out, from here on in she sure was going to try her damnedest to make the best of it.

For a long time she was too keyed up to sleep. She thought of Brianna and Colin and hoped that her sister found the same happiness with Colin that she and

Jayden had finally embraced. She smiled, thinking that crazy Colin and her sensible sister made an unlikely but adorable couple, and she had a good feeling the two of them were somehow meant to complement each other. When she thought of the trench coat incident, she almost laughed out loud, and had to bite her bottom lip so she didn't wake Jayden.

But after a while the soothing sound of the sea coupled with Jayden's steady breathing near her ear made her eyelids feel heavy and soon lulled her into a deep and well-deserved sleep.

Chapter Twenty-five

"What in the world are you doing?" Colin asked while he watched Brianna smack the boneless chicken breast with a big mallet.

"Flattening it out to about a half-inch thickness."

"Remind me never to make you mad," he commented when she continued to pound the meat.

Brianna laughed. "Yeah, I'm one mean mama with this mallet."

When she shook it at him Colin put his palms in the air and backed up a couple of steps. "Put the mallet down. I'll do whatever you want!"

Brianna wiggled her eyebrows. "I'll hold you to that."

"That's what I'm hoping," he admitted, then pulled up a stool to watch her. She worked with ease and he thought she looked incredibly cute in the denim apron that she must have found hanging in a closet somewhere. He took a pull on his longneck thinking that there was so much stuff in this house that he was totally unaware of and truly never cared about. It was fun to see Brianna finally make use of this big-ass kitchen. "So you obviously love to cook and know your way around a stove."

She bobbed her head with enthusiasm before giving the chicken another good whack. "In my dreams I'd be Rachael Ray. Writing is my passion but cooking comes in a close second . . . or maybe even a tie." She heated up a big skillet that Colin was pretty sure had never been used and then added some olive oil. After the oil sizzled and popped she drenched the chicken in a milk and egg mixture and then dipped them in bread crumbs before transferring the cutlets to the skillet.

Colin leaned his elbows on the counter and said, "Have you ever thought of combining the two . . . you know, writing and cooking?"

She looked up from browning the breasts. "You mean like a cookbook?"

He nodded. "Yeah."

"Ohh, that would be fun!" She turned the chicken with tongs and then sliced some mozzarella cheese. "Italian is my favorite cuisine." She tapped her cheek. "Hmm, a walking tour of Tuscany ending with a cookbook would be awesome. Of course, you get to drink plenty of Chianti along the way." She picked up her wineglass, gave him a salute, and took a sip.

"Let's do it." He didn't really mean to blurt that out but he realized that he wasn't kidding.

She almost choked on her swallow of wine and carefully set the glass down. "You're serious, aren't you?"

"I finally know what to do with all this damned money. Spend it on you."

She frowned. "Colin—" she began, but he stopped her.

"Don't even go there, cutie. I didn't mean to sound as if you were after me for that reason."

She shook her head firmly and then waved her hand in an arc. "Actually, I find it all a bit intimidating. Well, except for this kitchen, which is like a big playground for me."

"So do I."

"You find your own house intimidating?" She looked at him in confusion. "But this is your lifestyle . . . You earned it."

"Yeah, I know I earned it, but I never knew what to do with all this stuff." He stood up and came over to wrap his arms around her from behind. "Let's have fun with it . . . travel, whatever your heart desires. I love watching you in this kitchen. I had fun turning on the gadgets in my bedroom that I knew were there but never bothered to use. For the first time in my life I'm learning not to be so intense, so driven, and to simply have some fun."

"Wasn't racing fun?"

"Yeah, sometimes, but there was so much pressure." He kissed her neck. "You're making me . . . um, what is that silly saying?"

She angled her head to look at him. "You mean stop and smell the roses?"

"Yeah, that."

"It's not so silly." She twisted in his arms and put her hands up on his shoulders. "I needed to do the same thing, Colin. With my parents moved away and Alexia gone too, I immersed myself in my work. While I love the *Braxton Times*, I was missing out on a lot of living. You've taught me to open up and discover things about myself," she said, and rose on tiptoe to kiss him. "Thank you," she said softly. "I've never been happier."

"Me neither," he readily admitted. "Um, and speaking of discovering things about yourself?"

Seeing the look in his eyes made her grin. "Okay . . . what?"

"I have a confession to make. I bought you something."

"Am I supposed to guess?"

"No, just get that chicken Parmesan in the oven and I'll show you."

"Okay." She deftly slid the chicken from the skillet to a baking dish, placed two generous slices of cheese on the golden brown chicken breasts, and then poured spaghetti sauce over it all. She grated some fresh Parmesan and sprinkled it over the sauce before adding more mozzarella and then sliding it into the oven. "I'm all about the cheese."

"How long will it take to bake?"

"About half an hour or so or until the sauce is bubbly. Then I'll put the garlic bread in the oven and boil the spaghetti."

"Do I have a job? I thought I was supposed to be your something or other."

"Sous-chef. The second in command. You can toss the salad."

"That I think I can handle. Did I mention that I like it when you boss me around?" He took her hand and led her from the kitchen. "Now follow me."

"I thought I was the boss?"

"Okay, I'll follow you . . . to the bedroom."

Brianna laughed and let him lead her through the huge house. Lying on the bed was a trench coat. She turned to him and put her hands to her cheeks. "I still can't believe I did that."

"I spotted the coat at the mall and couldn't resist."

"Do you want me to put it on?"

"No, it just made me think of you. Of course, everything makes me think of you." He dipped his head and kissed her thoroughly. "I don't need props. All I need is you, Brianna. I know I must sound like a dork, but it's so true."

"Like you could ever be a dork," she scoffed with a shake of her head. She slid her hands beneath his shirt. "Mmm, we only have about twenty minutes left before the timer goes off."

He grinned at her. "Then let's make good use of it. Hey, what do you think Jayden and Alexia are doing right now?"

"I hope the same thing we're doing," she answered, and wrapped her arms around him. "I hate what Alexia went through but I really love having her back in Braxton and back in my life. You know, when I asked her how to deal with a broken heart she said that you just have to get back up, dust yourself off, and start over again."

Colin frowned down at her. "I won't break your heart, Brianna."

"You can't promise me that. But whatever happens between us, it's worth it. Alexia is an example that if you open your mind and your heart you will eventually find true love." She grinned up at him. "I know I just sounded like a dork but since I am one . . . or at least a nerd . . . I'm allowed."

"You're not a nerd."

She gave him a deadpan look.

"Okay, but a very sexy nerd."

"I'll take that," she said, and shrieked when he picked her up and tossed her onto the bed. She came up to her knees and crooked her finger at him. "Come on, sous-chef. Chop-chop."

"You don't—"

"Have to ask me twice," she said with him.

Knowing that the chicken would soon be bubbling, they tossed their clothes to the floor and then after Colin rolled on protection they tumbled together onto the bed. Laughing and kissing quickly sizzled into full-blown desire. With a moan, Colin scooted up against the pillows and pulled Brianna on top of him. She straddled his hips and sank down onto his erection with a satisfied sigh. Splaying her hands on his chest, she started moving slowly until he reached up and spanned her waist with his big hands, guiding and helping her.

"Oh . . . Colin!" With his help she rode him hard, with wild abandon, and nerd or not, she was a fire-cracker in bed. She felt so tight, so slick and hot that Colin had to hold back or immediately climax. She was so sexy with her eyes closed and her copper curls tumbling to her shoulders. When she moaned and then caught her full bottom lip between her teeth Colin clenched his jaw in an effort not to lose it. Her small but firm breasts jiggled and she let her head drop to the side. "God, Colin, you feel amazing," she said in a throaty, breathless voice that sent him over the edge. He thrust his hips upward and he felt her come right along with him.

She fell against him and kissed his chest, his neck,

and then his mouth. Colin held her close and said, "Bri, you know that I would rather cut off my right nut than hurt you."

"Thank you," she said, and then dissolved into a fit of laughter.

"Okay, I'm not very eloquent. Let me rephrase that."

"No, that was straight to the point," she assured him, and then became more serious. "Colin, I know how I feel but we're such an unlikely pair. This is happening so quickly that I feel as if I'm jumping off a cliff without a net."

He smiled at her. "I was going to say that I'd catch you, but that would be so corny . . . and then you'd just laugh at me again."

"I would not! Okay, maybe I would."

"This is fast and furious just like I ride and I'm loving every minute of it. Let's just take it one day at a time and see where this goes."

"Good idea."

"It's way too soon to be dropping the L-word."

She nodded.

"But you know what I say about that?"

"What?"

"Screw that. Brianna Spencer, I love you."

She gave him a slow smile that turned him inside out. "Again, straight to the point and well said." She leaned in and gave him a sweet kiss. "I'm in love with you too, Colin. I kinda like fast and furious."

"Does that mean you'll take a ride on my street bike?"

Her eyes rounded but then she shouted, "Yes! No, *hell* yes. I want to do it all!"

"Are you serious?"

"Yes!" she shouted, but then admitted, "Well, probably not, but it feels good saying it."

Colin laughed and pulled her into his arms. He liked to break rules and she liked to follow them. She was sensible and he was, by his own admission, a walk on the wild side. At first glance they seemed to be opposites, but Colin knew that they were bringing out facets in each other's personalities not yet tapped into and he was looking forward to finding out more.

"I'm dying to hear from Alexia and Jayden," Brianna said as she quickly tugged on her clothes. "I know you said that he arrived safely and that's good, but I want to know more."

"We could call."

Brianna wrinkled her nose. "I want to, but we should give them their space. I just wish that we'll hear some news soon . . . and I hope it's good."

Colin kissed her on top of the head. "I'm sure it will be." He sniffed the air. "Something sure smells amazing."

"Let's go finish, sous-chef. Maybe if we're lucky we'll hear from Alexia and Jayden before the night is over. I know this sounds odd but I have this weird sister radar thing going on that tells me that something is up. I'm going to put my phone here on the kitchen island so I don't miss her call."

"Good idea," Colin agreed, and did the same thing. "Okay." He rubbed his hands together. "Give me my orders."

"Take the romaine lettuce out of the crisper in the fridge, wash it, and then tear it into little bite-sized pieces for a Caesar salad."

"Gotcha."

Brianna bent over and opened the oven door filling the kitchen with the tantalizing Italian aroma. "Oh, the chicken Parmesan is ready." She removed it with big oven mitts that Colin didn't know he owned. "I'll get the garlic bread in the oven," she said briskly, and he grinned. "What?" she asked. Placing the big mitts on her slim hips, she tried to appear bossy, but with her hair sex-head messy and her rosy cheeks, it really wasn't working for her. "You aren't getting very far with your lettuce." She tried to wag a finger at him and then looked at the mitt and laughed.

"You're distracting me."

"How so?"

"Being you."

"Oh . . . Colin," she said, and put the mitts to her flushed cheeks, looking so cute that he had to leave the lettuce and come over to pull her into his arms. He leaned in and kissed her softly, and while he knew that their relationship was bound to have its ups and downs, he thought that moments like this would make whatever challenges life threw at them worthwhile. He could only hope that Alexia and Jayden had come to the same conclusion.

Colin pulled back and gave her a quick kiss on the tip of her perky nose. "Sorry, I had to do that. I'll get back to my task."

"I'll try not to distract you," she said with a laugh.

"Impossible."

Brianna giggled again and then they both stopped short when her phone rang. "Ohmigod, it's Alexia!" She was so excited that she tried to pick the small phone up with her oven mitts. With a little squeal she tugged them off and then tossed them over her head before pouncing on the phone. "Hey, Alexia, what's up? Yes, Colin is standing right here." She looked across the kitchen island and smiled. "Okay, I'll put you on speakerphone."

"Hi, Alexia," Colin said loudly. "Is Jayden with you?"

"Yes," Alexia answered, and sounded so emotional that Colin walked around the island to stand near Brianna, who frowned up at him.

"Is everything okay?" Colin asked, and took Brianna's hand.

"Yes," Alexia said, but her voice broke. "Oh, I wasn't going to tell you this until we were there in person, but . . . ," she began, and then said, "Oh, Jayden . . ."

"Alexia, what's wrong?" Brianna asked, and squeezed Colin's hand in a viselike grip, but he didn't care.

"Sweetie, you want me to tell them?" Jayden said gently in the background.

"No . . . ," Alexia replied, sniffed loudly, and said, "Oh, Bri . . . Colin, I'm . . ." She paused, sniffed again, and then said, *Pregnant.*"

"What!" Brianna looked at Colin with round eyes and then back to the phone lying on the counter. "But . . ."

"I know," Alexia said, "it wasn't supposed to happen, but somehow, we got lucky and beat the odds! Oh, Bri . . . ," she said, and then started to cry.

Brianna turned and buried her face in Colin's chest. He wrapped his arms around her and squeezed. "Congratulations, Alexia," he said, and couldn't keep the emotion from his own voice.

"Hey," Jayden said in the background. "I had something to do with this, you know."

Alexia and Brianna both did a laughing, crying combination.

"Oh, I'm so, *so* happy for you," she said in a shaky but ecstatic tone. "When are you coming home so I can hug you both?"

"We want to bask in the news and the Florida sunshine for a few days," Jayden answered.

"I don't blame you," Colin said, and hugged Brianna.

"We'll celebrate when you get home," Brianna promised. "Have you called Mom and Dad yet?"

"Not yet," Alexia said. "I'm going to call them as soon as we hang up."

"You pamper her," Colin ordered.

"You know it," Jayden answered.

"Call us when you're on your way and I'll have a huge dinner ready," Brianna said.

"We will," Alexia promised. "I love you both," she said, and Brianna could only nod and bury her face in Colin's damp shirt once again.

"We do too," Colin answered for her. "Talk to you soon," he said, and then ended the call.

"I can't believe it," Brianna mumbled into his shirt.

Colin pulled her head away from his chest and kissed her tenderly.

When the kiss ended Brianna looked up at Colin and said, "I'm so happy right now I think I could just . . . *burst.*"

He laughed softly, thinking how much he adored her. "I'm right there with ya." He reached down and swiped a tear away with the pad of his thumb. "You know, Jayden and Alexia's journey is testimony to the fact no matter what life throws at you, there's always hope if you just keep on pushing through and never give up."

"Well said, Colin."

He smiled at her. "I guess you're rubbing off on me."

"And you on me," she said before coming up on her tiptoes to kiss him. "Okay, now, sous-chef. Back to your task."

"Yes, ma'am," he agreed with a grin. The usually cold, pristine kitchen was filled with warmth from the oven and smelled of supper. Colin glanced over at his lettuce but then picked Brianna up and spun her around.

"Whoa!" She clung to him while laughing, and for the first time his big house felt like a home.

Turn the page for a sneak preview of LuAnn
McLane's next sexy and clever romance

Redneck Cinderella

In stores March 2009

Jolie Russell is a genuine redneck hillbilly, but when
she becomes a millionaire overnight, her beer-drinking,
music-blasting ways just don't cut it in her new social
circles. Southern gentleman Cody Dean steps up to be
her Prince Charming and gives the modern-day Cinder-
ella a crash course in country clubs, cocktail parties—
and a little bit of romance. Class lines are no match for
the sparks between them, and together they learn that
sometimes the best of both worlds truly is the best.

"I'll get it, Daddy," I shout from where I'm washing the supper dishes.

"Okay, Jolie," he calls back from his workshop just off the kitchen. He's busy whittling Christmas ornaments for a craft show, and I don't want to interrupt him. This year's drought hurt our tobacco crop, so what started out as a therapeutic hobby brings in much-needed income. Another sharp rap at the front door has me grabbing a towel and hurrying through the living room to see who might be coming our way on a cold night such as this.

"Hold your horses," I grumble. Our farm is miles from town, so it's not like we have visitors dropping in for a social call. After wiping my wet hands, I toss the dish towel over my shoulder and open the door. *Oh wow* rings in my head but doesn't reach my mouth. Now, I'm not one to be rendered speechless, but when I see who is on my doorstep, I get tongue-tied and flustered.

"Jolie Russell?"

"Ughaaaa." Forgetting about my tongue-tied situation, I try to respond and make a weird noise that I disguise as a sneeze.

"God bless you."

This time I'm smart enough to merely nod and rub my finger beneath my nose like I really did sneeze.

"Cody Dean." He extends his hand my way, and I give him a firm handshake just like my daddy taught me. Of course, like everybody else in Cottonwood, Kentucky, I'm already well aware of who he is. Cody, the oldest son of Carl Dean, is back from his fancy Ivy League education to take over his daddy's company. The Dean family is like royalty here in Cottonwood, with Cody being the prince. I also know that Dean Development has been buying up farmland for subdivisions all over Cottonwood, and I suddenly get light-headed at the prospect at why Cody is on my doorstep and I'm pretty sure it isn't to ask me out on a date.

No, I'm certain he isn't here to take little old me out to dinner. To say that he's out of my league would be the understatement of the year, which leaves me to wonder whether he's going to make us an offer to buy our acreage. My heart starts beating wildly, and I blink at him like an idiot.

"Sorry to have stopped by unannounced, but may I come in?"

"Oh . . . why, sure, where the hell are my manners?" I blurt out, and then wish my tongue had remained tied. "I mean, um, please, come on in," I amend softly, since I tend to shout when I get jittery, even when it's not necessary. With a nervous smile I step aside for him to enter. As he passes me, I get a whiff of expensive-smelling aftershave that makes me want to pant after him like a lovesick puppy. He's wearing a slick leather bomber jacket and fancy-looking black jeans, and don't ask me why, but I have a sudden, silly urge to take the dish towel from my shoulder, roll it up tightly, and zap him on the butt. "Take a load off," I offer, and gesture at the sofa. "Um, I mean, have a seat." God, I suck at this.

"Thank you," Cody says in his polite, refined tone, but the hint of amusement in his blue eyes has my chin coming up a notch. Did he know that I was ogling his backside? I make a mental note to keep my eyes on his face. Admittedly, I'm a bit lacking in social graces, having lost my mama at the tender age of seven. I'm more at home fishing and four-wheeling with guys than dressed up for a dinner date, not that shaking Cody's hand didn't give me a hot little tingle that traveled all the way to my toes. I might be a little rough around the edges, but I still have all my girl parts, and Cody Dean is making all of those parts stand up and take notice.

But when his gaze sweeps the room, pride stiffens my backbone. We might not have much, and although everything is old and outdated, it's clean and as neat as a pin.

"What brings you here?" My blunt question has a little more bite than intended.

Cody's dark eyebrows shoot up at my tone. "A business proposition," he answers smoothly. "Is your father home, Jolie?"

Oh, holy crap. I tamp down my don't-mess-with-me-attitude that tends to land me in hot water, and put a smile back on my face. "Why, yes, he is. I'll get him." I head out of the room but then pause and turn back to him. "Um, make yourself at home."

"Thanks." He inclines his neatly cropped head and

sits down on the ancient sofa. I hope he thinks it's an expensive antique instead of an old hand-me-down.

I walk toward the doorway but then stop and turn around again. "Would you like something to drink? Sweet tea?" I'm about to add crumpets just for fun, but I'm not sure what a crumpet is and I'm quite sure we don't have any. About the best I could do is Oreos, and that's if Daddy hasn't eaten them all. I'm trying really hard to remember the finer points of Southern hospitality, but in truth we rarely have visitors except for outdoor activities like four-wheeling, fishing, and such.

"No, thank you," he says, but then adds, "On second thought, a bottle of water would be nice."

Well, la-de-da. "Um, all I have is plain old tap water." My daddy thinks that buying bottled water is the dumbest damn thing ever imposed upon the American public. When Cody hesitates, I add, "We've had city water since last June."

Cody waves a hand at me. "That's okay. I'm fine. Don't go to any trouble."

I blink at him, and of course I'm going to bring him a glass of tap water just to be ornery. I'm bad that way. "I'll go and find Daddy."

I walk slowly out of the room, wishing I was wearing something better than worn jeans and a George Strait T-shirt, but when I get to the kitchen, I scurry into the workshop. "Daddy!" I say in a whisper for me but what is a normal tone for most folks. "Guess who is sittin' on our very own sofa?" Daddy blows sawdust off of an angel but when he opens his mouth to make a guess, I blurt, "Cody Dean!" I say the word _Dean_ so high-pitched that our old mutt, Rufus, lifts his head and whines.

"Ya don't say." Daddy frowns and looks down at the angel with a critical eye.

"He wants to talk to you!"

When Daddy doesn't move, I reach over and tug him by his shirt. "Hurry," I urge, and all but drag him from the room. While I love the farmhouse, I hate raising the very crop that's responsible for the death of my mama. I pause to draw a glass of water from the faucet and make a mental bet with myself as to whether Cody will drink it or not.

When we enter the living room, Cody politely stands up and shakes my daddy's hand. "Nice to meet you, Mr. Russell. May I have a few minutes of your time?"

Daddy nods, but I see the stubborn set of his jaw, and my hope plummets. He eases down into the overstuffed chair while I march over and hand Cody the glass of water.

"Thank you," he says, and while looking at me, drains half of the contents before setting it on the scarred coffee table. He gives me an I'm-on-to-you smile, and I can't help but grin back at him. His smile deepens, causing a little dimple in his left cheek, and I have to grab the back of Daddy's chair for support. I hang out with guys all the time, and while I've been sweet on one or two of them, no one had ever turned me inside out with a mere smile.

"So what brings you here?" Daddy asks even though we all know. Rufus, who must sense the excitement in the air, sits back on his haunches, and we all three look expectantly over at Cody.

After clearing his throat, Cody leans forward and rests his elbows on his knees. "There's no reason to beat around the bush, Mr. Russell. I'd like to make you an offer for your land."

"I'm not interested."

"Daddy, hear him out."

Cody shoots me a grateful glance. "I'm prepared to offer three million."

When my knees give way, I grab on to the back of the chair so hard that my fingernails dig into the nubby fabric.

"Sorry, Cody," Daddy says.

What! A little whimper escapes me.

"Three and a half million," Cody counters, and I breath a sigh of relief. Who knew that Daddy could bargain like this?

"Money isn't the issue, son. This here land is where I lived with my dear wife, Rosie. I'll never leave it."

Emotion clogs my throat. I can't argue with his reasoning, but I also have to think that Mama somehow has a hand in this sudden windfall.

Cody steeples his fingers and for a long moment remains silent, but then says, "You don't have to leave your land. I'll set aside your plot, and you can keep several of the wooded acres as well. Now, you would have to rebuild. Mr. Russell, this isn't going to be your average subdivision. I'm proposing a gated community with upscale homes. I might add that this would bring in much-needed tax dollars to Cottonwood."

Daddy shakes his head. "Who could afford homes like that around these parts?"

"Executives from nearby Nashville. Kentucky horse money. I've done my homework. These homes will sell quickly. Of course, we would build your house first."

Daddy slowly runs a hand down his face and then looks back at me. "Jolie? What do you think?"

I kneel down beside the chair and put a hand on his arm. "Daddy, I know that mama would want this for you. It seems like a good thing all around." I squeeze his arm. "But if you don't want this, I fully understand," I assure him, and then hold my breath.

Daddy looks up as if he's asking my mama for guidance, and then, as if getting his answer, nods slowly. He looks Cody Dean straight in the eye, extends his hand, and says, "Son, you have a deal."

Cody smiles and grasps Daddy's hand. "Congratulations, Mr. Russell." He looks at me and smiles, "Jolie. I'll have the paperwork drawn up tomorrow, but I trust in your handshake."

And suddenly we're millionaires.

LuAnn McLane lives in Florence, Kentucky, just outside Cincinnati, Ohio. When she takes breaks from writing, she enjoys watching chick flicks with her daughter and trying to keep up with her three active sons. Visit her Web site at www.luannmclane.com.